AMISH
CINDERELLA

BOOK 5 OF THE AMISH FAIRYTALE SERIES

ASHLEY EMMA

GET 4 OF ASHLEY EMMA'S AMISH EBOOKS FOR FREE

www.AshleyEmmaAuthor.com

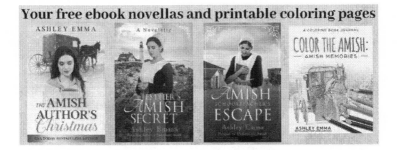

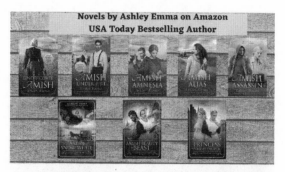

CONTENTS

PROLOGUE

"I want you to have this, but don't tell anyone. It's our secret." Esther Holt held out her trembling hand as she lay on the hospital bed, dropping a charm bracelet into Ella Ruth's palm. Normally Esther wore a white prayer *kapp* like all the other Amish women in Unity, but now she wore a plain fabric head covering to conceal the fact that she had lost all of her hair during chemotherapy.

Ella Ruth looked at her mother quizzically. "I've never seen this before, *Mamm*. It's yours?"

"No one knows I've had it all these years except your father," Esther said weakly, resting her head back on the pillow. "I've kept it hidden in a box in my closet. I told him I was going to give it to you. So, you can keep it, but you can't wear it." In their Amish community, jewelry was not allowed. "My sister Joanna and I each had one. After she left the church to marry an *Englisher*, she bought them and gave one to me. She said even though she was leaving the Amish and knew I could not wear it, she wanted me to have a token to remember we would always be sisters. They're friendship bracelets, and each charm means something special."

"What do they mean?" Ella Ruth asked.

"The book represents the love of reading I shared with my sister and passed on to you," Esther explained with a smile. "The horse charm represents my horse, Pumpkin, and the dog charm is for the dog we had when I was a child, Zeke. The apple is for when we would pick apples growing up. The little glass slipper shoe represents that we each have our own path to walk, and the Eiffel Tower is for how we wanted to travel together. The hot-air balloon is for how my sister and I always wanted to ride together in one, but then she left, so we never did, and we never traveled." Esther frowned. "Even still, my biggest regret was not seeing my sister and begging for forgiveness before she died. I didn't talk to her for years." Tears filled her eyes. "I suppose I'll get to do that soon."

"No," Ella Ruth choked out, clutching her mother's frail hand in her own. "Don't say things like that."

"Promise me," Esther said, her voice cracking as she peered into her daughter's eyes. "I want Pumpkin to be your horse, now. Take care of her for me."

"Of course, I will, *Mamm*," Ella Ruth choked out.

"Promise me you will chase your dreams. Pursue your writing. Travel. Find love. Do everything you want to do because one day you'll wake up and realize it's too late." Esther coughed, leaning back on the bed.

Ella Ruth's eyes burned at the thought of her mother not being able to travel and do the things she had dreamed of. "I'm sorry, *Mamm*. I wish you had done all those things."

"Don't be sorry for me," Esther said, patting Ella Ruth's hand. "I lived a wonderful life. I had all of you children, and I married my true love. That's what's most important. Not everyone gets to experience that in their life."

"I hope one day I will find love like you and *Daed* shared," Ella Ruth said softly.

Esther opened Ella Ruth's fist, revealing the charm bracelet that had been cutting into Ella Ruth's skin without her even realizing it.

"You will," Esther whispered. "I know in my heart you will, Ella Ruth. But remember, there is no such thing as luck or fairytales or fairy godmothers in this world, my dear. Don't wait for a prince to ride in and save you. It's all up to you. You have so many aspirations, and I know you will make all your own dreams come true. Just promise me you will."

Ella Ruth nodded, a tear crawling down her cheek. "I promise, *Mamm*."

CHAPTER ONE

Two years later...

Ella Ruth's fingers flew over the laptop keyboard as she tried to finish writing one last chapter before starting her morning chores. She rubbed away the sleepiness from her eyes, fidgeting as a piece of straw poked her in the back. It was stifling hot in the loft of the barn even though it was still early in the morning.

"Ella Ruth!" Priscilla, her stepmother, called from the house in a shrill voice.

Instinctively, Ella Ruth slammed the laptop shut and hid it behind a bale of hay. If anyone ever saw her with the laptop, she'd be in big trouble with the elders of the church, as electronics were not allowed in her community. Worst of all—her father would be disappointed in her.

But no, Priscilla wouldn't actually walk into the barn—it was much too stinky and dirty for her delicate self. Ella Ruth let out a long breath, retrieved it, then continued typing a few more sentences. She was finishing up the first draft of her third novel. Though she had queried dozens of literary agents and had even received some positive feedback, she still hadn't found one who would represent her. But still, she kept on writing. Her mother would want her to never give up.

"Ella Ruth?" Katie, Ella Ruth's teenage sister, asked from the barn below.

She jumped again. "Yes?"

"Priscilla sent me to come get you."

"I'll be right there. She saved her work and put the laptop in its case before hiding it behind the hay bales, then picked up her notebook from the hay, flipping through dozens of pages of handwritten stories and sketched illustrations. She loved drawing as much as she loved writing, and her dream was to write and illustrate middle grade fantasy novels about time traveling. Her detailed drawings of castles, princess warriors, and knights filled the pages of her notebook.

For now, it would have to wait. Maybe she would have time to draw and write more in the evening after she finished her chores.

She climbed down the ladder and dropped from the last step to the floor of the barn with a thud.

"What were you doing up there?" Katie asked curiously. "Writing?"

"*Ja*." Ella Ruth nodded. "And drawing. My new book is almost done."

"That's great!" Katie said. "Do you think you'll get it published?"

"I don't have an agent. It's so hard only being able to email them my query letters at the library or coffee shop," Ella Ruth admitted. "I might try self-publishing, but I heard it's a lot of work. But so is querying agents. I got some books about it at the library, and I've been studying."

"I'm sure you'll figure it out," Katie said.

"What does Priscilla want?" Ella Ruth was supposed to call her stepmother *Mamm*, but she didn't like to call her stepmother the same name she had called her own mother. Ella Ruth laughed when her horse, Pumpkin, nuzzled her back with her nose. Ella Ruth turned around, laughing. "Good morning, Pumpkin. Did Priscilla wake you up with her screeching?"

Pumpkin bobbed her head and snorted, causing them both to laugh.

"She wants you to come make breakfast. I'll help," Katie offered, "but I have to get to work soon."

"Thanks." Ella Ruth stroked Pumpkin's nose. "I need all the help I can get. She keeps me so busy. I'll see you later, Pumpkin."

"She and Amanda don't help with anything. If Lilly and I didn't work so much, we'd be able to help you a lot more," Katie added as they walked toward the house. Here in Unity, Amish children stopped school after the eighth grade. Katie and their sister Lilly were finished with school, so they worked full-time at their father's general store, where they sold items varying from tools to dry goods to fresh donuts.

"I'd appreciate that," Ella Ruth said, "But it's good for you to have a job, and *Daed* needs the help. I don't want you to quit because of me." She wished she could work there full-time instead of part-time, but she had to take care of Debra and Seth, their younger siblings, and she had so many chores to do at home.

They walked through the door and took off their shoes. Debra and Seth were playing with blocks in the living room, and their teenage sister Lilly was helping them.

"There you are!" Priscilla cried, fanning herself in the summer heat. "What were you doing out there? Daydreaming like you always do?"

"She was probably reading in the barn as always," Amanda said with a smirk as she flounced into the kitchen, her long purple skirt flapping behind her. "We're starving. When will breakfast be ready?"

"Maybe if you weren't so lazy, selfish, thoughtless, and disorganized, breakfast would be ready by now, Ella Ruth," Priscilla chided.

Ella Ruth sighed and pulled a cast iron skillet out of the cabinet and held back a retort. Her father, Irvin, had asked all of his children to be respectful of Priscilla. For his sake, she held back what she wanted to say. Instead, she said, "It'll be ready soon."

Katie walked over to stand next to her at the woodstove and began cracking eggs into a bowl, giving her sister an apologetic look.

"Good morning, sleepyhead," Priscilla said snidely as her daughter Sadie meandered into the kitchen.

"I didn't sleep well last night," Sadie said, rubbing her eyes. Her disheveled red hair peeked out from under her prayer *kapp*.

Ella Ruth gave her a sideways glance. She often saw the glow of the battery-operated lantern on in Sadie's room late at night, but she didn't know why. Ella Ruth had asked her about it in the past, but Sadie always had some excuse.

"You're just as lazy as your stepsister," Priscilla snapped, then turned to Ella Ruth. "That reminds me. I need one of my dresses mended, and I need you to wash our sheets and give the entire house a good top-to-bottom cleaning."

"She just did that recently," Katie interjected.

"Do not speak unless you are spoken to." Priscilla's head whipped around toward Katie.

Irvin Holt walked into the kitchen and kissed his wife. "Good morning."

"Good morning, dear," Priscilla said in her artificially sweetened voice that she always used around him, plastering on a smile as she stood up to greet him.

"How is everyone this morning?" Irvin asked in his usual cheerful voice.

"Just wonderful," Priscilla answered for everyone, casting Ella Ruth a warning glance.

Katie handed Ella Ruth the bowl of eggs. "I'll set the table."

"Thanks," Ella Ruth said, setting the eggs on the counter beside the woodstove. She turned to grab the salt and pepper, and as she did, Amanda quickly stood up and intentionally knocked the bowl of eggs onto the floor when Irvin wasn't looking. The runny yellow liquid ran from the counter onto the floor, dripping off the counter.

"Oh, no, Ella Ruth," Priscilla said, shaking her head and clicking her tongue. "Do try to be more careful next time." She shared a knowing look with Amanda.

I bet they planned that, Ella Ruth thought, scowling.

"Accidents happen," Irvin said with an understanding smile. "Katie is busy setting the table. Amanda, will you help her clean it up?"

"Me?" A look of panic flashed across Amanda's face as she fell into one of the chairs at the table. "I have a terrible headache. Sadie, would you be a dear and do it for me?"

Sadie, who had seen what had happened, frowned. "Fine." She grabbed a towel off the counter and began cleaning up the eggs.

"Thank you," Ella Ruth said as she knelt down to help.

"She shouldn't have done that," Sadie whispered, shaking her head. "I'm sorry."

"It's not your fault," Ella Ruth whispered back.

"Stop dawdling and finish up so we can eat," Priscilla ordered, then gave a fake smile when she realized Irvin had heard her. She changed her tone from sharp to soft and sweet. "We don't want your father and Katie to be late for work."

Sadie took her dirty towel and rinsed it out in the sink as Ella Ruth cracked new eggs and began cooking them. Soon, she had breakfast on the table.

As Irvin and Katie walked out the door, Ella Ruth hurried to follow them.

"*Daed*," she said. "Wait."

"I think I know what this is about," Irvin said with a sigh.

"It's not fair that Ella Ruth does most of the work and Priscilla, Amanda, and Sadie do nothing to help," Katie interceded. "I would help more, but I'm at work with you all day, which I am happy to do."

"I want to come to work full-time with you and Katie," Ella Ruth said. "We could bring Debra and Seth until school starts. They would have fun at the store, and they could help us."

"We've talked about this. I need you to stay home and do the chores, and they can help you."

"They're so young, and it's summertime. I want them to enjoy their summer," Ella Ruth said. "They do help me with some things, and so does Sadie, but she often doesn't know what to do to help."

"I'm sorry most of the work falls on you, Ella Ruth. Priscilla gets very tired," Irvin said, "And so do her daughters. They are not as energetic as the rest of us because they aren't used to this lifestyle. They can't handle too much physical work. They lived a very different life before."

Ella Ruth wanted to roll her eyes. Amanda and Priscilla claimed that they had chronic fatigue, but they only did what they wanted to do and didn't think about anyone else. They were lying to him to get out of helping with the chores.

"I know Amanda and Priscilla can be a bit..." Irvin's voice trailed off.

"Difficult?" Ella Ruth interjected. *Bossy? Cruel?* she added inwardly.

Irvin frowned. "I know you miss your mother, and no one will ever replace her."

That was for sure.

"Still, I want all of you to respect Priscilla no matter what and be kind to Amanda. Understood?" Irvin added.

Ella Ruth nodded, though her stomach roiled. She hated the way Priscilla spoke to not only her but all of her siblings. However, for some reason, Priscilla seemed to single Ella Ruth out, making her the most miserable. But Ella Ruth would rather it be her than one of her younger siblings. She could handle it.

If Priscilla ever started mistreating them, Ella Ruth would put her foot down. After Katie and Lilly were kidnapped by sex traffickers a few years ago and almost lost forever, Ella Ruth vowed to herself after they were rescued that she would always be more protective of all her siblings. Thank the Lord that they had been rescued before being sold, but still, they had been held in a warehouse with other survivors.

Even though they had been in captivity for only a few days, Katie and Lilly were never the same after being kidnapped, but they were healing. However, Priscilla's harsh personality wasn't helping the process. Ella Ruth still didn't know what truly happened to her sisters during their time in captivity or what they had seen.

What had happened to Priscilla in her past to make her want to belittle everyone else around her?

"The Singing is tonight," Ella Ruth said. "I was hoping to go with Katie and Lilly. Priscilla might not want me to if I don't finish all the chores."

"You can go," Irvin said. "Even if you don't finish them all."

Katie and Ella Ruth smiled, looking forward to the event.

"We need to get going, Katie," Irvin said, and Katie gave her sister a sympathetic look.

As they began their short walk down the lane to the Unity Community Market, Ella Ruth sighed and turned around to face the house. "And I'll be here," she muttered, walking inside to start cleaning up from breakfast.

"What on earth was that?" Priscilla demanded as Ella Ruth walked through the door.

Ella Ruth froze. "I was just talking to my father." She turned to Debra and Seth, who were still playing in the living room. "Children, go outside, please."

This could get ugly, and she didn't want them to witness it. Her younger brother and sister agreed enthusiastically, put on their shoes, and ran out the door.

"You were talking to your father about me," Priscilla snapped. "I could hear you through the open window. You were complaining about me."

"I think it would only be fair if you and Amanda helped more with the chores. Sadie does help me sometimes," Ella Ruth said. "If you did, I could help my father more at the store. He needs the help."

"You ungrateful, selfish brat," Priscilla sneered. "I bring your father happiness after his wife died. You are the oldest one living at home now that your older sisters have married and moved out. It's your responsibility to do the work, not mine, and certainly not my daughters' responsibility."

"But—"

"If I hear one more word about you complaining about me to your father, I will tell him all about your little secret." An evil glint glimmered in Priscilla's eyes.

No, Ella Ruth thought as panic snaked down her spine. *Does she know? How did she find out?*

"I followed Katie out to the barn this morning to fetch you for breakfast and overheard your conversation about your writing, so I went up to the loft to find your laptop hidden in the hay bales," Amanda said, strolling into the kitchen.

Ella Ruth's stomach plummeted to her feet, and her heart froze in her chest. "What did you do to it?" she cried, taking a step closer to Amanda.

"Nothing, for now," Amanda said with a smirk.

"We will leave your laptop alone and keep your secret as long as you do whatever we ask and don't talk to your father about us," Priscilla said.

"As far as he knows, we are frail and get tired easily, so dear Ella Ruth can handle our chores for us," Amanda added, hands on her hips.

Sadie came into the kitchen, her eyebrows drawn together in concern.

"And what about you, Sadie?" Ella Ruth asked. "Do you know about this too?"

"Yes, I know about their plan, and I think this is unfair to you," Sadie said, and Ella Ruth's eyebrows shot up in surprise.

Priscilla whirled around to face her daughter. "You are just as un-grateful as she is. I am your mother, and you will do as I say. After everything we have been through, I have always taken care of you and Amanda. You must do this for me."

Ella Ruth looked at her stepmother. "What do you mean by every-thing you've been through? What happened to you?"

"My past is none of your business," Priscilla retorted, throwing her hands up.

Sadie gave her an apologetic look. Maybe she would tell Ella Ruth what happened.

"It would break your father's heart if he knew you own a laptop," her stepmother spat out. "He's already lost so much. You wouldn't want to hurt him, would you?"

Unfortunately, Priscilla was right. It would break Irvin's heart if he knew Ella Ruth used a laptop.

No, she could never let that happen.

"If you care about your father at all, you will do as we say," Priscilla said. "Starting with mending my dress after you clean up from break-fast. Understood?"

Amanda crossed her arms and tapped her foot, giving her a sinister look.

"Understood," Ella Ruth said with a defeated sigh.

Chapter Two

After cooking, cleaning, doing laundry, and gardening all day long, Ella Ruth walked with Lilly and Katie to their friend's house down the lane where the Singing would be held that evening.

"It's so nice to get out of the house and have some free time," Ella Ruth said, enjoying the cool night air as they walked. When they arrived, their friend Laura Miller greeted them at the door.

"Hello!" she cried. "So glad you made it. Come on in. I'm looking forward to eating some of your famous popcorn."

"And we are looking forward to eating your famous donuts," Lilly added.

"Who is that?" Ella Ruth asked, noticing a young woman talking to some of the young men. Her dark hair was pinned up neatly under her prayer *kapp*, and she wore a long dark blue dress.

"I heard that her name is Esther. She just moved here with her cousin," Laura explained.

Lydia, Laura's more serious older sister, came over. "They're helping Boaz with the wheat harvest."

Ella Ruth set out a large container of the popcorn she had already made on the counter as Jake, one of the young Amish men, came over with Esther. "Let me introduce you to everyone," Jake said. "Esther, this is Ella Ruth, Laura, and Laura's sister, Lydia."

"Hi! Nice to meet you! We heard you were coming," Laura said cheerfully.

Ella Ruth smiled at their new friend, sensing that they would become close. Esther shared the same first name as Ella Ruth's mother. "So glad to have you here in town. Popcorn?"

"Sure. Thanks so much," Esther said, taking a bite of the seasoned popcorn. "Wow, this is great. What's on it?"

"Nutritional yeast and some other seasonings. It's my own recipe." Ella Ruth smiled proudly.

"Wow. It's so good," Esther said. "That's the best popcorn I've ever had!"

"Glad you like it. Here, take a bowl for yourself." Ella Ruth chuckled and poured some into a smaller bowl and handed it to Esther.

As Jake whisked Esther away to meet his friends, Ella Ruth turned to Laura. "I like her. I hope we get to know her better. Is she staying?"

"I think so. She seems adventurous." Laura lowered her voice to a whisper. "Maybe we should invite her on one of our movie theater outings."

Ella Ruth chuckled. "We haven't done that in so long. It would be fun, though."

When the Singing began, everyone sat at the large dining room table and took turns choosing songs. One person would begin to sing a song, and then everyone would join in, and they took turns choosing songs in random order. Ella Ruth loved the way the voices filled the room, each note vibrating in her heart.

After the Singing was over, they continued to eat snacks and talk with one another. Esther approached them again.

"So, what do you two do for fun?" she asked.

Ella Ruth gave Laura a questioning glance, wondering if Laura would ask her about going to the movies with them.

"We like to go to town and secretly go to the movie theater," Laura whispered. "We dress in *Englisher* clothing so no one stares at us. You know how people are."

"Really?" Esther said, intrigued. "That sounds like fun. And yes, I know what you mean, how people stare at us in our 'quaint' clothing."

"Well, when you're wearing *Englisher* clothing, you can pretend to be anyone you want to be."

Esther sighed wistfully. "Actually, that sounds amazing. I used to do it sometimes back in Smyrna, but it's been a long time since I have. I'll admit, I often get curious about *Englisher* life."

"You should come with us next time," Ella Ruth said.

"We haven't gone in a while, Ella," Laura said, turning to her friend.

"I've been so busy with chores at home. My stepmother expects me to do everything while she and her daughters do nothing." Ella Ruth said with a frown.

"That's not fair," Laura piped up.

"Your stepmother and stepsisters don't help you with the chores?" Esther asked.

Ella Ruth shook her head. "Sadie helps somewhat, but not Amanda and Priscilla. If only my father knew, but they said that if I tell him, they'll tell him I've been writing my stories on a laptop. I couldn't bear to break his heart after he's lost so much already." Her mind went back to their conversation that morning, and she ignored the sick feeling in her stomach.

"That's not right, Ella." Laura shook her head.

"They're taking advantage of you," Esther added somberly. "Is there anything we can do?"

"No, it's just the way it is." Ella Ruth sighed. "Well, anyway, I'd love to go tomorrow night. I'll get my chores done early."

"I'd love to go, too," Esther said, her heart aching for her friend.

"What about you, Esther? Do you ever do other things that aren't allowed?" Laura asked, her eyes twinkling with excitement.

"Well, not yet, but I do really want to travel. I want to go on a plane and travel to Europe. I think it would be incredible. There's so much history there. I just want to see it all! Especially the castles," Esther said with a sigh.

"Me too!" Laura cried so enthusiastically that several people stopped talking to look.

Ella Ruth laughed. "Shh!"

Laura lowered her voice. "Sorry. I'm very passionate about traveling."

"It's all she ever talks about," Ella Ruth added, rolling her eyes.

"I haven't gone on my Rumspringa yet, but I could never afford a ticket to Europe," Laura said dismally. "It's so expensive."

"It really is. Besides, when we lived in Smyrna, I would have hated to leave Mordecai at home all alone. That's why I like to read travel books and novels set in other countries," Esther said. "I guess it's the next best thing."

"Me too," Laura agreed, and Ella Ruth nodded.

"I do too, when I'm not busy taking care of my family and doing chores," Ella Ruth said. "There's always so much work to be done, and ever since my sisters' terrible experience, they can't help as much as they used to."

"What happened?" Esther asked.

Ella Ruth wrapped her arms around herself, lowering her voice so that her sisters across the room wouldn't hear her. "My two younger sisters were kidnapped by traffickers and held in an abandoned warehouse for a few days. It must have been terrifying. Even though they were rescued and they try to act like their old selves, I can tell they're not the same people they used to be. They don't like to talk about what happened to them, and they still cry sometimes, so I don't want them to have to do work if they don't want to."

"Ella is the most hard-working person I know," Laura added solemnly. "Honestly, you do the work of ten women."

"I just want them to be happy. They're improving, but still, more work has fallen on me as a result. I don't mind, though. I just hope they get better," Ella Ruth explained. "And they are, one day at a time. Or, at least they would be even better if my stepmother wasn't so hard on us."

"Wow, I'm so sorry," Esther said, stunned. "How horrible."

"It was a few years back," Laura added. "Thank the Lord they were rescued just in time and brought home."

Esther shook her head slowly. "I'm so sorry your family had to suffer that. You're so sweet to take care of them. You deserve a night out with us, though. Right, Laura?"

Ella Ruth shifted her weight nervously. What if her stepmother wouldn't let her go out? What if she didn't finish all her chores on time?

"What do you say? Do you want to go to the movies tomorrow night?" Laura asked Ella Ruth, her eyebrows going up and down playfully. She turned to Esther. "You'll come, won't you, Esther?"

"Of course! And Ella Ruth? What about you?"

She would have to try to finish all her chores. Even if she didn't, maybe her father would still let her go.

"Okay. That does sound like fun. But I can't stay out too late. I have to get to bed at a reasonable time to wake up early and do the laundry and cook breakfast," Ella Ruth said.

And have time for writing and drawing, she added inwardly.

Laura smiled, sighing. "Ella, does anyone ever call you Cinderella?"

Ella Ruth chuckled. "No, of course not. That's just a silly fairytale."

"Maybe they should call you that," Esther agreed.

"Well, I'll pick you up in my family's buggy tomorrow night after dinner," Laura said. "Don't forget your *Englisher* clothes to change into. See you then?"

Esther grinned, eager to get out on the town, disguised as an *Englisher*, and escape the Amish life for just a few hours. "See you then."

CHAPTER THREE

The next evening, Ella Ruth thumbed through racks of dresses at the local thrift store along with Laura and Esther. Their evening had taken an unexpected turn. Outside the movie theater, on their way inside, a handsome stranger had bumped into Esther and had given them three invitations to a formal gala happening at his friend's mansion the next week. Now they were searching for dresses and shoes for the event, also something that could be transformed into a matching mask. Fortunately, they all knew how to sew well enough to make any necessary alterations, and the thrift store was nearby. They made this detour before the movie, thrilled with this once-in-a-lifetime opportunity to be adventurous, disguised as *Englishers*.

"Who knew this would happen?" Laura said as she held up a shimmering blue dress. "We just thought we were going to the movies tonight, but we just got invited to the social event of the year."

Ella Ruth laughed. "I don't even know why I'm looking for a dress. My stepmother, for some reason, seems intent on making my life miserable. If she ever found out, she'd never let me go."

"Do you think she'd really tell your father about the laptop?" Esther asked.

"I think she would, yes, but for now, she is enjoying holding the secret as a means to keep me in line." A shiver snaked down Ella Ruth's spine at the thought.

"Why is she so cruel? I've heard rumors that she wasn't always Amish. People say things around town." Laura shrugged. "Maybe it's not true. I also heard that she was married before that to an abusive drunk *Englisher*. So, who knows? Have you ever asked her about her past?"

"We have, but she never wants to talk about it," Ella Ruth said. "She said something yesterday, making it sound like they'd been through hard times."

"Even still, it's no excuse to mistreat you. Oh!" Laura cried, grabbing a dress off the rack and holding it up. "This is the one for you, Ella Ruth. It would bring out the blue in your eyes. Go try it on, won't you?"

"That would look great on you," Esther agreed, nodding.

"Okay, I'll try it on," Ella Ruth agreed, taking it and heading toward the changing room. She tried it on and looked in the mirror, stunned by what she saw. She'd never worn anything so beautiful in her life after only wearing long, plain dresses for so long. The long, light blue chiffon material flowed around her legs and ankles, and with some altering, she could make it into the dress of her dreams. However, she felt uncomfortable wearing a strapless dress, so if she bought another dress, perhaps she could use the material to add straps and ruffles to this dress.

"Let us see it!" Laura cried outside the changing room.

Ella Ruth chuckled and opened the door to see her friends gaping at her.

"You look beautiful, Ella," Esther cried.

"It's amazing," Laura added.

"I need to add sleeves to it," Ella Ruth said, feeling half-dressed without any sleeves. "I think I could make it work."

"You definitely could," Laura agreed. Ella Ruth found another dress that was a close fabric match she could use for sleeves and a mask. They were each also able to find shoes to go with their gowns.

"Come on," Laura said, motioning to the others, "We've all found our dresses, so let's pay and get to the movie theater. We can still make the next showing."

That evening, after impromptu shopping and the movies, Laura dropped Esther and Ella Ruth off at home.

When she got home, Ella Ruth first went into the barn and hid her dress behind a loose board in one of the walls of the barn. No one would ever find it there, and at night she could sneak out to the loft to work on it.

After she hid the dress, she sneaked through the front door, knowing everyone would be in bed at this time.

Throughout that next week, she used whatever spare time she had to work on her dress. Whether it was early in the morning or late at night, she would go up to the loft and work on it by the light of the rising sun or the illumination of a battery-operated lamp.

Finally, the night of the gala came. After Ella Ruth pretended to go to bed, she prepared to leave. She pulled a box down from the top shelf in her closet, which had been hidden by other boxes. Inside was the charm bracelet her mother had given her before she died. Ella Ruth carefully put it on, deciding to wear it to the gala. She'd never worn it out before, only sometimes trying it on in her room, secretly wishing she could wear it.

Everyone in the house went to bed around eight-thirty as usual, and soon after that, Laura picked her up. Ella Ruth kept her gown concealed in an oversize bag and would change later. Just in case someone saw her, she didn't want to be caught in her formal dress. She crept down the stairs and hurried out into the night, breathing a sigh of relief when she realized she'd made it out of the house unnoticed.

She tossed her bag in the back. "I just have to be home by midnight or else."

"Or else what? You'll turn into a pumpkin?" Laura joked, laughing.

"No, silly. I'll be exhausted tomorrow. Who am I kidding? I'm going to be exhausted tomorrow, no matter what." Ella Ruth fell back against her seat, removing her prayer *kapp* and unpinning her long, blonde hair, which fell far past her waist.

"It will be worth it, though," Esther said. "Even though tomorrow is a Saturday, I still have to harvest wheat all day. We have to get it finished. Still, I don't care if I'm tired tomorrow. Tonight is going to be incredible. I know it."

Laura grinned at them. "We get to escape our lives and be someone else for just one night. Let's make the most of it."

Before reaching the mansion, Laura parked the buggy down the street where the horse would wait for them. They each went into the back of the buggy and changed into their dresses one at a time.

Laura changed into a sequin-covered pink dress, and Esther wore a dark green dress.

Ella Ruth changed into her light blue, ruffled chiffon dress with a full skirt. On the way there, she pinned her long blonde hair into the best updo she could manage without a mirror. When she emerged from the buggy, her friends' eyes went wide.

"Oh my!" Laura cried. "See? You do look like Cinderella."

Ella Ruth felt her cheeks heat at the compliment. "Oh, Laura."

"Really, you look beautiful, Ella Ruth," Esther said.

Ella Ruth pulled on her heels and had no idea how she would walk in them, let alone dance with them. They walked up the hill together and through the open gates. Even from down the hill, they could hear the loud music playing from the mansion.

"We've never danced before," Ella Ruth said. "What if we make fools out of ourselves?"

"Oh, just have fun and stop worrying. Come on!" Esther cried, hurrying toward the open doors where the music was booming louder. "Oh, wait. We have to put on our masks."

They each put on the masks they had made, which matched each of their dresses. Ella Ruth had made a light blue mask with sequins on it that matched her dress. She had tied a piece of string around it, which held it in place on her head. Once they each had theirs on, they stepped up to the door.

"Invitations?" the man at the door asked, and they handed him their invitations. "Please proceed," he said, motioning for them to go inside.

Ella Ruth gazed up at the tall pillars as they walked through the large door. Once they were inside, the pop music was so loud, it vibrated in her chest. They walked through a hall where several people were mingling, then stepped through another set of open doors to reveal the massive ballroom, which had been elegantly decorated with white and gold streamers. The room was filled with dancing guests. There was even a photographer taking people's photos—something not allowed in the Amish community. A tall cake stood on a table in one corner along with a long table covered in food, and ice sculptures decorated other corners of the room. Every young woman wore a colorful, beautiful dress, and each young man was dressed in a formal suit. Everyone laughed and smiled, so carefree. The formal party was the complete opposite of her plain life in the community, with its rigid rules on everything from clothing to music.

"Want to dance?"

Esther turned to see a young man holding his hand out to Ella Ruth, who blushed fiercely. Laura elbowed her.

"Oh, yes. Thank you." Ella Ruth gave her friends a nervous smile before taking the young man's hand and following him onto the dance floor.

CHAPTER FOUR

He was tall with dark, wavy hair and warm, brown eyes that made her stomach flip when he smiled at her.

What am I doing? Ella Ruth wondered as other people bumped into her as they danced. She had no idea how to dance. She studied everyone around her, trying to copy their movements, but she only felt awkward and clumsy as she swayed and stepped to the fast music.

"I'm sorry," she yelled over the music. "I'm a terrible dancer."

"So am I!" The young man began bopping to the music just as awkwardly as she was, making funny faces. Ella Ruth laughed out loud at his attempt to make her feel better. She knew her dancing was awful, but he was so much worse that she no longer cared what anyone else thought of her. All she could do was laugh at his silliness and be silly along with him.

A moment later, the song ended, then a slow song began to play. *Now what?* Ella Ruth wondered.

She stood there awkwardly, realizing that each couple held each other close, slowly swaying to the music. She gulped, ready to turn and run.

"Here, let me show you," the young man said, gently pulling her closer. He put her hands on his shoulders and slid his arms around her waist, holding her close to him. "Is this okay?" he asked into her ear, making her heart pound even harder.

She nodded, glancing up into his face. He smiled at her; his warm brown eyes searched hers. Somehow, she knew in her heart she could trust him, even though she didn't even know his name. How was that possible? She was usually so guarded, so cautious...

Ella Ruth let her hands slide up to clasp behind his neck, and she rested her head on his shoulder, closing her eyes as the music washed over her. As they danced, everyone else around them slowly faded away, and it felt like they were the only two people in the room, dancing alone.

When the song ended, she was abruptly pulled from her reverie as another fast pop song began to play.

"Want to go for a walk?" the young man asked loudly over the music.

Ella Ruth nodded. "Sure."

They walked out of the room into the hallway, where they could hear each other better.

"I'm James," the young man said, extending his hand.

Ella Ruth shook his hand. "I'm...nobody," she blurted.

"Nobody?" He chuckled. "You're not going to tell me your name?"

"No. I'm sorry. I can't." It wasn't like she was ever going to see him again.

"Why not?"

"It's complicated. I think it's better if you don't know my name. That's all," she said with finality.

"Well, it's nice to meet you," James gave a crooked smile.

Ella Ruth chuckled. "Nice to meet you, too."

They walked out a side door toward the gardens, where some people had gathered to talk away from the loud music. "You seem to know your way around here," Ella Ruth observed.

"This is my friend's house."

"Really?" Ella Ruth looked around in awe at the fountains, stone pathways, and rows of flowers, all lit by twinkling lights and moon-light.

"Oh, yes. Xavier is my best friend. We just went to Rome together."

"Rome?" Ella Ruth turned to him with wide eyes, then sighed. "I'd give anything to go there. How was it?"

"It was incredible!" James exclaimed. "The Colosseum was breath-taking. Just imagining all the history that was made there...it was glorious." He glanced at her. "Do you think you'll ever go?"

Ella Ruth laughed mirthlessly. There was no chance she'd ever make it anywhere across the ocean. In her community, they were not allowed to ride on airplanes, and she was terrified of traveling by boat. "No. I would love to go to Europe, though. Especially Germany, where there are beautiful castles. It would be a dream come true, but that's not going to happen for me. I'll never be able to go to Europe or anywhere overseas."

"Why not?"

"It's so expensive to travel, and my family needs me. I can't leave them now. Everything would fall apart." He would never understand, and she couldn't tell him the full story.

"Surely they could manage without you for a few weeks."

Ella Ruth shook her head. "No, I'm afraid they wouldn't. My mother died a few years ago, so I take care of all the household chores while my father and two of my sisters manage the family business. I work there part-time. I wish I could work there full time, but there is so much cooking and laundry and dishes to be done at home. Not to mention the gardening." Ella Ruth winced. Sure, *Englishers* gardened too, but that had been too much information.

"I'm sorry about your mother," James said. "My older brother died a few years ago."

"Really? I'm so sorry," Ella Ruth said, her heart going out to him. "I can't even imagine losing a sibling."

"He was going to take over the family business," James said. "Now it's being passed on to me, but I can tell that my father doesn't think I'll ever measure up to my brother."

They stopped to sit down on a marble bench in front of a fountain. Ella Ruth set her purse on her lap.

"I'm so sorry," Ella Ruth said, at a loss for words. Her father loved her and all of her siblings equally, so she couldn't relate to his pain at all. "That's incredibly unfair."

"To be honest, I'm not sure I want the business. My sister, Eliza, would be so much better at running the company, but my father is set on handing it down to me. I want to be a middle school English teacher, actually. I want to teach students how to write."

"That's a wonderful dream," Ella Ruth said.

"I have my degree. My parents thought if I went to college, I'd get it out of my system, I suppose, but I know it's what I want to do with my life. I just love writing, and I want to pass it on."

"You should. Have you considered applying for a job at one of the local schools?" she asked.

James sighed. "I'd have to quit working for my father, and I have to admit that I'm scared of disappointing him. I actually got accepted into a summer teaching internship in New York. It's coming right up."

"Congratulations on being accepted. That's quite an accomplishment. How many got in, and how many applied?" Ella Ruth asked curiously.

"Thank you," James said. "They accepted only a few dozen out of thousands of applicants. I have my degree already, but I wanted to do this to prepare myself even more for teaching."

"Teachers are some of the most important people in the world, I think. Maybe one day they will realize that being a teacher was the right path for you once they see how great you will be at it."

He looked down and smiled at her. "My mother is more open to the idea, but I don't think my father would ever witness me teaching."

"You never know. People can change their minds. I hope one day your father realizes how vital teachers are and that it's a wonderful career choice," Ella Ruth says.

"I doubt it. He wants me to be wealthy like him, but I don't care about money. I just want to do what I love. I want to help children learn to read and write, and I get excited about it."

"I feel the same way," Ella Ruth said. She would write books until the day she died, even if she never made a dollar from it, only because she loved it so much.

"My brother was my father's favorite. I'll never be like him." James sighed.

"How did he die, if you don't mind me asking?" Ella Ruth asked.

"I wrote a screenplay that had been used in a local play. On opening night, my brother wanted to go see the play with me even though the roads were icy. Even though there were snow tires on the car, when we hit black ice, the car skidded..." James shuddered at the memory. "We hit a tree, and it slammed into his side of the car. I still feel like it was my fault. I was driving. If he hadn't been sitting in the passenger seat, he might have survived."

"It's not your fault at all, James," she said.

James slowly shook his head. "My sister always told me it wasn't my fault, but I think my father will never forgive me for it. It was opening night, so he wanted to go with me, but we could have gone a different night when it wasn't snowing. It is my fault." James shook his head, blinking. "I'm sorry. I have no idea why I'm telling you all of this and being such a downer." He gestured to her wrist. "I like your bracelet. What do all the charms mean?"

Ella Ruth smiled. "This was my mother's bracelet. The shoe represents how she and her sister each had their own path to walk. The book was because she loved to read, like I do. There is a dog charm because my mother had a dog named Zeke as a child, and there is a horse charm because my horse's name is Pumpkin. My mother gave Pumpkin to me before she died."

"Wow, you have a horse?" James asked curiously.

She nodded. "My mother wanted me to take care of her. Pumpkin is like a member of the family."

"Pets are often like members of the family," James agreed. "What do the rest of the charms mean?"

Ella Ruth continued, "The apple charm is for when my mother would pick apples growing up. My mother always wanted to go on a hot-air balloon with her sister, so she added a hot-air balloon charm. She wanted to travel, so that is what the Eiffel Tower charm is for. But she never got the chance to go."

"I bet she would want *you* to travel," James said. "You should, you know, in memory of her."

"Even if I could get away, I could never afford it." Ella Ruth sighed as she touched each of the charms lovingly. "I've accepted that it's not in my future."

"I won't accept that." James shook his head. "One day, if you really want to travel, I think you'll do it. You seem like the kind of person who can do anything you set your mind to."

Ella Ruth grinned. "Thanks." Could it be possible? Would she travel to places like Paris or Rome one day as she'd always dreamed of? "My mother and her sister each had one of these bracelets. They were friendship bracelets."

"So, they were close," James said.

"They were, until..." Ella Ruth's voice trailed off. "My aunt left town one day, and they had a big argument. After that, they didn't speak for years." There was no way Ella Ruth could explain to him what really happened, how her mother was assaulted and gave birth to twin girls. Ella Ruth's mother convinced her sister Joanna to raise them for her, then missed her babies so much that she asked to have the babies back. Ella Ruth's mother and Joanna decided it would be best to each keep one baby, but they never spoke again after that. One twin was raised Amish, and one was raised *Englisher*. They were Leah and Charlotte, Ella Ruth's older sisters.

But she couldn't tell James any of that without giving away that she was Amish.

"It must have been a terrible argument for them never to speak again," James said.

"Yes, it was devastating. They've both passed away now, but yes. Once upon a time, they used to be close."

"It's not right when families are ripped apart like that," James said, shaking his head. "Anyway, tell me something about you. What do you like to do for fun?"

"I like to write," Ella Ruth told him.

"What do you write?"

"Science fiction and fantasy novels."

"Really?" James asked in surprise. "Wow."

"Well, I'm not published yet, but I've written several manuscripts. My last three are in a series. It's a young adult fantasy and science fiction series. I've tried to get an agent for four years, and I've had some interest, but no one has agreed to represent me yet."

"Oh, don't give up. It took my aunt ten years to get an agent, but now she has four books published. She said she's going to start self-publishing though because the publishers aren't paying as much as she expected. She has built up a following for herself on social media and email, so she wants to sell directly to her fans."

"I've actually been thinking about self-publishing. I don't know how, though. I have a lot to learn either way."

"That's incredible," James said. "Can I read some of your work? Do you have anything written in that notebook?"

Ella Ruth laughed nervously, realizing the corner of her notebook was sticking out of the purse on her lap. "Well, yes, but it's not done yet. I'm writing a short story in it, and I draw illustrations for my stories. Well, I have several short stories in it."

"Can I read one? Maybe my aunt could give you some advice on publishing. You should send her your book, and maybe she will give you some feedback."

"Wow, that would be great." Ella Ruth didn't have anyone to talk to about publishing in her life except for the local librarian, so she would take any help she could get. She found herself removing the notebook and handing it to him. "Remember, this is just a rough draft. I like to handwrite things in here and then type them into my laptop and edit them after."

"Easy, tiger." James laughed. "It's just me. Don't worry. I'm sure it'll be great." He flipped through some of the drawings. "Wow, these are beautiful!"

"Thank you." Ella Ruth smiled.

He started reading the story. After a few minutes, Ella Ruth continued to wait impatiently, tapping her foot on the ground.

"Well?" she asked, running her fingers over each charm on her bracelet and fiddling with the clasp.

"Sorry." James blinked. "I was completely sucked in. I forgot you were even sitting there. This is amazing. I read all the time, but this is the best thing I've read in a long time."

"Are you just saying that?" She looked at him quizzically, trying to figure out if he was lying.

"No. I'm being completely honest. You need to publish this." He held up the notebook and handed it back to her. "I think readers would love it. And you have three novels in a series?"

She nodded. "This short story goes along with that series."

"I'm going to tell my aunt about you," James said. "Maybe she can point you in the right direction."

"I'd appreciate that," Ella Ruth said.

"I love science fiction and fantasy, but I also love mysteries and thrillers, too," he said.

"Me too. Those are my favorite genres."

"So, how many siblings do you have? You mentioned your siblings earlier," James asked.

"I have five sisters, one brother, and two stepsisters," Ella Ruth said.

"Wow! That's a lot. That must have been fun growing up," James said, laughing.

"It really was. There was always someone to play with. Although, my stepsisters have only been with us for a year, since my father got remarried."

"Still, that's a big family. I always wished I had more siblings. My brother and I were close, so it was hard when he died. At least I still have my sister, but it might have been a bit easier if I had more brothers or sisters," James said.

"We are always there for each other, that's for sure."

They continued to talk for hours until Ella Ruth heard someone yelling her name.

"Ella! We have to go!" Laura called.

"Now?" Ella Ruth asked, filled with disappointment. She felt as though she had only been talking to James for a few minutes, but it had been hours. Still, she didn't want to leave now. She had so much more she wanted to talk to him about.

"It's almost midnight," Esther said. "Also, there are other reasons. It's a long story."

"I'm sorry," Ella Ruth said to James. "I have to go."

James grabbed her hand, but she forced herself to turn away and follow her two friends out of the mansion.

"Why did we have to leave in such a rush?" Ella Ruth demanded. "I was having the night of my life."

"Who was that man?" Laura asked. "He looked head over heels for you."

"He said his name was James, but he wouldn't tell me his last name. We danced and talked all night. He's a friend of Xavier Carnegie. He told me all his hopes and dreams, and I told him my hopes and dreams, but I left out that I'm Amish. He's incredible," Ella Ruth said with a sigh. "Who were you talking to, Esther?"

Esther told her about her night talking to Xavier. His family had hosted the ball. Esther had embarrassed herself by insulting him, not realizing that the man she was talking to was Xavier himself because he had given her a fake name when they'd met. While talking to Xavier, who she thought was someone else, she had said that she didn't think Xavier had done anything to earn taking over the family business since he spent all his time traveling. "He must think I'm so conceited. How can I ever face him again?"

"Well, you don't have to if you don't want to. Why would we ever run into him again?" Laura asked.

"It's a small town," Esther said.

"But he's always traveling. He's hardly ever around. We've never run into him before, have we?" Ella Ruth asked.

"If I did, somehow I never noticed," Laura said somberly as they walked down the hill.

"Wait!" a voice called behind them.

They turned to see Xavier running toward them, waving his hands.

"Let's just go," Esther said, starting to turn away.

"Why? Don't you like him?" Ella Ruth whispered.

"Oh, yes, I think you do," Laura added with a playful smile as Esther blushed.

"I just completely embarrassed myself in front of him," she argued.

"Just wait to hear what he has to say," Laura encouraged her.

Esther sighed as Xavier ran up to her. As they began talking, Laura told Esther they were going just beyond the gate, where the buggy was concealed by the cover of trees and darkness. After a few minutes passed, Laura stuck her head out from behind the gate.

"We have to go!" she called, and Esther ran down the hill, leaving Xavier behind with a puzzled look. His expression reminded Ella Ruth of how confused and stunned James had looked when she'd run away from him.

They ran around the corner toward where they had left the buggy, climbed in, and Laura began driving.

"Wow, that was the best night of my life!" she cried, rubbing her feet. "But those shoes were horrible. When am I ever going to wear high-heels like this again, anyway?"

Esther laughed out loud. "They really are uncomfortable. I don't know how *Englishers* wear these. I prefer my plain old black sneakers, thank you very much."

"I'm so glad we did this. Now we just have to sneak back inside our houses without getting caught," Ella Ruth said gravely.

Chapter Five

James ran after Ella Ruth as she hurried out of the mansion with her two friends, but suddenly an up-beat song started, and a crowd of people began moving toward the dance floor, blocking his way.

"Excuse me! Excuse me," he called out, but the music was so loud, he doubted anyone could even hear him. He pushed his way through the crowd of dancing guests and finally made it out of the ballroom, then ran toward the door. Once he was outside, he could just make out the form of a young woman running down the hill and then disappearing through the gate.

Ella was gone. He didn't even know her phone number or even her name. How would he ever find her? And because she was wearing a mask, he didn't even know what her face looked like!

"Did you see the girl I was talking to all night?" James asked Xavier, who was standing there, frozen, as he stared at the gate.

"She just went home with the woman I was talking to all night," Xavier told him. "They're friends."

"Really? Maybe you can help me find her. She didn't even tell me her name. I have no idea who she is." James' shoulders slumped. "She was the most amazing girl I've ever met."

"If Esther comes back, I can ask her for you."

"Thanks. I'd appreciate it." James sighed.

"So, you don't know her name or what she looks like? How do you think you're going to find her?" Xavier let out a small chuckle.

"This isn't funny," James muttered. "I need to find her. All I know is she has blonde hair and blue eyes, and she's an incredible writer."

"I'm sorry, James," Xavier said, clearly feeling guilty for joking about his friend's plight. "You're my best friend. I'll help you find her if Esther comes back for the week-long event. They're friends. Maybe she'll tell me her name and where she lives."

"I don't know. She seemed like she didn't say anything about her name or where she lives for personal reasons. She was so secretive." He stared at the ground, defeated and discouraged.

"I know they live around here. She was with Esther when I bumped into them in town outside the convenience store."

"What if they're just here on vacation?"

"No, Esther said she lives here. If they're friends, they must both be from here."

James sighed. "Maybe you're right. This is a small town. How hard could it be to find her?"

"Don't worry about it, man. We'll find her." Xavier clapped his friend on the back.

"Xavier!" a shrill voice called.

Xavier groaned and turned to see his mother hurrying toward him with his father.

"Who was that woman you were talking to all night?" Mrs. Carnegie asked, slightly out of breath.

"All I know is her name is Esther, and she works on a farm in town," Xavier said, shrugging. "She didn't say very much about who she is."

"A farm?" Mrs. Carnegie asked, eyebrows raised. Xavier didn't miss the look of disappointment on her face.

"Just like the woman I talked to," James added softly. "She didn't say much about herself either."

Who were they? Did they live here in Unity, or were they visiting from somewhere far away? His mind swirled with questions.

"Well, don't worry, son. We've invited plenty of the young women back, all from wealthy and successful families," Mr. Carnegie said, patting his son's shoulder. "You will have many women to choose from."

"I'm not interested in any of them. I'm only interested in Esther. I gave her an invitation to come back," Xavier said. "I sure hope she does."

"You did? But if she works on a farm, she's not from a high-class family," Mrs. Carnegie pronounced, fanning her face.

"So? I don't care about that," Xavier said.

James' heart went out to his friend. He hoped his parents would soon understand how Xavier felt about marrying someone he didn't love.

"See you later, Xavier," James said, bowing out of the conversation and returning to the mansion, not wanting to intrude on the family's conversation.

How would he find his mystery woman? Perhaps if he searched for her in town and asked if anyone knew a young woman with long, blonde hair, he might find her. Someone had to know her.

He wandered back to the garden to the bench where he had sat with Ella, where she had shown him her story and let him read it. He'd been completely captivated by her writing. She was truly talented. He could tell it wasn't easy for her to share her unfinished work with him, but she'd bravely done so.

James sat down on the bench and sighed, letting his head fall in his hands. He closed his eyes.

"Please, God, help me find her. I need to find her," he prayed out loud, then opened his eyes.

On the grass near his feet, something twinkled in the moonlight. He bent down to pick it up and felt cool metal in his hand. It was Ella's silver charm bracelet. It must have fallen off when she'd been nervously fiddling with it while he read her story.

"Thank you, God," he whispered. He could use this to find her. If he hosted another ball, maybe she would come, and if other women claimed to be her, he could just ask them to tell him what the charms on the bracelet were and what they meant.

Could it work? Would she show up? It had belonged to her deceased mother, so he knew she would probably like it back.

"Thank you so much for driving me," Ella Ruth said as she stepped down from the buggy, which they had stopped around the corner behind some trees so that no one would see or hear them approaching.

"Any time," Laura said.

"See you later," Esther said, and the buggy rumbled down the lane as Ella Ruth walked the distance to her house. She carefully opened the door, which they kept unlocked, and went inside. She took off her shoes by the door and tiptoed into the kitchen.

"Where were you?"

Ella Ruth held back a shriek, her hand covering her mouth as her heart leapt in her chest. "Oh, you scared me."

Priscilla sat at the kitchen table, tapping her fingernails on the wood surface. "I knew you were hiding something. What do you think you are doing? Why are you sneaking around late at night?"

Ella Ruth bit her lip, not wanting to get her friends in trouble.

"Tell me where you were, or I will tell your father about your secret laptop in the morning. He's already lost so much. Just think of how disappointed he would be if he knew," Priscilla said, slowly shaking her head and frowning. "What's in your bag?" She stood up, walked over, took it from Ella Ruth, opened it, and pulled out the hem of the sparkling gown.

"What is this? Tell me. Where were you tonight?" Priscilla demanded.

"I went to a gala," Ella Ruth said with a dejected sigh. She stared at the floor. "It was just down the road at the mansion on the hill. I wasn't there very long."

"How did you get there?"

"I went with my friends. I don't want them to get in trouble."

"Who went with you? Tell me, or I will tell your secret." Priscilla shoved the bag back into Ella Ruth's arms.

"Laura and Esther. Please don't tell anyone," Ella Ruth begged.

"Fine. I won't tell as long as you stop sneaking out," Priscilla said. "You are a young Amish lady. You should not be attending galas and wearing fancy ball gowns. I'm sure there was dancing there as well, which is also not allowed. What would your father say?"

Of course, Irvin would be disappointed in her. She already knew that, but she certainly wasn't the only young Amish woman who broke the rules.

"Did you drink?" Priscilla asked. "Was there alcohol there?"

"No." Ella Ruth adamantly shook her head. "I didn't drink. I wouldn't do that."

"So, you agree to stop this foolishness?"

Ella Ruth nodded.

Priscilla shook her head in disapproval. "Look at you, wearing jewelry and makeup. You better wash that off right away."

"I will." She was planning on it, anyway. Her hand went to the necklace around her neck, then her wrist, to feel her bracelet.

When she felt nothing, she looked at her wrist. Panic shot through her. The bracelet was gone.

"Where's my bracelet?" she cried softly, not wanting to wake anyone up as her stomach churned. "Where is my mother's bracelet?" She looked on the floor, her eyes trailing toward the door, but it was nowhere to be seen. Maybe it was in her bag. She emptied it out on the table, searching the pockets.

"Perhaps this is for the best," Priscilla said. "We aren't allowed to wear jewelry, anyway. I always wondered why your father allowed you to keep that thing."

"It was my mother's. Aunt Joanna gave it to her after she left the Amish. They each had one. They were friendship bracelets. Now that my mother and aunt have both passed on, that's all I have left to remember them by," Ella Ruth said as her heart clenched and her eyes filled with tears.

"It's just a worldly possession," Priscilla said, putting her hands on her hips. "We don't need things to help us remember people."

"I know, but it was important to me." Ella Ruth wiped away a tear. Perhaps it had fallen off in the buggy or in the driveway or on the porch. In the morning, she would go look, but there was nothing she could do now this late at night.

If it wasn't here or in the buggy, then maybe it had fallen off at the gala or in the garden when she had talked with James. If so, she knew there was no way she'd ever get it back.

It was most likely gone forever.

"Go to bed, Ella Ruth. We're both going to be exhausted tomorrow," Priscilla said, walking down the hallway. "And we have chores to do."

We? Ella Ruth wanted to scoff. *I'm the one who does all the chores.*

Ella Ruth wiped another tear from her eye as she walked up the stairs to her room.

Lord, please help me find my bracelet, she prayed. *But if I don't, then it is Your will. And I know it's not likely, but please let me see James again, even if it's only for a moment.*

Even though I know nothing can ever happen between us.

She changed into her nightgown and climbed into bed. As she tried to fall asleep, tears came to her eyes once more as she grieved the loss of her mother's bracelet.

Her mind wandered back to the day when Amanda had found the bracelet hidden in Ella Ruth's closet.

"Look what I found, *Mamm,*" Amanda said with a sneer as she flounced into the kitchen, where Ella Ruth had been washing dishes. She showed the bracelet to Priscilla, who had been sitting at the table.

When Ella Ruth turned around and saw her mother's bracelet in Amanda's hands, terror gripped her body. What was she going to do with it? Would her stepmother make her throw it away?

"Where did you get that?" Priscilla asked.

"In a box in Ella Ruth's closet," Amanda replied, glaring at Ella Ruth. "Why do you have jewelry? And why are you hiding it?"

"Good question," Priscilla said. "Does your father know about this?"

"Yes, he does," Ella Ruth said, drying her hands with a towel. "And he allows me to keep it. He knows my mother gave it to me before she died. I only have it to remember her by. I don't wear it, of course.

That's not allowed." She tried to keep her voice even to not give away the fact that she was trembling inside with fear.

"Exactly," Priscilla said. "Having this in your possession, even if it is stowed away in a closet, may tempt you to wear it. I think the bishop would agree with me."

"No, no," Ella Ruth said. "It's never been a temptation. I only keep it because it was my mother's."

"Well, we wouldn't want the bishop to know about this, would we?" Priscilla asked, earning another smirk from Amanda.

Ella Ruth ignored her look. "No, we wouldn't." What would the bishop do if he knew? The bishop was a very reasonable, kind man, but Ella Ruth wasn't sure what kind of trouble she would be in, and she didn't want to find out. Most of all, she didn't want to embarrass her father or hurt him in any way. He'd been through enough already.

"Then you will do as I ask," Priscilla said. "I think you should get rid of it."

"My mother gave it to me," Ella Ruth protested. "It's one of the few things I have left to remember her by."

"We don't need possessions to remember people by," Priscilla said.

"Well, yes, but it's important to me," Ella Ruth said. "My father knows I have it, and he has let me keep it."

"Go throw it away, Amanda," Priscilla ordered, pointing her finger toward the trash can. Amanda hesitated, seeing the distress on Ella Ruth's face.

"But—" Amanda began.

"Do it, Amanda," Priscilla said.

Amanda frowned and walked toward the trash can.

"But my father said I could keep it!" Ella Ruth cried.

"Yes, I did," Irvin said, stepping into the room. "I couldn't help but overhear. Priscilla, Ella Ruth's late mother gave that to her, and she will keep it. Why make her get rid of it when I already told her she could keep it? Yes, I know we are not allowed to wear jewelry, and we don't need possessions to remember people by, but after all we've been through, it would be cruel to take it from Ella Ruth. And you should not have threatened to tell the bishop when I already gave her permission, and I already spoke to the bishop about it two years ago. Amanda, please give it back to her." Irvin waved his hand, a calm expression on his face.

Priscilla was as white as freshly fallen snow.

"Please do not go behind my back again, Priscilla," Irvin said in a firm yet gentle tone. He waited until Amanda put the bracelet back into Ella Ruth's hand, then briefly touched Ella Ruth's shoulder. "It's all right, Ella Ruth. Go put it back in your closet."

Ella Ruth breathed a sigh of relief. "Thank you, *Daed*." For a moment, she felt as though she wasn't battling her stepmother alone anymore, but she knew she couldn't tell her father the truth about Priscilla—or else he would find out about her laptop and take it away.

He nodded, then she turned to walk to her room. She didn't miss how Priscilla's eyes had narrowed slightly at her before she had left.

CHAPTER SIX

James searched for the mysterious woman all over town. He went to local businesses and asked if anyone knew a young woman with long blonde hair, but no one did.

Meanwhile, one evening at dinner, he spoke with his parents about hosting a ball in their home. If he couldn't find the mystery woman by asking around, then maybe she would see a flyer and come to the ball and meet him there.

"What a wonderful idea, son!" his mother, Lois, cried. "Maybe you will find a special young woman?"

"I already have," James said and explained what had happened. "I need to find her, and I hope she will come to the ball."

"I agree. This is a good idea," Richard, his father, said. "You will be taking over the company soon, and it would be good if you had someone to help you. Xavier's parents won't even let him inherit the company until he gets married."

Eliza, his younger sister who was twenty-one, scoffed. "I say that's absurd." She took a sip of coffee. "It's antiquated."

"They want him to prove he is responsible," Richard said. "All he seems to care about is traveling." James' father turned to him. "Just like all you seem to care about is your writing. Please tell me you've given up on that silly dream of yours. You can't be an English teacher while also running the company, James."

"Being an English teacher is not a silly dream," James said, setting his glass down on the table with more force than necessary.

And I'm not so sure I want to run the company, he thought but didn't dare to voice his feelings out loud. It wasn't the right time yet. He knew his younger sister would be so much better at running the company than he would, and she wanted the job more than anything, but their father insisted that James should take over because he was the oldest.

Or, at least, he was the oldest child who was still alive. His older brother would have taken over the company, but he had passed away.

"You need to get your priorities straight," Richard grumbled, taking a bite of steak. "Nicolas would have his priorities straight," he muttered so quietly that James almost didn't hear him, but his father's words cut straight to his heart.

"That's why this ball is such a good idea," Lois interjected, giving her husband a warning look. "This ball could help you find the woman you will marry someday."

Richard noticed the look on his wife's face and nodded, understanding what she was trying to say. If James got married, he might be more likely to want to take over the company. "Very well. We shall host this ball, and hopefully you will find your mystery woman. Do you know much about her?"

"I don't know her name, but she has long blonde hair, blue eyes, and is very sweet and caring. She's a writer. A wonderful writer," James said, sighing as he remembered the night they shared talking under the stars.

"Aw," Eliza grinned. "That's so romantic. You both love writing. No wonder you had such a connection."

"She let me read one of her short stories in her notebook, and it was incredible. I wish you could have read it. I know you'd agree with me. She deserves to be published, Eliza. I just have to find her. She was the most interesting, captivating woman I've ever met." The mystery woman's mask-covered face flashed in his mind.

"Wow." Eliza raised her eyebrows. "I've never heard you talk about any woman like that before. You must really like her."

"Yes, I do. I must find her."

"Then we will need to spread the word of the ball all across town," Lois said. "We will post it on social media and post flyers on the streets."

"That's the thing," James said. "I'm not sure if she lives here in town, but she does have friends here."

"Well, maybe they will hear about it and let her know," Eliza offered.

"I hope so," James muttered, pushing his scalloped potatoes around on his plate. "We will have to get as many people to share it on social media as possible."

"I'll help you with the planning and getting the word out." Eliza grinned.

"So will I," his mother offered.

"Thank you," James said gratefully. "I need all the help I can get."

Little did he know that Ella Ruth wouldn't be seeing the announcements on social media.

After dinner, Eliza approached him in the hall.

Eliza smacked his arm playfully. "That was pathetic. You need to talk to him. Tell him I want to run the company, then you can be free to become a middle school English teacher. You already have your degree in English. Why not use it?"

His parents had encouraged him to go to college and get a degree in business, but he had disappointed them when he decided to switch majors.

"You know it's not easy to talk to him. His eyes are so intense. It's like they're seeing right into my soul," James said, shuttering.

"Clearly, he's not seeing into your soul, or else he would realize how much you want to be a teacher," Eliza said.

"He's always disapproved of me, no matter how hard I try to impress him," James said, shaking his head. "It wasn't like that with Nicolas. Dad was always proud of him, even when he made mistakes."

"That's because Nicolas did everything Dad wanted. Nicolas wanted to run the company and won Dad's favor."

"Thanks a lot." James sighed. "I think Dad blames me for his death."

"What? Are you serious?" She stared at him with wide eyes.

"Yes," James said. "I was driving us to see my play, after all." James had written a screenplay that had been used in a local play.

"It's not your fault at all, James. The roads were icy. You couldn't have done anything differently." Eliza patted his arm gently with a soft look in her eyes, opposite of how she had smacked him moments ago.

James briefly squeezed his eyes shut, blocking out the memories. He could still feel the wheel jerking uncontrollably in his hands.

"We could have decided not to go see the play that night," James said with a sigh.

"Nicolas wanted to support you. He was so proud of you. You couldn't have talked him out of going," Eliza said. "So, there's nothing you could have done."

"I wish I wouldn't have written that play, then."

"How can you say that?" Eliza demanded. "Writing is a part of you. Nicolas would be devastated if he were here to hear you say that. The play was a huge success." She shook her head. "You have to believe everything happens for a reason and that this was God's plan. Otherwise, you'll drive yourself crazy."

"I do believe that," James argued, furrowing his eyebrows. "But I still feel guilty. When Dad gives me that look with disappointment in his eyes, I can't help but feel ashamed."

Eliza sighed. "If Dad really thinks it was your fault, that's on him. It's not right. Hopefully, God will show him that one day. Still, we need to talk to him about the company. How do you want to tell him?"

James frowned. "I don't want to, but I know we have to. I'm just afraid he'll never agree to it. He's always believed the oldest should run it."

"I think we can change his mind," Eliza said. "Maybe I can change his mind. But I need your help."

"I'm not ready," James said, shaking his head.

"You're scared," Eliza taunted.

"Yes. Yes, I am. You know how he is."

"When will you be ready?"

"I don't know," James said, walking out the door toward the garden as she followed him outside.

"When you are, please let me know."

***

Ella Ruth walked across the yard in the warm summer air, taking in the sunshine as she approached the garden with her sisters Lilly and Katie. She smiled at the sight of the enormous pumpkin that she was growing for the contest at the Common Grounds Fair, which took place in Unity at the end of every summer. She'd been growing and caring for this pumpkin for months as if it were her own baby.

"You'll definitely win this year, Ella Ruth," Lilly said.

"*Ja*," Katie agreed. "It looks like it weighs a thousand pounds!"

"I'm not sure it's that heavy," Ella Ruth chuckled. "But thank you."

"But Fanny Montgomery's was eleven hundred pounds last year, and yours looks even bigger than that!" Katie insisted.

"Really? You think so?"

Katie and Lilly nodded.

"Fanny wins every year," Ella Ruth said with a sigh.

"Not this year. You'll definitely win!" Katie cried.

Ella Ruth smiled at the thought. The grand prize was a thousand dollars for the heaviest pumpkin, and she would love to use the money to buy a new laptop. The one she had now was used and terribly slow with a very short battery life, which made writing without outlets in her home even more difficult. She had to charge it at the coffee shop down the street, but she couldn't write there in case anyone saw her, so she had to take it home to write in secret, but the battery only lasted a few hours. If she had a newer one, she could write so much more.

Fanny Montgomery, a sweet elderly *Englisher* farmer down the road, had won for the past three years, but Ella Ruth was determined to win this year. By the looks of it, she just might.

"It's so big that you could make a carriage out of it like in the story Cinderella," Lilly said with a giggle. "You could just hollow it out and add wheels. After the contest, of course."

Ella Ruth laughed at the idea. "What a silly story," she muttered, shaking her head. "And so unrealistic."

"I like the story," Katie said with a sigh. "It reminds us there is such a thing as happily ever afters."

"Of course, there are," Ella Ruth said. "But there aren't any fairy godmothers in this world. It's all up to us. We have to make things happen."

"I suppose you're right." Lilly stepped around some of the other pumpkins and patted Ella Ruth's massive one. "I think we should name it."

"Name it?" Ella Ruth smiled. "Okay. Any ideas?"

"How about Gertrude?" Katie offered, and Lilly laughed.

"I love it," Ella Ruth said. "Gertrude the pumpkin."

"It suits her." Lilly smiled. "I can't wait for the fair. I look forward to it every year."

"Me too," Ella Ruth said. "It'll be here before we know it."

"And the best part is that Priscilla and Amanda leave us alone to do what we want while they go off on their own," Katie said in a low voice. Lilly nodded in agreement.

"I still think that it's not fair that they made you give up your room," Lilly said. "It's a bit crowded with all three of us in that small room upstairs. It's not fair."

"*Daed* said it was the right thing to do, and he's right," Ella Ruth said somberly. "We shouldn't complain. They've been through a lot."

"Have they really? They never talk about it," Katie added. "Whenever we ask them about their past, they clam up."

"That might mean they don't want to talk about it because it's too painful," Ella Ruth said. "Remember right after you were rescued from the traffickers? You didn't want to talk about it either."

"It brought up terrible memories," Katie said, staring off into the distance. A shiver came over her, and she wrapped her arms around herself as Lilly came over to her and hugged her.

"It still does," Lilly added softly. "And it always will."

Ella Ruth's heart clenched at the mere thought of what her sisters had endured during their time in captivity. "I think Priscilla is so bitter because she faced hardships, too. We lost our mother, so we should be more understanding. I know it's hard because she is so cold, but we should try harder. We just don't know what really happened to them."

"All we know is that Priscilla's husband died," Katie said.

"And they weren't always Amish," Ella Ruth added. "I wonder what Sadie and Amanda's stepfather was like. Was he loving like our father, or was he cruel?"

Lilly shrugged. "Maybe we will never know what happened to them."

"I know I am guiltiest of this, but we should make more of an effort to be more compassionate toward them," Ella Ruth said, kicking a pebble under her foot.

"Sadie is nice. It's just too bad that she doesn't defend you when Priscilla and Amanda are mean to you," Katie said.

"Maybe she's scared of what her mother will say. Still, we should be kind to all three of them. *Daed* would want it, and God commands it." Even as she said the words, she felt like an absolute hypocrite. Ever since they had moved in and asked her to give up her room, she'd felt bitter toward them, but she couldn't help it.

Or could she? If she asked God for help and tried harder, could she be kinder to them?

If she was honest with herself, did she even want to?

Her mind wandered back to when Priscilla, Amanda, and Sadie had moved in after the wedding.

Amanda had walked into the house like she owned the place, looking around with a wrinkled nose. "So, where's my room?"

"You and Sadie can have a room upstairs," Irvin said. "Ella Ruth, will you show them?"

There were three bedrooms upstairs. The youngest children, Debra and Seth, shared the smallest room.

Before Ella Ruth had shared a room with her older sisters, Charlotte and Leah, but they had both moved out after getting married. Since three of them had shared it, it was by far the largest.

Katie and Lilly had always shared a room, which was smaller, though Ella Ruth found herself spending the night in their room with them on most nights because of the nightmares of their kidnapping that plagued them. She offered for them to move into her larger room, and they gladly accepted. Now when they cried at night, Ella Ruth was there in an instant, climbing into the large bed they had shared since childhood, hugging them and comforting them. She'd sing them lullabies late into the night like she had when they were children afraid of the dark.

So, now the three of them shared the largest room.

"This is your room," Ella Ruth told Amanda and Sadie, gesturing to the medium-sized room.

Amanda wrinkled her nose. "Oh, this won't do."

Ella Ruth raised her eyebrows. "Why not?"

"Can't we have your larger room?" she asked, pointing to the largest room.

"I share that room with Katie and Lilly," she said. "There are three of us in there. That's why it's the largest."

"Why do the three of you share a room?" Sadie asked.

Ella Ruth hesitated, not sure if Katie and Lilly would want them to know about their nightmares yet. But if they did, perhaps they might want to tell their new stepsisters themselves. "We just like to be together."

"Well, can't we switch rooms?" Amanda asked, giving her a mournful look that reminded Ella Ruth of a begging puppy.

Irvin and Priscilla came up the stairs, holding bags, followed by Katie and Lilly.

"Are you settling in?" Irvin asked.

"We would like the larger room," Amanda said as Sadie shook her head briefly.

"I don't need the larger room," she said softly.

"But *Daed*, in our old house, the bedroom we shared was so tiny, and we would love to have such a large bedroom," Amanda insisted, clasping her hands together in front of her chest.

"That's fine, Amanda." Irvin smiled and looked at Ella Ruth. "Ella Ruth, Katie, and Lilly, I want you to move into the medium-sized room together."

"All three of us in there?" Lilly protested. "That will be crowded, won't it?"

"Oh, we would appreciate it so much," Amanda said with a wide grin. "Wouldn't we, Sadie?"

Sadie turned pink, looking as if she wanted to crawl under one of the beds to hide. "I still don't need the largest room. The smaller room is fine."

"Nonsense," Amanda said, waving her hand. "We would love the large room. She's just being shy. But only if you're sure."

"Of course," Ella Ruth said, noticing the frowns on Katie's and Lilly's faces. They would just have to make do in the smaller room.

After moving their things over, Irvin approached them, putting a hand on their shoulders.

"Thank you, girls. I know you didn't want to give up your big bedroom, but it was the right thing to do," Irvin said. "I don't think they had a nice house before like we do, so I'm sure it means a lot to them."

"Really?" Ella Ruth asked. "Where did they live? I thought they were from Smyrna." Smyrna was Unity's sister community in northern Maine.

"Priscilla is originally, but she didn't always live there. They weren't always Amish."

"Really?" Lilly asked.

"Yes, but all that matters is that they're here now. They've been through hard times, but they don't like to talk about it. So, I am glad you girls were so generous. We should be thankful for the large home we have. There are many less fortunate than we are," Irvin said.

The three sisters nodded, but a small seed of resentment toward Amanda had been planted in Ella Ruth's heart that day no matter how much she wanted to ignore and deny it. When Priscilla threatened to tell the bishop about her bracelet, that's when the seed of resentment toward her stepmother had been planted. Sadie had done nothing mean to Ella Ruth and her siblings, but she didn't take their side, either. She seemed to just reluctantly go along with whatever Amanda and Priscilla wanted.

Ella Ruth hoped that one day Sadie would find her own path, but most of all, Ella Ruth wanted to love Amanda and Priscilla more, no matter how hard it was. Maybe with God's help, one day she would.

CHAPTER SEVEN

Suddenly, Ella Ruth was jolted back to the present as Debra and Seth ran out of the house, laughing and yelling as they played a game of tag. They scampered over to the garden, where Ella Ruth stood with Katie and Lilly.

"Watch out for the vegetables!" Ella Ruth cried, laughing as her younger brother and sister scampered around the edge of the garden.

"Lift me up!" Seth hollered. "I want to sit on the giant pumpkin."

"Okay," Ella Ruth said. "I'll lift you up, but you better be careful."

"I will."

She hoisted her brother up. "Wow. You're heavy. What have you been eating? Bricks?"

He giggled as he plopped down on top of the pumpkin. "Look at me!" he yelled, raising his hands.

"I want a turn!" Debra said, jumping up and down.

As they all laughed at Seth, who was making funny faces, Ella Ruth didn't notice Sadie walk out of the house and approach them.

"He's so funny," Sadie said softly.

"Yes, he is," Ella Ruth agreed.

"I always wanted a brother when I was younger. Well, I wanted more siblings in general. You're so blessed to have all your siblings."

Ella Ruth gave a small smile. "I'm very thankful. When our mother died, we helped each other get through it. I don't know what I would have done without them. I'm sorry about your father. It must have been hard."

A thoughtful look came over Sadie's face. She was about to say something, then hesitated. "Not in the ways you might think."

Ella Ruth wanted to ask her what she meant, but Debra tugged on her arm, saying, "My turn! My turn!"

After Ella Ruth lifted her little sister up onto the pumpkin and turned around to ask her stepsister what she meant, Sadie had already walked back toward the house.

***

The next morning, Ella Ruth knelt in front of the fireplace, cleaning out the ashes.

"We want to go into town and run some errands. Can you take us, Ella Ruth?" Amanda asked behind her. "*Daed* told me to ask you to drive us in the buggy. We don't know our way around yet very well."

Ella Ruth backed away from the fireplace and turned around to face Amanda, who laughed at the sight of her.

"You're covered in ashes," Amanda said, covering her mouth. "You look ridiculous."

Sadie, who stood behind Amanda, whispered, "That's not very nice, Amanda."

"Well, someone has to clean the fireplace," Ella Ruth muttered. "But yes, I can take you. I wanted to run some errands in town as well."

"You better go get cleaned up first. Otherwise, we'd be the laughingstock of the town," Amanda crooned, and Sadie shook her head at her sister.

"I'll get cleaned up as soon as I finish this chore. I wouldn't want to go out like this," Ella Ruth said, now sweeping up the last of the ashes and dusting off her skirt. A few minutes later, she returned and walked to the bathroom to wash her face and hands. She'd need a clean dress, too.

"We'll come along too," Katie said, gesturing to Lilly. Debra and Seth were playing with their friends at the neighbor's house.

After she changed and hitched up the horse, Ella Ruth drove everyone in the buggy down the driveway and then down the dirt lane that led to the main road.

"Thank you for driving us, Ella Ruth," Sadie said from the back. "I'm afraid we might get lost if we drove on our own."

"Exactly," Amanda said. "It's not like we have a GPS like the *Englishers*."

Ella Ruth chuckled. "I'm happy to drive you. I wanted to go to the bookstore, anyway."

"Oh?" Sadie asked. "What do you like to read?"

"I like mysteries," Ella Ruth said. "Clean ones with nothing inappropriate, of course. It's not forbidden."

"I like reading, too," Sadie said. "I like clean romance."

Amanda rolled her eyes. "She's a hopeless romantic. It's not like real life at all."

"That's the point," Sadie said. "Reading is about escaping real life, even for a moment."

Surprised, Ella Ruth raised her eyebrows. "Well, maybe you'd like some of my books. Feel free to borrow them anytime. Both of you."

"Thank you," Sadie replied. "I'd love that."

"Thanks," Amanda added.

They arrived at the bookstore, and Ella Ruth parked the buggy in front of it. They all climbed out and walked into the store, and Ella Ruth smiled at the scent of the thousands of pages that held hundreds of stories calling out to her.

"Hello, Ella Ruth," Debbie, the owner, called out. She pushed her wire-rimmed glasses higher up on her nose. "Looking for a new mystery? How was the last one?"

"It was wonderful, but I read it in only a few days, so I need a new one," Ella Ruth said.

"We have some new arrivals, and I added more to the clearance shelf," Debbie said, waving her hand with a smile. "Have fun."

Ella Ruth immediately walked to the mystery section to look. She liked going to the library as well, but she bought books so that she could read them over and over again any time she wanted.

As she ran her finger over the spines, she heard the bell on the door chime.

"Hello, do you have any new mysteries?" a deep voice asked.

She'd heard that voice before. Was that him? No, it couldn't be. Could it? Ella Ruth peered over the edges of the books on the shelf to see a young man with dark, wavy hair talking to Debbie.

"Oh, yes. I just got some new arrivals. It's the last shelf on the right. Would you like me to show you?"

"No, that's okay. I see it. Thank you," he said, then turned around and started walking toward Ella Ruth.

It was him. It was James! She turned to walk the other way, but another customer was blocking her escape, so she was stuck. James rounded the corner.

"Hello," he said politely with a nod and a smile.

"Hello," she squeaked out, busying herself with looking at the books so that she didn't have to make eye contact. She only nodded in his direction.

She wanted to tell him who she was more than anything, but her stepmother would then reveal her secret. Besides, if she did tell him, he would want to pursue a relationship with her, which could never happen.

She couldn't even think about leaving her siblings behind with her stepmother. If Ella Ruth was gone, would Priscilla make them miserable instead?

"You like mysteries as well?"

She nodded. "They're my favorite."

"I always like to try to figure out who the culprit is before the end," he said. "But I'm usually wrong."

"I've figured it out a few times, but it takes a skilled writer to keep readers guessing until the end. Unless, of course, the culprit is someone who wasn't mentioned in the story until the end. But I think that's a bit unfair for the author to write it that way."

"Well, what if they were mentioned a few times intentionally but the reader missed it or forgot until the end?" James argued.

"Then that's on the reader for not paying close enough attention," Ella Ruth said. "It's hardly ever the person I most suspect or the person I least suspect."

"I find that it's usually the person who is right in the middle of my suspicions, if that makes any sense at all." James chuckled.

Ella Ruth couldn't help but turn to face him, and she was struck by how handsome he was, even though every moment they had spent together at the gala would be etched in her memory forever. "No, I know exactly what you mean, and I agree with you."

"So, do you recommend any of these? I haven't been here before."

"You haven't? Oh, you've been missing out."

"I've been meaning to, but I've been busy lately. Well, I'm here now, and I need some distraction."

"Why is that?" Ella Ruth asked, her stomach turning into one large knot. Could it be what she thought?

"I met a young woman, and I can't get her out of my head. I also can't find her because I have no way to contact her. I've been looking all over town," he said with a dejected sigh.

"I'm sorry to hear that," she managed to choke out, attempting to swallow the lump of cotton in her throat. He was thinking about her? Looking for *her*? Her heart pounded in her ears so loudly that she struggled to hear him.

"Thanks. Well, I'm hosting a ball in my home on Pembrooke Lane next Saturday evening, and I am hoping she will come. I'm inviting all the young women in town. You're welcome to come." He hesitated, taking in her prayer *kapp* and long, brown dress. "I'm sorry. Is that against your customs?"

"There are many things that are against our rules, but that doesn't mean that the rules aren't broken sometimes," she said softly, thinking of the laptop she kept hidden and her lost bracelet. "Don't tell anyone I said that."

"Your secret is safe with me," he replied, hand over his heart. "What kind of rules do you break, if you don't mind me asking?"

"I write stories on a laptop," she blurted out in a whisper, then clamped a hand over her mouth. Why had she told him that? Would it give her away?

"How scandalous," he said with a chuckle, then he frowned. "I'm sorry that's not allowed. I also love to write, and I'm not sure what I'd do without my laptop. Maybe I'd get a typewriter."

"A typewriter? That's a novel idea."

He laughed out loud. "Nice pun."

"Oh, come on. That was corny." She waved her hand, a blush creeping over her face. Did he actually find her funny?

"I like corny." He grinned at her, then gestured to the books. "So, have you read any of these?"

"Oh, yes. I read this one last week. It will definitely keep you guessing until the very end." She pointed to a paperback titled *Come Find Me,* then pointed to another titled *The Disappearance at Huckleberry Hill.* "But this one was excellent, too. It kept me up reading late into the night until I finished it."

"That can be a good thing and a bad thing, can't it?" he asked with a twinkle in his eye. "That means a book is written extremely well, but it's not so fun to lose sleep."

"But it's worth it to be tired the next day if the story is good, isn't it?" she asked, chuckling.

He paused as his eyes searched hers, then he furrowed his brows and tilted his head. "Have we met before? You seem familiar."

"No," she said quickly, grabbing a book off the shelf and flipping through the pages. "Do you know other young Amish women in town? Maybe you have me mixed up with someone else. We all dress the same, after all."

He smiled at her joke. "No, unfortunately, I don't know any other Amish women well, or any of them, for that matter. I've talked briefly with the Amish in stores and on the street, but I wish I knew them better. Still, even if you all dress similarly, I think I'd remember you. You're different. In a good way."

Her heart fluttered at the way he was looking at her so intently, and she couldn't help but notice how long and dark his eyelashes were.

Realizing how close she was to him, she took a step back. "Well, if that's true, then I think you would remember if you met me before."

He was about to ask her something else when Amanda came barreling around the corner. "Oh, hello," she said flirtatiously, batting her eyelashes.

CHAPTER EIGHT

Ella Ruth rolled her eyes. Could Amanda be any more obvious?

"Who is your friend, Ella Ruth?" Amanda asked.

"I'm James Baldwin," James said, extending his hand to each of them. Amanda shook his hand first, then Ella Ruth. "Sorry. I should have introduced myself earlier," he said to Ella Ruth.

"James Baldwin? As in Baldwin Auto Sales?" Amanda asked curiously. His family-owned multiple local car dealerships in the next town over and across New England.

"Uh, yes. That's my parents' company," James said modestly.

"It will be yours one day, won't it? At least, that's what I've heard," Amanda said, clearly not noticing when James hesitated. He was about to say something when she cut him off. "I'm Amanda, and this is my stepsister, Ella Ruth."

"Nice to meet you both," James said. "The woman from the gala I'm looking for also had blonde hair like you both do." Even though they wore prayer *kapps,* a few inches of their hair was still visible in the front. "Do you know any other young women with long blonde hair?"

"It couldn't be Ella Ruth." Amanda laughed and waved her hand. "She would never sneak out of the house to go to a gala. She's too devout."

Amanda shot Ella Ruth a warning look, and Ella Ruth froze. By now, Sadie, Katie, and Lilly had come around the corner to see what the commotion was all about.

"Well, I'm hosting a ball in my home next Saturday on Pembrooke Lane, as I was telling Ella Ruth." He glanced at Ella Ruth, and she noticed how he looked a bit puzzled. "You're all welcome to come. I'm inviting all the young women in town. The theme is classic literature like Shakespeare, fairytales, Jane Austen..."

"Sounds divine," Ella Ruth murmured, earning a warning look from Amanda.

"Yes, it sounds wonderful," Amanda interjected.

"Do any of you know a young woman with long, blonde hair who is also a wonderful writer? She left behind a charm bracelet, and I want to find her so I can give it back to her and get to know her. Everyone was wearing masks, so I never saw her face, and I don't know her last name."

Katie's and Lilly's eyes went wide, and Sadie gave Amanda a questioning glance.

Lilly raised her hand as if she were in a classroom. "Oh, she's—"

"We don't know her," Amanda interrupted a bit too loudly. "But thank you for your invitation to the ball, James. We are all quite devout, so I don't think we will be able to come."

"I understand. Well, if you change your mind, you are welcome to come," James said, selecting the two books that Ella Ruth had recommended and pulling them off the shelf. "I'm going to go pay for these. Have a nice day."

He looked at Ella Ruth once more with something in his eyes that she couldn't place. Was it confusion? Longing?

Did he suspect that she was the one he had spoken with at the gala?

James paid for his books, and as soon as he walked out of the store, Amanda whirled around to face her. "My mother told me you went to the gala, but you never told us that you met James Baldwin. You're the one he was talking about, aren't you? He's looking all over town for you. You like to write, and you lost your charm bracelet. It's you. Don't deny it."

"Okay, yes, he's looking for me. So what?" Ella Ruth shot back. "It doesn't matter. He's an *Englisher,* and I'm Amish, and I'm not going to leave my family for some man I barely know."

Even if we did have a connection, she added inwardly.

"Do you know how wealthy his family is?" Amanda asked.

Ella Ruth shrugged. "So?"

"So? So, any girl in town would gladly trade places with you right now," Amanda said with her hands on her hips. "I'm going to the ball, and I'm going to take your place."

"What? Why?" Ella Ruth demanded, her stomach sinking. Yes, maybe she could never actually date James Baldwin or even reveal who she was to him, but the thought of Amanda pretending to be her made her feel sick to her stomach.

"Because I want to marry into wealth and get out of here," Amanda said. "I'm not meant for the simple Amish life. I want to be rich with mansions and nice things, and the only way I can get that is if I marry someone rich. He's my ticket out of here."

"What about your mother? What would she think? Wouldn't she be devastated if you left the church?" Ella Ruth asked.

"My mother wants more for me as well. She would support my decision," Amanda said. "I'm sure she'd miss me, but she would be happy if I married into wealth."

Ella Ruth blinked in surprise.

"And you three better not tell anyone, or else everyone will know Ella Ruth uses a laptop to write," Amanda whispered harshly to Sadie, Lilly, and Katie.

"That's unfair," Katie said, crossing her arms.

"Life is unfair," Amanda said, huffing and turning around. "Let's go. I need to find a dress."

"I'm so sorry," Sadie said, frowning. "My sister is completely unreasonable sometimes."

"Sometimes?" Lilly scoffed.

"Most of the time," Sadie corrected herself. "I don't want you to get in trouble."

"Thanks," Ella Ruth said. "I'm sorry she wants to leave the church."

Sadie shrugged. "I always knew it would happen. I've gotten used to the idea."

"What do you have there?" Ella Ruth asked, gesturing to the large book Sadie held.

"It's about fashion design." She smiled sheepishly.

"Are you thinking about leaving to become a fashion designer?" Katie asked, wide-eyed.

"Well...yes. I'm also not so sure I want to stay Amish forever, but I don't want to leave my mother if Amanda does. So, I'm not so sure. Either way, I love to learn about fashion design," Sadie said, hugging the book.

"Well, let's go pay before Amanda has a fit," Lilly said, causing them all to chuckle.

James walked down the street after leaving the bookstore, puzzled. Why did he feel like he had met Ella Ruth before? Surely, he would remember a woman like that. He could see that she had blonde hair because her white prayer *kapp* didn't hide all of it, and she did have blue eyes, but so did many other young women he knew. She did say she liked to write. But she was Amish, so she couldn't be the one from the gala, could she? Amanda also had blonde hair, but she didn't seem familiar to him.

Would an Amish woman really sneak off to go to a gala dressed in an *Englisher* gown? James wished he knew more Amish folks better so he could ask them and find out more, but he supposed it was a touchy subject. Besides, would any of them reveal if they knew someone who had broken the rules in that way?

"I guess the only way to find out is to see if she comes to the ball," he muttered to himself as he walked to the nearest coffee shop to read one of his new books and get lost in the story.

After they arrived home, Amanda pulled her mother aside in her bedroom.

"You won't believe what I discovered today," she said, then told her mother all about what she had found out at the bookstore. "So, what do you think?"

"I think you should go," Priscilla said, taking Amanda's hands. "Ella Ruth had a gown that she wore to the gala. She must have hidden it somewhere. We can get her to give it to you so you can wear it. You both have long hair, so with that dress, you'll look enough like her since everyone was wearing masks."

"It just might work," Amanda said, clapping her hands.

A serious look crossed Priscilla's face. "This has to work. You re-member when we lived in poverty? We lived in that shack with a leaky roof, and we barely had any food to eat. It was horrible, wasn't it?"

Amanda nodded slowly.

"I regret it more than anything, but there's nothing we can do about that now. All we can do is improve our future. Your future. If you have the opportunity to make something of yourself and marry into wealth, then you should take it, my dear. I want your life to be far better than mine. I haven't been able to give you the things I have wanted to. I know you have been thinking of leaving the church anyway, but it's expensive to live on your own. Maybe this is your ticket out of here," Priscilla said.

"That's exactly what I was thinking. But won't you miss me?" Amanda cried.

"Of course, I will. But I can go visit you, or you can visit me. You haven't been baptized into the church, so you wouldn't be shunned if you left."

"What about Sadie?"

"She could go with you or stay here with me," Priscilla said.

"What if you both come with me?"

"I married Irvin, so I will honor my vow to him. He's a good man. But that doesn't mean you can't go live the life you've always dreamed of. I want so much for you and Sadie." Priscilla lovingly touched Amanda's cheek.

"Maybe we're getting ahead of ourselves. What if James doesn't fall in love with me?"

"You said he was head over heels for Ella Ruth, right? So, all we have to do is make him believe you are her, the woman he got to know at the gala. He was only with her for a few hours. I think you could easily convince him that she was you."

"He mentioned Ella Ruth left behind her charm bracelet, and I already know all the charms. I'm just not sure what they mean."

"Well, then, you'll have to ask Ella."

"And what about her stories? He said she was a good writer. Does that mean he read her stories?"

"Maybe. You'll have to find her laptop and read them in case he asks you about it. Remember, you have to be just like her. You need to know everything about her writing and her bracelet," Priscilla said.

"I have to read everything she's written? I once heard her say that she's written three novels. That will take forever to read." Amanda groaned.

"Well, then, I guess you better go start studying."

When they heard the stairs creak, they opened the bedroom door to see Ella Ruth coming up the stairs.

"Just the person I wanted to talk to," Priscilla said. "Amanda told me everything about how you made an impression on James at the gala. You left that part out."

Ella Ruth crossed her arms defensively. "I didn't see the need to tell you since I figured I'd never see him again."

"You might not ever speak to him again, but Amanda will. She needs to know everything about your charm bracelet and your stories so she can pretend to be you and win him over," Priscilla said. "You will go to the ball with her to help her in case she needs help or has a question, but you will not reveal who you are to him. Understood?"

"Even if you learn everything about me, it's going to take a lot more than that to get him to fall in love with you, Amanda," Ella Ruth said. "I shared a connection with him. What if he doesn't feel that with you?"

"He will if he thinks I'm you," Amanda insisted.

"How long do you think you'll be able to keep up that charade?" Ella Ruth asked, throwing her hands up.

"Until we get married, of course," Amanda said with a snicker.

Ella Ruth wanted to roll her eyes. Why on earth did Amanda think James would marry her when she was such a cold, manipulative person? He surely had better judgment than that. It would never happen. She hated to see him get hurt, but hopefully he would figure out this foolishness before it went too far.

"If you don't help her impersonate you, I will tell everyone about your laptop," Priscilla said, not that Ella Ruth needed the reminder. "Your father would be so disappointed. And what would the bishop say?"

"Fine," Ella Ruth said, letting out a long breath. "I'll tell you what the charms on my bracelet mean and what we talked about that night, and you can read my stories."

"Thank you." Amanda grinned with narrowed eyes.

"Good girl," Priscilla said, patting Ella Ruth's shoulder as she brushed past her. "You've made the right decision, Ella Ruth. Now go get the gown that you wore to the gala."

With a sigh, she turned and trudged to the barn where she'd hidden her blue ball gown in the wall. She felt as though she was about to give away a piece of herself she might never get back.

A knot of regret was already tangling up in her stomach, but what choice did she have? She couldn't bring any more pain into her father's life. He'd endured enough already.

With that, she turned and walked toward the house to give her gown to Amanda, each step more difficult than the one before.

What would James think of her if he ever discovered the truth?

Why do I care what he thinks about me? Ella Ruth thought. *I barely know him. It's not like we're in love. It would never work between us, anyway.*

CHAPTER NINE

The evening of the ball arrived quickly, and because Priscilla had kept Ella Ruth so busy with chores all week, she had barely any time to alter the dress she'd bought at the local thrift store. It was blue, and though she loved the fabric, she didn't like the style and had planned on improving it. Also, it was too big for her, so it had to be taken in, but she hadn't been able to work on it for several days. It was nowhere near ready to wear. She hadn't touched it in days.

What on earth could she wear to at least blend in at the ball?

"I know you didn't have time to work on your dress, so you can borrow the dress that I bought before I realized it would be better to wear the one you wore to the gala," Amanda said, shoving a hot pink, ruffly dress into Ella Ruth's arms.

Ella Ruth wrinkled her nose. *Not my style at all,* she thought.

"It's not like you're trying to impress anyone," Amanda said, packing her bag with a secret stash of makeup.

Maybe I could cut off some of the frills, but it will still be hot pink, Ella Ruth thought, and the ball was that night. She wouldn't have time to work on it. "Thanks."

"It's the least I can do," Amanda said, smiling at herself in the mirror. Ella Ruth shook her head and walked out the door.

A few hours later, Laura came over and dragged Ella Ruth up to her room.

"So, what's happening? Are you still going along with your stepmother's evil plan?" she asked. They'd met earlier in the week, and Ella Ruth had told her everything.

"I have to," Ella Ruth said.

"I'm sure your father would understand if you told him you write on a laptop. It could be a lot worse."

"I'm just not sure what kind of trouble I'd get in with the bishop. Most of all, I just don't want to embarrass or disappoint him. I don't care what happens to me."

"Either way, you have to go tonight, right? I wish Esther could come with us." Esther was at a week-long event at Xavier's mansion, trying to befriend him and gain his trust so that she could convince him to stop his family's land development company from building a strip mall right next to their Amish community, which would bring tourists and disrupt their peaceful way of life.

"I know. I wish she could come too. I just hope she can convince Xavier to stop the strip mall from being built." Ella Ruth said as they both sat on her bed.

"Me too. Did you get to finish working on the dress you bought?"

"No. It's not ready. Priscilla kept me busy all week. I think she did it on purpose so I wouldn't have time to alter my dress."

"Of course, she did. Well, then, what are you going to wear?"

Ella Ruth opened her closet to reveal the hot pink, frilly dress. "Amanda was gracious enough to let me borrow this," she said sarcastically.

"Ugh. My eyes are burning." Laura shielded her eyes from the offending dress. "I should have sewn a dress for you, but we both know how terrible I am at it. I barely fashioned a mask to go with my gown. I'm so sorry."

"Don't feel bad. As Amanda said, it's not like I'm trying to impress anyone."

"You're going to wear it?"

"I don't have anything else to wear. She's wearing the gown I wore to the gala."

"Ella, seriously?" Laura shook her head. "Does she really think James is going to fall for this?"

"She does," Ella Ruth said.

"Did you hide your laptop just to be safe?"

"What, do you think they'll delete my books?" Ella Ruth asked.

"I wouldn't put it past them," Laura said.

"I keep it hidden somewhere they'll never find it," Ella Ruth said. "Just to be safe."

"This entire thing isn't right. They're blackmailing you. I'm going to tell your father," Laura said, standing up.

Ella Ruth shot up and grabbed her arm. "No! Please, don't."

Someone knocked on the door, and Ella Ruth opened it to see Sadie holding a box containing shimmering light blue fabric in her arms. The sheer outer layer looked as iridescent as a butterfly's wing, changing shades of blue depending on how the light hit it.

"What's that?" Laura asked, wide-eyed.

"I finished working on the dress you bought to wear to the ball. I know you don't want to wear that obnoxious fuchsia frilly thing Amanda gave to you, and I know you didn't have time to alter yours," Sadie said. "So, I made some improvements to it. I added more layers of fabric. I hope you like it."

When she shook out the gown, Ella Ruth and Laura gasped as Katie and Lilly ran into the room. It looked like something out of a romance novel set in the Middle Ages. The fabric looked soft as silk but light as air, fluttering daintily as it unfurled in multiple layers in a dozen shades of blue. They blended together like watercolor paints on a canvas, ranging from sky blue to navy to cyan. Hundreds of tiny gems and sequins had been sewn into the fabric, and there was a layer of lace added to the bodice, which only added to the romantic, medieval look. The back laced up with ribbons in a corset style.

"It's gorgeous!" Lilly cried.

"It's magnificent!" Laura added.

"It's the most beautiful dress I've ever seen," Katie gushed, clasping her hands together. "It looks like Cinderella or Juliet's dress."

"You made this?" Ella Ruth asked. "For me? It must have taken you hours and hours."

"I love designing and sewing clothes. Especially gowns." Sadie shrugged and smiled. "It's the least I could do to make up for how they're treating you. I know you like blue, and this will look beautiful on you."

"It's her favorite color," Laura said.

"Yes, it is," Ella Ruth murmured.

Sadie handed Ella Ruth the box. "I know you didn't have time to get shoes, so I found these at the thrift store and got them for you."

Ella Ruth opened the box to reveal heeled shoes made of white lace, covered in sequins and crystal beads. They sparkled in the light like shards of glass in the sun.

"I sewed on the sequins and beads," Sadie said, grinning.

"Those are incredible," Laura cried.

Ella Ruth threw her arms around Sadie. "Thank you so much. You have no idea what this means to me."

"I think once James sees you, he will know it's you," Sadie said.

"If he does, everyone will know about my laptop," Ella Ruth said. "So hopefully not. I barely know the man."

Sadie handed Ella Ruth the dress. "Well, we'll see. Now go and try it on."

"Yes! We all want to see it," Lilly cried, clapping her hands. "We'll turn around."

Ella Ruth smiled at their enthusiasm, and as they were turned around, she quickly changed. This was safer, so she didn't have to risk anyone else seeing her in the hallway on her way back from the bathroom.

"I wish Lilly and I could go to the ball." Katie flopped onto the bed as Ella Ruth changed.

"I'm sorry. I wish you could come, but you're both under twenty-one," Ella Ruth said. "It said ages twenty-one and over on the invitation. There might be alcohol, but I won't be drinking, of course."

"So not fair," Lilly added.

"I'll stay with you," Sadie told them. "We can play games. It'll be fun."

"You're twenty-two, right? You sure you don't want to come, Sadie?" Ella Ruth asked.

"I'm sure." Sadie shook her head. "All those people... That makes me nervous just thinking about it. I'd rather stay here with Katie and Lilly."

"Thanks." Katie smiled at Sadie.

"Okay, you can look now," Ella Ruth said.

When they turned around, they all gasped again, and Laura cheered.

"Shh!" Ella Ruth put a finger to her lips. "Priscilla is downstairs."

"You look beautiful. I have no words," Laura said, fanning herself as her eyes filled with tears.

"Oh, stop it," Ella Ruth said, waving her hand.

"Look in the mirror," Katie said, rushing to grab the only mirror they had in their room, a small one they kept on the dresser. In their community, mirrors were allowed, which surprised some people. Katie held it up for Ella Ruth, backing up so she could see better.

Ella Ruth couldn't see the entire length of the dress in the mirror, but she saw enough to make her eyes widen in surprise. "Wow. I don't even know what to say. Sadie, you're incredibly talented! This should be in a magazine."

"Thank you." A blush crept over Sadie's face.

"You should start your own fashion design company. You could specialize in gowns, wedding dresses, and prom dresses," Laura offered.

"I wish I could, but I'd have to leave the church. I don't want to leave my mother," Sadie said. "I'm not sure I could."

"I'm sure she just wants what's best for you," Ella Ruth said, putting a hand on her arm.

"But how would I even start my own company? I would need investors, not to mention a college degree. And money, which I don't have." Sadie sat on the bed. "For now, this is all I can do."

"Oh, just this?" Lilly laughed.

"You're like her fairy godmother," Laura added. "Like in the fairy-tale."

"I just wanted to help," Sadie said, then frowned. "What they're doing to you is unfair. I hope this helps."

"It does. Thank you, Sadie." Ella Ruth smiled. "And if anyone asks me about this dress, I'm going to tell them you made it. Do you have business cards or anything I can give them?"

"No," Sadie said. "It's not like I have a phone number they could call without other people finding out."

"Katie and I answer the phones at the store," Lilly said. "Just write down the store phone number."

"Really? Okay." Sadie scribbled her name and the Unity Community Store phone number on a few pieces of paper and handed them to Ella Ruth, shrugging. "It's better than nothing."

"Thanks. I'm sure I'll hand out some of these tonight," Ella Ruth said, tucking them into a small pocket Sadie had sewn into the dress.

"We need to leave, Ella," Laura said. "Come on. Let's go. We will get ready on the way. Put the dress in my bag and put the pink one in yours in case Amanda or Priscilla decide to check."

They scurried around to get ready. Ella Ruth tucked her notebook and pen in her purse so she could write or draw in case she got bored at the ball.

When it was time to leave, Ella Ruth climbed into the buggy with Amanda and Laura, and they drove to the Baldwins' mansion. Irvin was already sleeping, and if he happened to wake up, Priscilla would cover for them and say they slept over at Laura's house.

"I'm going to talk to James as soon as we get there," Amanda said, fluffing her hair as they rode in the buggy. She'd taken off her prayer *kapp*, and now her long blonde hair fell down her back. Ella Ruth had to admit that it looked similar to hers. "Park the buggy out of sight, and I want you to stay out of sight as well. Go wait in the garden, and I will come to you if I have a question about your story or your bracelet. Understood?"

Ella Ruth sighed. "Fine."

Laura scowled in the front seat.

She won't get away with this, Ella Ruth thought as she drove the buggy. *Her plan will fail. And if it doesn't, I'll find some way to reveal the truth to James without her knowing.*

When they arrived, they each took turns changing in the buggy. Ella Ruth went last, and when she stepped out in the gown Sadie had made her, Amanda gasped in shock.

"Where is the pink dress I gave you?" she demanded.

"The wedding cake, you mean?" Laura scoffed.

"I'm wearing this one instead," Ella Ruth said defiantly.

"Where did you get this? There's no way you had time to work on it. We made sure of it," Amanda blurted. "Who made it for you?"

"I knew it," Ella Ruth said. "You gave me all that extra work for this very reason. And I'm not telling you where I got it."

"Go change into the pink dress right now." Amanda pointed her finger at the buggy.

"No." Ella Ruth crossed her arms. "We're here now, and you can't do this without me. Either I wear this or I'm leaving, and you can trick James all on your own without my help."

Amanda scowled, throwing her hands up. "Ugh. Fine. Let's go."

The music was already booming from where they stood outside the gate. They followed a crowd of young women who approached the mansion, giggling and chattering the entire way. Some of the young women clearly didn't get the memo about the theme or just didn't care because many of them wore flashy, revealing dresses.

As they moved toward the mansion and walked through the door, the women in front of Ella Ruth and her friends began shrieking and jumping up and down, and Ella Ruth craned her neck to see why. What was all the fuss about?

"James! James! I'm your Cinderella!" one of the young women in front of them cried.

"No, it's me! I'm the one you're looking for!" another shouted, followed by several more similar proclamations.

Finally, the crowd parted just enough for Ella Ruth to catch a glimpse of him. He wore black pants and a blue doublet over a ruffled white shirt, complete with a sword in a sheath strapped to his hips. He looked like he came right out of a Shakespearean play.

In fact, his outfit matched her dress perfectly.

"Good evening. Please write down your answers on a slip of paper and drop it in this box," James said, clearly uncomfortable with all the attention. "Thank you for coming."

When the group ahead of them finally stopped fawning over James and moved along, Laura, Amanda, and Ella Ruth approached.

"Thank you so much for inviting us," Amanda said, fanning herself. "I'm Amanda. We met at the bookstore."

"Oh, yes, Amanda. Thank you for coming. Ella Ruth, how are you?" he asked, briefly turning to Ella Ruth, who felt as though her heart had launched into her throat.

"Good. This is my friend Laura. She was also at the gala," Ella Ruth said.

"Nice to meet you. Thank you all for coming. As you may know, I'm looking for a special young woman who captivated me at Xavier's gala. She left behind her charm bracelet. If someone here can tell me what the charms were and what they mean, she is the one I'm looking for," James explained. "Feel free to write down your answer here and put it in the box."

"No need," Amanda said, shaking her head as she set her eyes intently on James. "My bracelet had seven charms: a dog, a horse, a shoe, an apple, a hot-air balloon, a book, and the Eiffel tower."

James froze, then turned slowly to Amanda, his eyes wide. "That's... That's right. What do the charms mean?"

"My mother had a dog named Zeke when she was younger, and my horse is named Pumpkin. The book is because my mother loved to read. She always wanted to travel, but she never got the chance. That's what the Eiffel Tower represents. The shoe represents how she and her sister each had their own path to walk. The apple is for when she would pick apples growing up, and the hot-air balloon is for how she always wanted to ride in a hot-air balloon with her sister, but she never did," Amanda said, feigning a sorrowful look. "I didn't tell you my name because I was nervous. My name is Amanda."

"And your hair," he said, gesturing to Amanda's long curls that reached past her waist, much like Ella Ruth's. Tonight, Ella Ruth wore her hair up to hide its length. A wide grin spread over his face like a child on Christmas morning.

Ella Ruth suddenly felt sick to her stomach. A ball of regret and dying wishes knotted up in her stomach. She hadn't expected to be so devastated over a man she barely knew.

Yet, even after talking with him for one night, she felt as though she'd known him all her life.

"It's you. It's really you!" James cried, taking Amanda's hand and leading her into the ballroom. "Will you dance with me, Amanda?"

CHAPTER TEN

"I'd love to," Amanda said, giving him a coy smile as she walked with him to the dance floor. A slow song played as they danced.

"Wow," Laura said. "That was fast. I'm so sorry, Ella."

Ella Ruth shook her head. *Don't cry. Don't cry,* she told herself as her eyes stung with tears. "It is what it is."

"Wow!" someone cried behind them. They turned to see a young woman in a shimmering ball gown who was staring wide-eyed at Ella Ruth's dress. "Where did you get that dress? It's the most beautiful dress I've ever seen!"

"My sister made it," Ella Ruth said.

"I want to hire her to make one for me," the young woman said.

"Here's her phone number. Her name is Sadie. Just call this number and leave a message. It's a store phone number, but this is the best way to reach her," Ella Ruth said, handing her one of the slips of paper Sadie had given her.

"Wow, thanks! I'll definitely give her a call," the young woman said with a grin, then walked away.

"I hope she orders a dress," Ella Ruth said.

"Me too. Listen to me, Ella. You can still change this situation with Amanda," Laura said, grabbing Ella Ruth's arm. "You can go tell him it was you."

"Like all the other women here? She already told him what the charms were. She knows my story. He'd never believe me," Ella Ruth said with a sigh. "It's over."

"So, talk to him about your story before she does. No matter how much she read it, she can't know it like you do. And so what if Priscilla and Amanda tell your father about your laptop? What's the worst that can happen?" Laura asked. "You haven't been baptized, so you won't be shunned."

"My father would be so disappointed," Ella Ruth said, looking out at the colorful, swirling skirts that filled the ballroom as couples danced.

"He knows how much you love to write. I don't think he'd be as disappointed as you think. Priscilla is gaslighting you," Laura said, grabbing Ella Ruth's shoulders. "You care about James, don't you? You had a connection."

"Yes, I do care about him. We did have a connection."

"Make a stand. Go tell him the truth! Look." Laura pointed to Amanda, who had taken a break from dancing to get a drink. "Now is your chance."

"You're right," Ella Ruth said, standing up straighter. "I'm going to do it."

"That's it. Go!" Laura playfully shoved Ella Ruth, almost causing her to trip over her dress, but she quickly regained her balance and walked confidently toward James. Before she could reach him, two other young women flocked to him. As she drew closer, she could hear bits of what they were saying.

"The bracelet had a hot-air balloon and the Eiffel Tower on it because my mother loved to travel..." one was saying.

"And a horse and a dog," the other one said. "It's my bracelet."

"No, it's mine!" the other woman said.

"Ladies," James said, raising a hand. "I've already found my Cinderella. I'm sorry. Please enjoy the ball."

The two young women harrumphed before stomping away, scowling.

James sighed, then turned and walked out the door to a balcony. Ella Ruth cautiously followed him.

Why would he believe me now when those women just told him what was on the bracelet? They must have overheard Amanda tell him what the charms were, Ella Ruth thought dejectedly. Still, she had to try.

"James?" she said softly.

James was leaning against the railing and turned toward Ella Ruth. "Good evening," he said. "I suppose you're here to tell me what charms were on the bracelet. I've already found the woman I'm looking for."

For a moment, Ella Ruth froze, at a loss for words. "I was the one you talked to in the garden the night of the gala, James. It was me, not Amanda."

"Every other woman here is saying the same thing," James said, sounding a bit flustered and discouraged. He stared at the floor.

"Everyone is trying to convince me it was them. I never meant for that to happen. I was just hoping to find the woman I was looking for."

"But I can prove I'm the one you're looking for," Ella Ruth said. "You read my story, and you said that you'd contact your aunt to give me advice on getting it published. I said I was thinking about self-publishing it. You told me your sister would be better at running the company and that you want to be an English teacher. You told me about how your brother died and how you felt like you'd never measure up in your father's eyes—"

"There you are!"

Ella Ruth froze at the sound of Amanda's voice behind her. James stared at Ella Ruth in confusion.

"I was looking for you, James," Amanda said, sidling up beside him. "Is my stepsister bothering you like all the other desperate young women here?"

"No," James said, staring at Ella Ruth. "She was just telling me everything we talked about at the gala in the garden."

"Oh, poor Ella Ruth," Amanda said, feigning a sorrowful look and shaking her head slowly. "When I got home that evening, I told my stepsister everything that you and I talked about in the garden. She must have just repeated it all back to you. And she knows the charms on my bracelet because she's seen it in my room. Ella Ruth, I trusted you. How could you do this?"

"But I'm the one who wrote the story," Ella Ruth insisted, her eyes burning with unshed tears. She would not cry in front of Amanda.

She wouldn't let her win. "Ask me anything about the story. I can prove it."

"She reads my work as well," Amanda told James. "So, she knows it inside and out. She's my biggest fan. Or, at least, I thought she was. I never thought she'd betray me like this. Excuse me, James. I need to talk to my sister for a minute."

"Of course," James said, nodding with a perplexed look on his face.

Amanda walked over to Ella Ruth and grabbed her arm, steering her back into the ballroom. They walked toward the other end of the room where no one would hear them.

"This is your last warning," Amanda said, holding up a finger with jealous flames in her eyes. "If you try something like that again, I won't just tell Irvin about your laptop, I'll tell the bishop how Laura sneaks out to the movie theater with you at night. I know you two have been doing it for a long time."

"How do you know about that?" Ella Ruth demanded.

"I've heard you two giggling and talking about it in your room. And I've seen you sneak out at night."

"Why haven't you told anyone?" Ella Ruth asked in surprise.

"Because I knew one day I'd need something from you and a reason for you to do it. Laura has been baptized into the church, unlike you. If the church elders found out that she goes to the movies, she could be shunned. You would only get reprimanded and embarrass your father, but she would have much more serious consequences. What would her parents say? Her family would be so embarrassed."

"How dare you threaten her," Ella Ruth said, a tear escaping her eye and coursing down her cheek. She swiped it away, anger churning in her stomach. "Leave her out of this."

"Clearly, you don't seem to care about getting in trouble yourself and upsetting Irvin, but it seems as though you are very protective of your friend. Stay away from James, and no one will know her secret. Do you understand?" Amanda demanded.

Ella Ruth sighed. "Fine. But he's going to figure it out that it wasn't you, you know. He's going to realize it was me."

"I only have to keep him convinced until we get married."

"What kind of marriage would that be? It would all be based on lies."

"I don't care, and why should you? If you want to protect Laura, keep your distance. Stay by the food table in case I need you. I might have questions about what you two talked about at the gala. Now, if you'll excuse me, I need to get back to my prince." Amanda hiked her chin and walked away, her skirts trailing behind her. Ella Ruth hated seeing Amanda wearing her dress.

He didn't believe me, Ella Ruth thought as more tears slipped from her eyes, slowly at first. Once she found a secluded hallway, she began to weep.

After Amanda and her stepsister walked away, James stood on the balcony even more puzzled than he was before. Amanda's story made sense, and she did know all the charms on the bracelet, but which one of them was lying?

Clearly, the other two women who had approached him just before Ella Ruth had only known the charms because they'd overheard Amanda when she'd told him. He'd seen them lurking down the hall nearby, eavesdropping. Besides, they were both brunettes, and the woman he was looking for had blonde hair.

It was Amanda, wasn't it?

"So sorry about that," Amanda said, walking toward him and fluffing her hair. "My poor sister. Ever since her mother died, she's never been the same."

"I thought you said your mother died," James said. "You said at the gala that your mother gave you the charm bracelet before she died."

"Oh, yes. Well, her mother died too," Amanda rushed to say, putting her hand on his arm. "We've both been through so much. That's why I love to write. It's an escape from reality. It helps me feel closer to my mother."

"In one of your stories, your character's mother had died too. Is that why you wrote it that way?" he asked.

"Yes," Amanda said. "I feel a deep connection with my character. That's why her mother dies. I almost feel like she is like me, in a way."

"Well, I only read part of your story, but I do get that sense," James said. "I'd love to read the rest of your story some time."

"That would be great." Amanda grinned.

Why hasn't she asked for her charm bracelet back yet? James wondered. *Isn't it really important to her?*

He decided to wait and see if she would ask for it. He didn't want to give back the charm bracelet until he was sure he had the right woman.

"What if we wrote a short story together?" James suggested. Surely if Amanda was lying, she wouldn't be as good of a writer as the woman he was looking for.

"Oh, I would love to," Amanda said. "You mean here? Right now?"

"Well, sure. Why not?"

"I'm Amish. I never get to come to parties like this."

"So, the night you came to the gala, you sneaked out? And you sneaked out tonight?" James asked. "Could you get in trouble?"

"Well, yes," Amanda said. "We aren't allowed to wear gowns like this or attend such worldly parties, but I had to see you, so I came anyway. The night of the gala, I only wanted to get away for one night and forget about my mundane life. I mean, I love my family, but my life is quite boring."

"Why is that?" James asked curiously. "I would never guess that from your writing."

"At home, I'm always the one doing all of the chores. I do all the laundry, all the cooking, all the dishes, and all the cleaning. I just want to escape my life for just one night."

James' eyebrows shot up. "Your stepsister doesn't help you?"

"She's still so sad over the death of her mother. I couldn't bear to ask for her help. My sisters Katie and Lilly have jobs, and my younger siblings are a bit too young. My father works so much. So, it all falls on me."

"I'm sorry to hear that," James said, his heart going out to her. "That's unfair."

Amanda shrugged. "I can't complain. I do like being Amish, but since we don't have dishwashers or washing machines, dishes and laundry take so long to do. But I shouldn't complain. I have a good life." She sighed, clasping her hands together as if she were praying.

James asked, "How do you find the time to write?"

"I stay up late or get up early. I lose sleep, but it's worth it." She smiled, shrugging.

"You're committed. I admire that." He smiled at her, admiring her determination.

"Thank you." She grinned. "Can't we just dance for a while?" Amanda pleaded, grabbing his arm and leading him to the dance floor. "Come on. It will be fun!"

"Okay, okay," he said, laughing as he let her pull him along. An up-beat song played, and Amanda danced energetically but terribly. James didn't mind, though—he wasn't a good dancer either. When she stepped on his toes, she apologized.

"It's okay," James said.

"I suppose I'm much better at writing than dancing," Amanda joked, and he laughed.

"I have to agree with that," he said. "But I think the same is true about me, too."

A slow song came on, and Amanda wrapped her arms around him. Several other young women watched jealously as they danced, and he noticed Amanda smiling at them haughtily.

"They're jealous of you," he said. "You look beautiful."

"They're only jealous because I'm dancing with the most handsome and successful young man in town," Amanda said with a coy smile.

He smiled back at her, but as they danced, he wondered why he didn't feel the same connection with her that he'd felt the night of the gala. Maybe it was that he was so caught up in the whirlwind of finding the one he was looking for, and it was all happening so fast. With so many others claiming to be his Cinderella, he had to admit he felt confused and flustered.

"Don't worry about anyone else," Amanda said soothingly. "Just focus on us. I'm so glad you found me."

James smiled down at her. "I'm glad I found you too."

He *had* found the one he was looking for, hadn't he?

After they danced, his sister Eliza walked over to them.

"So, is this the famous Cinderella I've been dying to meet?" Eliza asked.

"Yes, Eliza, this is Amanda, the mystery woman I met at the gala. Amanda, this is my sister, Eliza," James said.

"Nice to meet you," Amanda said.

"James talks about you all the time," Eliza said, waving her hand. "I can see why."

"I know," Amanda said with a dramatic sigh, flipping her blonde hair over her shoulder. "How could he not?"

"Uh..." Eliza glanced at James with a confused look. "Are you serious?"

"What? No, no," Amanda stammered. "I don't know why he would talk about me. I don't know why I said that."

"You are beautiful, kind, and talented," James said. "She's going to send her book to Aunt Adeline to get her feedback."

"My writing is amazing. I'm sure she will love it," Amanda said haughtily, hiking her chin.

Eliza blinked. "Well, you're confident, that's for sure." She turned to James. "That's one word for it."

James looked at Amanda with confusion. The woman he met at the ball wasn't so...self-absorbed.

"Can I talk to my brother for a minute?" Eliza asked Amanda, already walking away with James to the other side of the room. "James, are you sure that's the woman from the gala?"

He drew his eyebrows together with confusion. "She proved it was her by naming the charms on the bracelet and telling me what they represented, so it must be her. But the woman I met at the ball was humble and kind, not so..."

"Full of herself?" Eliza asked, shaking her head. "I don't think that's her, James. I think she found out that information somehow and is lying to you."

"Several women have tried to tell me it was them, but I ignored them," James said, remembering how Ella Ruth had approached him. His stomach clenched with guilt. "What if I turned away the real Cinderella?"

Eliza sighed. "I'm not sure what to tell you right now, James, but maybe the real Cinderella is someone Amanda knows, and that's how she found out those things about the bracelet. Keep your eyes and your heart open." She glanced toward the dance floor. "I have to go. This is my favorite song."

James laughed as his sister danced away.

"Ella!" Laura called. "There you are. I've been looking for you. What happened?"

Ella Ruth slowly turned toward her friend, revealing her reddened eyes.

"Are you crying?" Laura threw her arms around Ella Ruth. "What did she do? Did you tell him?"

"I tried to tell James it was me, but he didn't believe me. I even told him the things we talked about at the gala, but then Amanda found us. She said she told me everything the night of the gala and that I was just repeating what she'd told me about that night." Ella Ruth's shoulders slumped. "Before I walked up to him, two other women told him what the charms were on the bracelet. They must have overheard Amanda. He didn't believe me."

"But what about the story? Did you tell him you wrote it and you know everything about it?" Laura asked.

"Amanda said that I read her stories, so that's why I'm so familiar with them." Ella Ruth sighed. "Ugh. She was so convincing. How can I ever prove it was me?"

"Amanda is vile. Sorry to say it, but she is. Her true personality will show through soon enough, and he will figure it out. How could he not realize she's not the one?"

"She says she's going to keep this up until they get married."

"Trust me. It won't get that far," Laura said, looping her arm through Ella Ruth's. "We're at a ball, Ella." She grinned. "Let's have some fun."

Laura pulled Ella Ruth on to the dance floor, and they danced to an upbeat song, laughing.

Ella Ruth smiled at her friend through her tears. What would she do if Laura ever got in trouble because of her? What if she was shunned because of her?

She would never be able to forgive herself. Laura's friendship meant so much to Ella Ruth. She didn't even want to think about what would happen if Laura was shunned.

CHAPTER ELEVEN

"Let's go get some food," Ella Ruth said, remembering what Amanda had said about staying near the refreshments in case she needed help.

"Food is always a great idea." Laura chuckled.

They walked over to the refreshments and filled their plates with tiny sandwiches and other fancy appetizers. She could see Amanda slow dancing with James, but she turned away so she wouldn't have to watch as it caused a physical ache in her chest.

"This is delicious," Laura said, her mouth full of crab cakes.

Ella Ruth nodded, then overheard some ladies a few feet away talking over the music.

"So, James found the girl he was looking for. Did you hear about how he looked for her all over town? She didn't even tell him her name. How can he know for sure that he found the right woman? What if she is an imposter?" one asked.

"I saw some other girls telling James what the charms were on the bracelet. What if she just overheard the real Cinderella and was only repeating the information back to him like they were? I'm not convinced she's the one." The brunette shook her head. "If the real Cinderella didn't tell him her name, and he didn't see her face, then you're right—she could be anyone, and he has no way of knowing for sure."

"The woman from the ball sure made an impression on him," the other woman said. "Apparently, she's an excellent writer and artist. She wrote three novels and let him read part of the story. He said it was like nothing he'd ever read before. I heard him telling his mother about it."

Ella Ruth smiled as she took another crab cake.

"What?" Laura asked her quizzically.

Ella Ruth nodded her head toward the two talking women. "Listen."

Laura noticed them and drew a little closer to eavesdrop.

"So, if that woman who is dancing with him right now is not the real Cinderella, why hasn't the real Cinderella come forward?"

"Maybe she doesn't love him."

"Who wouldn't love James Baldwin? I'd marry him any day of the week. I think every woman here would say the same."

"Well, if that woman he's with now isn't the one he is looking for, that means you and I still have a shot, right?"

"Absolutely." They clinked glasses. "Except I can't draw to save my life. Can you?"

"No."

"And are you an excellent writer?"

"No. Are you?"

"I failed English. And no, I can't even draw a stick person. I guess we don't have a shot after all. He'd figure it out."

"Do you think that woman can write and draw well if she's not the one?" The young woman gestured to Amanda.

"If she can't, then he's going to figure it out eventually, isn't he?" Ella Ruth nodded in agreement, catching Laura's eye.

"I told you. He will figure it out when he realizes how awful she is," Laura said. "He should know it's you." A look of determination crossed her face. "I'm going to tell him." She began to march forward.

"Laura, no!" Ella Ruth grabbed her arm.

"Why not? He didn't believe you, but he might believe me."

"If you tell him, then I'll get in trouble."

"We already talked about how that's not a big enough reason for you not to tell him. What is the real reason you don't want me to tell him? What are you hiding from me?" Laura demanded. "I know you so well that I can read you like a book, and I know you're keeping something from me. Out with it. Tell me. What else did Amanda threaten you with? Just tell me, Ella."

Ella Ruth sighed, defeated. "She said that if I tried anything else to let James know I am the one from the gala that she would tell the elders and your parents that you've been sneaking out to the movie theater with me. You could be shunned, Laura. I can't risk that. I love you too much to let you get in trouble because of me."

Laura's eyes widened. "She'd really do that?"

"Of course, she would. She's not bluffing. I don't want to ruin your chances with your boyfriend. I know you two want to get married soon. If you are shunned, it will ruin your reputation. I can't do that. You are such a good friend, Laura. Please don't tell James. It's not like I'm in love with him. We barely know each other, anyway."

"But what if he's your soul mate?"

Ella Ruth laughed. "If he is truly my soul mate, then I believe we would end up together no matter what. But he's probably not."

Laura frowned, stomping her foot. "Ugh. How dare she?" She sighed, biting her lip as she let out a growl of frustration. "I do want to get married soon. It would ruin everything if I were shunned. I won't tell him, but I hate that she's doing this to you. To us."

"Me too."

"I can't believe her!" Laura punched the air. "I can't believe she did this. So, that's why you've been going along with this the entire time?" Laura threw her arms around Ella Ruth. "You're such an amazing friend. I can't believe you did all of that for me."

"What are friends for?" Ella Ruth smiled as Laura pulled away. "I didn't tell you because I was afraid you wouldn't care about yourself and convince me to tell James the truth, anyway."

"You're right. I would have," Laura said. "Look on the bright side. Once Amanda gets married and moves out, we won't see her very much anymore." Laura grinned mischievously.

"*If* she gets married. According to your theory, James will figure it out."

"What if he doesn't? You wouldn't let him marry her, would you?"

"I hope his judgment isn't that flawed," Ella Ruth said. If it came down to it, would she risk Laura getting shunned so she could tell James the truth?

She'd have to make that decision when the time came because right now, she honestly had no idea what she would choose.

After another song ended, James took a step back from Amanda. "I need a drink. Can I get you one?"

"Oh, yes, thank you. I'm going to the restroom while you do that. I'll have some punch. Thanks!" Amanda called and then walked away.

James headed over to the refreshment table and poured punch into a cup for Amanda, then a cup of water for himself. He downed it quickly and was about to pour another when he noticed Ella Ruth a few feet away talking to her friend. She was facing away from him, so she didn't see him approach, but her friend's eyes grew wide when she noticed him.

"Hello, Ella Ruth. Your dress is beautiful," he said, noticing the multiple layers of airy fabric in several shades of blue. The back laced up, giving it a Shakespearian feel. "It looks like a waterfall."

"I have to get some more food," Laura blurted, then darted away. James noticed her plate was already full, so she was probably just making an excuse for Ella Ruth to be alone with him. He smiled at her loyalty.

Ella Ruth's hair was pinned up in an elegant, effortless updo with a few blonde curls brushing her neck. The woman he spoke with at the gala had the exact same hair color.

Amanda was the one from the gala. Wasn't she? Yet he couldn't help but wonder how long Ella Ruth's hair was. The woman at the ball had long blonde hair far past her waist, but so did Amanda. They both normally wore a prayer *kapp*, and even though Ella Ruth wasn't now, he had no way of knowing because her hair was pinned up.

Ella Ruth slowly turned around to face James. He blinked rapidly, struck by how beautiful she was. Her eyes were framed by long eyelashes that almost brushed her cheek. When she slowly looked up to meet his gaze, he couldn't breathe. She had the most vivid blue eyes he'd ever seen, and he remembered the woman from the gala also had bright blue eyes behind her mask. However, Amanda also had blue eyes.

"Thank you," Ella Ruth said softly.

He couldn't help but let his eyes drop to her lips, which were perfectly pink. The mask had only hidden the top half of the woman's face at the gala, but now he was having trouble remembering what she'd looked like. It was hard to piece together a face in his mind when he'd only seen part of it.

Still, the woman standing before him was stunning. The gauzy blue neckline of her gown brushed against Ella Ruth's collar bone and shoulders, and the hundreds of sparkling gems and sequins caught the light with each movement she made.

Now he couldn't even remember what he'd just said to her. "Are you dressed as a specific literary character? Juliet, perhaps? I suppose we don't really know what their clothing looked like, but I imagine Juliet might have worn a dress like that."

"Thank you. My stepsister Sadie made it for me," Ella Ruth said. "However, my favorite literary character is Roxane."

"Roxane? From the play *Cyrano de Bergerac* by Edmond Rostand?" James' jaw dropped in awe. "You know that play?"

"Know it? I love it!" Ella Ruth exclaimed.

"I actually dressed as Cyrano de Bergerac tonight, but I didn't think anyone would know of that character. You're the only person I've met who does," James said, smiling at her with admiration.

Ella Ruth grinned. "I once snuck out with my friends to see it performed at the local theater. It was phenomenal."

"It's my favorite," James said. "Everyone talks about Shakespeare and Charles Dickens, but Edmond Rostand was also a legendary writer. I feel like not enough people know about his work."

"I agree," Ella Ruth said. "I love Roxane because she was a bit shallow at first, but then her character grew. Even though she was drawn to Christian's handsome outward appearance at first, ultimately, she was in love with Cyrano's exquisite writing. Cyrano was afraid to tell Roxane how he felt because he was too afraid she would reject him. When she realized that he was the true author all along, the words he wrote for her were the truth that set them both free."

James stared at her in awe, unable to speak for a few moments.

CHAPTER TWELVE

"Are you okay?" she asked.

He nodded, stunned by her compelling words. Who was this woman? He felt as though he could talk to her for hours about literature, listening to her insightful observations.

Was Amanda as knowledgeable about literature as her stepsister? Would he be able to speak with her about it in the same way? At the gala, the woman he spoke with was just as intelligent as Ella Ruth, but surely Amanda knew just as much about classic literature.

"I'm sorry. I'm just impressed by your observations and your insights," he stammered.

"Oh," Ella Ruth shrugged, looking at the floor. "Thanks."

"I have to apologize for how I treated you earlier," he said, overcome by guilt. "It's just that so many women have claimed to be the one from the gala, and I'm feeling confused and a bit overwhelmed."

"I understand," Ella Ruth said. "It must be overwhelming, having all these women throw themselves at your feet. Or maybe you think it's fun." Was that a bit of sarcasm in her voice?

James cringed. "It's really not fun at all, but talking to you is," he blurted.

A slow smile spread across Ella Ruth's face. A slow song began to play, and she sighed.

"I love this song. Adam McKenna is my favorite. His lyrics are so deep," Ella Ruth said. "He's so talented, but not as many people know about his music."

"I'm surprised you know his music," James said. "He's my favorite, too." They had so much in common, and he had only spoken a few brief times. What else did they have in common?

He held out his hand. "Amanda is in the restroom. Would you like to dance?"

"Do you think she'd mind?"

James shrugged. "You're her stepsister. I'm sure she won't mind. Come on. We both love this song. It would be a shame to let it go to waste."

She smiled and set her plate down on the refreshment table along with the purse she'd been holding. She took his hand, and he immediately felt a surge of warmth spread through his arm and throughout his entire being.

That's strange, he thought. He hadn't felt anything like this when he'd danced with Amanda, but it had been a whirlwind of a night. Maybe it all happened so fast that he didn't have time to think about how he felt about her yet.

Ella Ruth and James walked out onto the dance floor. He put one hand on her back, the bumpy sequins and beads beneath his fingers.

He put his other hand in hers and felt her other hand on his shoulder. His heart began to pound as they began to slow dance.

"You must be so glad that you finally found the mystery woman from the gala," Ella Ruth said.

"Yes, I am. It's too bad I have to go away for a few weeks, though. I won't be able to see her for a while."

"Where are you going? Traveling to Europe again?" she asked, then bit her lip and looked away.

"How did you know I just went to Europe?" he asked.

"I overheard some of the other women talking about it." She shook her head.

"Well, no, I'm not going back to Europe this time. I have a summer teaching internship for a few weeks in New York. I'll be teaching reading and writing to inner-city middle school students. I applied and was accepted, and I can't miss this opportunity, so I have to go. The timing isn't the best, but I've been looking forward to going for months," he explained. "I want to be a middle school English teacher."

"Wow, the internship sounds marvelous," Ella Ruth said. "Congratulations. Your parents must be so proud of you," Ella Ruth said. "That's an admirable occupation."

"Thank you. My parents don't approve. They want me to take over the company, not be a teacher."

"Maybe one day they will change their minds."

He nodded slowly. "I doubt it, but thank you. The thing is, I haven't completely decided if I will be a teacher or take over the company. I feel like it's my duty to do what my father expects of me, but I also want to follow my heart." He chuckled. "That sounds corny."

"No, it doesn't. You need to do what you think is right."

"It's silly because I already went to college and got my degree. I was so sure, but now I am having second thoughts. My parents want to retire soon, and I don't want to let them down."

"So you might actually still take over the company?" Ella Ruth asked.

"I'm really not sure."

"Maybe the internship will help you make your decision."

"Maybe. I hope Amanda doesn't mind my leaving for a while."

Ella Ruth scrunched up her nose and looked away.

"What? You think she will be upset?"

"I... Uh... I'm not sure. Hopefully she will understand," Ella Ruth stammered.

"I asked Amanda to write and illustrate a story with me, just for fun," James said. "I'm thinking we could write a middle-grade book."

Ella Ruth held back a laugh, then looked away.

"What? You don't like middle-grade?" James asked.

"It's not that," Ella Ruth said. "I love middle-grade and young adult books."

"Do you write too?" he asked curiously.

"Oh, no. I don't know anything about writing or drawing." She shook her head.

"Do you think Amanda is good at writing and drawing?" he asked, watching her reaction.

She suppressed a smile. "It depends on how you define good. I'm sure it will be interesting."

"Yes. I'm really looking forward to it. When she let me read her story from her notebook at the gala, it was incredible. I wanted to read more, but she had to leave suddenly. I can't wait to read more of her work."

Ella Ruth frowned and looked away.

"What's wrong?"

"Nothing."

"May I cut in?" a voice behind them asked. Amanda had walked up to them and was holding out her hand to James.

"Of course," James said, and Ella Ruth quickly turned and walked away.

"Sorry if she stepped on your feet," Amanda said, rolling her eyes. "She's a terrible dancer."

"She didn't step on my feet," James said, rushing to her defense. "She wasn't terrible at all."

"I'm sorry she threw herself at you. You didn't have to dance with her out of pity. She's always been jealous of me."

"Actually, I asked her to dance with me," James said and noticed jealousy flicker across Amanda's face, but only for a brief moment. She quickly replaced it with a smile.

"How...gentlemanly of you," she said.

"Well, shall we dance?" He held out his arm, and they stepped out onto the dance floor.

"I was just telling Ella Ruth that I have to leave for a few weeks for a summer teaching internship in New York. I hope you won't be too disappointed that I'll be gone for a while," James explained. "I know the timing is poor since we are just getting to know each other. I know I will miss you."

"What? You're leaving?" Amanda asked, stunned, then blinked rapidly. "A teaching internship? What do you mean?" Amanda was so shocked that she tripped over James' feet, then caught her balance. "Aren't you going to take over the car dealership?"

He held her hand so she wouldn't fall. "I'm not sure yet. I want to be a middle school English teacher. I already have my degree, but this will help prepare me even more for teaching."

"I want to do what I love, but I also don't want to disappoint my father. I'll make the decision after the internship."

"Why wouldn't you want to inherit and run a multi-million-dollar company?" Amanda cried.

James frowned. "Because teaching is my dream, and I want to do what I love. Don't you agree that spending your life doing a job you love is so much more important than being wealthy?"

"Not at all." Amanda shook her head, then noticed the shocked look on his face. "I mean...yes. I do agree. So, you haven't decided yet?"

"No. I think I need to do this internship and actually teach in a summer school to get a glimpse of what it would be like. Then I can make my decision."

Amanda stared at the floor. "I see."

"If you want, I could meet you halfway on the weekends. Oh..." He paused. "I'm sorry. I forgot. Of course, you don't own cars."

Amanda nodded. "I would hire a driver, but that's really far. And I don't think my parents would let me go on the bus alone to see you. They need my help at home. I'm sorry."

"I understand. Well, I'll see you when I get back. I hope you won't mind me leaving for a while. I know you don't have a cell phone, so we can write letters to keep in touch, if you'd like," James offered. "I love writing letters. It's too bad that no one our age does it anymore."

"That sounds great," Amanda said. "I understand that you have to leave. I will miss you, but we will keep in touch."

"I knew you'd understand. And when I get back, we can get to know each other more in person." He smiled.

"I would love that."

After they danced for a few songs, Amanda and James took a break to get a drink. James noticed the purse Ella Ruth had been holding and picked it up.

"Ella Ruth left her purse behind. I'll go find her and give it back to her," he said and started to walk away.

"Oh, that's mine. She was holding it for me while I was in the bathroom," Amanda said, holding out her hand. He handed it to her. "Thank you."

James scanned the room but didn't see Ella Ruth anywhere. Where had she gone?

The song ended a moment later as he mulled over his sister's words in his head. It was time to figure out if this was the true Cinderella with a test. "Amanda, I think we should write a story together. Right now. What do you think? You could even illustrate it."

"Write a story with you? Right now?" Amanda stammered. "Okay, sure. I'll be right back."

She darted away, leaving James confused again.

"Who was that woman you were dancing with before Amanda?" Eliza asked, sashaying over to him.

"Her stepsister, Ella Ruth," James said, recalling the magical dance they shared.

"It seemed to me like you have a real connection with her, not Amanda," Eliza said. "I saw how you two were looking at each other while you were dancing."

"Ella Ruth isn't the one from the gala, Amanda is... I think," James said. "I'm about to find out for sure. Amanda and I are going to write a story together right now."

Eliza chuckled. "That'll be interesting."

Chapter Thirteen

Ella Ruth hurried away after Amanda cut in and began dancing with James. She felt as though she couldn't breathe, as if all the guests were closing in around her. The music felt overwhelmingly loud, and her heart pounded in her ears.

Dancing with James had been one of the most beautiful moments of her life, but Amanda had put an end to it. Did she have any idea how devastating that was?

"What's wrong?" Laura asked, catching up to her. "I saw you dancing with James, then Amanda cut in."

"I had to get out of there. I couldn't stand to see my stepsister dancing with the man I'm falling in love with," Ella Ruth blurted, then clamped a hand over her mouth.

"Falling in love with? I thought you said you barely knew him."

"I do barely know him, but I feel like I've known him my entire life. He's so easy to talk to. I thought if I convinced myself that I didn't care about him, it might be easier to help Amanda deceive him, but I have to admit to myself that I am falling in love with him. What is wrong with me?" Ella Ruth cried, sitting on a chair on the balcony. Laura sat next to her.

"You're falling in love! Nothing is wrong with you," Laura insisted. "I knew it. That's why we have to put a stop to this."

"I can't," Ella Ruth said, shaking her head. She couldn't bear to let Laura get shunned. "I'm going to the bathroom. I'll be right back."

"I'm going to get more food," Laura said.

Ella Ruth walked down the hall to the bathroom, where it was quieter. The upbeat music continued to thump from the ballroom, but at least she could hear herself think here.

She turned a corner and bumped into someone. "Oh, I'm sorry."

"Don't worry about it. I wasn't watching where I was going. I'm Eliza, James' sister," said the young woman with long brown hair and warm brown eyes. She looked quite a bit like James.

"I'm Ella Ruth."

"You were dancing with my brother a minute ago, right?"

"Yes, but it was nothing," Ella Ruth lied.

"Didn't look like nothing to me," Eliza said. "You're the real Cinderella from the gala, aren't you?"

Ella Ruth's heart lurched. "What? No. It's not me. It's my stepsister, Amanda."

"Are you sure? Because I could tell you and James shared a connection when you were dancing. I can't say the same about Amanda. She's very..." Eliza cleared her throat. "She doesn't seem like someone my brother would be interested in. You tried to tell him you were the one he was looking for, didn't you? I saw it."

"You saw that?" Ella Ruth asked, her heart hammering. Was everything about to fall apart? If Eliza knew the truth, would she tell James and get Laura shunned? "No, I was lying. I was just jealous of my stepsister. It's silly, really."

"You shouldn't be jealous of her. Trust me." Eliza snorted a laugh.

"Well, I've never had a boyfriend, and she gets boyfriends so easily," Ella Ruth went on, inwardly cringing at the lie. "I just wanted to see if James would believe me. But I was wrong to lie about it. I feel bad now. I shouldn't have done that. I'm not the one from the ball. Amanda is. I took her bracelet out of her room to look at it and asked her what the charms meant. And I read her story." Ella Ruth sighed soberly for effect. "I feel sick with guilt just thinking about it. I shouldn't have lied to him. I hope he forgives me."

"Wow. Okay, okay. I'm sure he will forgive you. My brother is quite a catch. A lot of the women here tried to tell him it was them," Eliza said, touching Ella Ruth's arm. "Don't feel bad."

"Can you tell him I said I'm sorry?" Ella Ruth asked, frowning.

"Sure," Eliza said. "He'll forgive you. Don't worry. My brother is a very forgiving person."

"Thank you. I feel so much better." Ella Ruth smiled with mock relief.

"It was nice to meet you," Eliza said, then continued down the hall.

"You too." Ella Ruth stepped into the bathroom, and a few minutes later, she was walking toward the refreshment table, where Laura was still standing with her plate of food.

"Ella Ruth!" Amanda cried, barreling around the corner. "I've been looking everywhere for you! James wants to write a story with me. I need your help." Amanda grabbed her hand and pulled her toward the balcony as Laura followed them. "Just stay here, and I'll put this plant between us. Help me."

Ella Ruth helped her slide a large potted plant closer to where she'd been sitting, which hid her almost completely. On the other side of the plant were two empty chairs, where Ella Ruth supposed James and Amanda would sit.

"You sit there, and I'll sit here, on the other side of the plant. Then you can whisper your ideas to me," Amanda said.

"That is the most ridiculous idea I've ever heard," Laura said flatly. "Even for you, Amanda."

"Shhh," Amanda whispered. "Here he comes."

"You left your drink and purse on the table," James said, walking over and handing her a cup of punch and Ella Ruth's purse, which matched the dress Amanda was wearing—the dress Ella Ruth had worn to the gala. What was she doing with Ella Ruth's purse?

Ella Ruth felt her heart drop. Her notebook was in that purse. Was that why Amanda was saying it was her purse? Laura gave her a wide-eyed look, confirming her suspicions.

"Oh, I'm such a scatterbrain. Thank you for getting it for me," Amanda said. "Come sit with me." She patted the chair beside her.

Ella Ruth peeked through the leaves of the plant to see James sitting down in the chair farthest from her.

"So, what should our story be about? I know you only let me read part of your story, but you said you've written three young adult fantasy and science fiction novels. What are they about? I mean, I read the story in your notebook, but I don't know what your other three books are about."

"Well, the first one is about Naomi going on a school field trip to Europe, where she finds a magic diary in the wall of an ancient castle. She goes back in time with it to the Middle Ages, where she finds out she's a princess. She had amnesia, so she never knew where she came from. The second one is about her best friend coming back in time with her and falling in love, but then she gets sick, and Naomi has to travel to the future to get medicine for her. The third one is about... Uh..." Amanda reached behind her through the plant and tapped Ella Ruth's arm.

"It's about Naomi refusing an arranged marriage and falling in love with a commoner, but then she's kidnapped by the enemy kingdom and realizes that man was a spy," Ella Ruth whispered. With the music blaring from the ballroom, James couldn't hear her.

Amanda repeated Ella Ruth's summary.

"But she escapes and finds her way back to the castle, then convinces her father to call off the arranged marriage," Ella Ruth added, and Amanda repeated it.

"A magic, time-traveling diary? That sounds interesting," James said. "What if we wrote a prequel to your series? You said Naomi has amnesia, right? What if we write about how she got to the future in the first place and how she got amnesia? Or is that already explained in the first book?"

Amanda froze.

"It starts with her waking up in the hospital after she gets hit by a car. When she travels through time, she lands in the road and gets hit. That's how she gets amnesia. But then it skips forward a few years to the field trip, so we could write about her life in between. What was it like for her to get adopted and not know who she was or where she came from?" Ella Ruth whispered through the plant.

"...That's how she gets amnesia. But then it skips forward a few years to the field trip...and...and then..." Amanda stammered, then reached behind her, batting at the leaves of the tree.

"So, we could write about her life in between, like what it was like for her to get adopted and not know who she was or where she came from," Ella Ruth whispered, and Amanda repeated it back to James with a fake smile.

"Are you okay? Why do you keep hitting the plant?" James chuckled. "What, you don't like plants?"

"What? No. I love plants," Amanda said, awkwardly patting one of the branches as Ella Ruth held back a laugh. "I'm fine. I'm just nervous. I'm afraid you won't like my weird ideas."

"Weird? No, I love your ideas," James said, leaning forward. "I think your writing is brilliant."

"Oh, thank you," Amanda said, flipping her hair over her shoulder.

Laura rolled her eyes and imitated Amanda, causing Ella Ruth to laugh accidentally, but only for a moment until she caught herself.

"What was that?" James asked, looking around. "Is that plant...laughing?"

"No. It's nothing. Just me laughing," Amanda said, forcing a laugh. "I just can't believe you think my writing is brilliant."

"Of course, I do. That's one of the reasons why I like you so much," James said, causing Ella Ruth's stomach to churn with an unpleasant emotion.

Was that...jealousy she was feeling? If she was honest with herself, it was. She was jealous of Amanda, and she hated it. She peeked through the branches to see Amanda leaning forward. Was she trying to kiss him? James was writing something down, oblivious.

Before she could stop herself, Ella Ruth reached through the plant and poked Amanda in the side, causing her to jump and shriek.

"What's wrong?" James asked.

"I...saw a spider. Sorry. I'm terrified of spiders," Amanda said, swatting Ella Ruth's hand away.

"Where?" He looked around.

"It's gone now. Don't worry. Now, where were we?" she asked, leaning forward to kiss him again.

Laura shook her head, scowling, then walked around the plant. Ella Ruth tugged on the skirt of her gown to stop her, but Laura ignored her.

"You should draw an illustration for the book, Amanda," Laura said, then smiled apologetically. "Sorry. I was sitting over there and couldn't help but overhear. She's a talented artist. Aren't you, Amanda?"

Ella Ruth let her head fall into her hands. Amanda couldn't even draw a stick figure, and Laura knew it. Wasn't she worried about Amanda ruining her reputation? She didn't seem to care at the moment.

"What an excellent idea," James said, handing her a pencil. "Please. I would love to see more of your drawings. Would you draw what your character Naomi looks like? Or maybe the castle from the field trip in Europe?"

"Uh, sure," Amanda said, taking the pencil and opening Ella Ruth's notebook. She flipped through several pages, looking for a drawing of Naomi or the castle. "You're putting me on the spot here, James. I'm a bit nervous."

"Don't be nervous," James said. "It's just me."

"You're just being modest," Laura said with a grin, then turned to James. "You won't believe it when you see her drawing." She turned back to Amanda. "Go ahead."

Ella Ruth looked at her friend, shaking her head. *What is she thinking?* she wondered.

Amanda found a drawing of Naomi's face and pretended to draw for a few minutes. James leaned closer and noticed the drawing.

"I saw that one at the gala, silly," he said with a chuckle.

"Why don't you draw a new one?" Laura asked.

James nodded. "I'd love to see a new one."

Amanda held the pencil to a blank sheet of paper and began drawing, then furiously erased it. "I...uh...have to go to the bathroom. I'll be right back." She abruptly stood up and walked toward the ballroom, and while James was talking to Laura, Ella Ruth used the distraction to hurry around the corner and go into the ballroom through another doorway.

"Here. Draw your character or your castle from the story or whatever," Amanda demanded, shoving the notebook into Ella Ruth's arms. "I was afraid if I passed it back to you that he would see it."

"Probably," Ella Ruth said, sighing as she took the pencil and began sketching another drawing of the face of Naomi, the character from her story. On the next page, she drew a new drawing of the ruins of a castle. Amanda went to the bathroom and returned.

"Are you almost done?" she asked, tapping her foot. "He's going to think I left. What is Laura talking to him about out there?"

Ella Ruth's stomach dropped at the thought. Would she tell James the truth? She shouldn't have left her with him. She quickly finished the drawing and handed it back to Amanda.

"Just use your pencil to trace some of the outlines when you sit down to make it look more like you drew it," she said. "Tell him you were too nervous to draw in front of him."

"Great. Thanks." Amanda pivoted on her heel and walked back toward James, sitting on the balcony. Ella Ruth went through the other door and crept back over to her spot behind the plant.

"I'm sorry I left like that, James," Amanda said. "I was too nervous to draw in front of you." She opened the book, and James' eyes went wide.

"You drew that so quickly," he said in awe. "It's incredible. Look at the detail."

Amanda went over the outline of Naomi's face with her pencil but accidentally made it crooked. She then tried to erase it, but it only made it worse. Ella Ruth cringed, and Laura walked through the ballroom, through the other door, then crept over and sat down next to her.

"She's ruining your drawing," Laura whispered. "It's so obvious she can't draw. He's going to figure it out."

Ella Ruth sighed. "What did you say to him while we were gone? Did you tell him anything?"

"No. I knew you'd be angry with me if I did," Laura said in a low voice. "I just told him about how you're growing a massive thousand-pound pumpkin, and he should come to the Common Ground Fair to see you win the contest. He said he will be gone for a few weeks, but will be back by then. He said he'd have to have Amanda come along with him as his date."

Ella Ruth smiled. "At least he will see my pumpkin."

"He's going to see you win. I have no doubt."

Chapter Fourteen

"Here. Will you write the opening to the story? It's based on your world," James said to Amanda on the other side of the plant. "You know it better than I do."

"You're putting me on the spot again, James," Amanda said with a nervous laugh. "I have to...go get a drink." she started to get up.

"Your drink is right there next to you. I know you're just making excuses because you're nervous, but I want you to feel comfortable around me. Here, how about I write the first paragraph, then you write the next one?" he said, taking the notebook from her.

"I guess it's more than fair, since I drew the illustrations," Amanda said, obvious relief in her voice.

"You're right. It was unfair of me to ask you to do both," he agreed, then began scribbling away in the notebook. A few moments later, he handed it back to her, and she read it.

"That's really good," she said.

"Your turn. You did say you want to write a story together, right?"

"Oh, yes, I do."

"We both know you're a great writer. Just write from the heart and pretend like I'm not here," he said gently, and Ella Ruth peeked at him through the leaves of the plant, smiling. He was so kind.

Amanda held the pencil and hesitated, then finally wrote something down and handed it back to him. James read it slowly.

"I'm sorry. It's not very good. It's just because I'm nervous. I'll make it better when I go home," Amanda stammered.

"Don't worry. We'll edit it and make it even better," James said. "How many chapters do you think we can write tonight?"

"Chapters?" Amanda asked, gulping. "Uh... I have to go. I'm sorry, James."

"You have to go already?" James asked.

"It's midnight," Ella Ruth realized in a whisper as she noticed the clock through the door in the ballroom. "We do have to go."

"Yes. I have so many chores to do early in the morning. I have to get up before dawn to feed the donkey," she said, gathering up her skirts and the purse.

"We don't have a donkey," Ella Ruth whispered to Laura, and they both held back a laugh.

"Wait. Will you come to the Common Ground Fair with me next month after I get back from the internship? Laura said Ella Ruth grew a giant pumpkin, and she's entering it into a contest. It sounds like fun. I'm sure there will be many things to do there."

"The fair? With all those stinky animals?" Amanda asked, then plastered on a smile. "Oh, yes. I love animals. And pumpkins. I want to support Ella Ruth in her endeavors. I'd love to go with you."

"Can I pick you up?"

"No, no. I don't want anyone to see me with you. Let's meet there. I'm risking a lot to be with you, but it's worth it." She batted her eyelashes. "I'll have to wear a disguise to the fair, too, so no one recognizes me."

"Oh, because of the rules. I understand."

"Sounds wonderful," Amanda said. "Have a nice time in New York."

"Here." He took the notebook and wrote down an address. "You can send me letters to this address. Can you write down your address for me?"

She tore off a corner of a blank page and wrote down her address, then handed it to him. "I can't believe we have to wait until next month to see each other."

"Absence makes the heart grow fonder," he said with a smile.

"What?" Amanda blinked.

Ella Ruth had to turn away to hide her laugh.

"Don't worry, Amanda. It will go by quickly, and when I get back, we can spend time together and get to know each other," James said.

"I'll see you then. Goodbye." She stood on her tip toes, kissed his cheek, then turned and hurried away. Ella Ruth and Laura went in the other direction, following her toward the road.

"Here. Take your stupid notebook," Amanda said, thrusting it back into Ella Ruth's arms. "I made a complete fool out of myself. How can I ever write a whole chapter of a story with him, let alone several? He's going to figure out that I can't write well or draw."

"*Ja*, he is," Laura said with a wry smile. "And when he does, you'll make an even bigger fool of yourself then."

"Oh, stop it, Laura," Amanda snapped. "Let's just get out of here. And by the way, he's leaving until next month, and he might give up being a millionaire so he can become a teacher!"

"I know," Ella Ruth said. "So, are you still going to keep up this charade?"

"He hasn't decided yet. He doesn't want to let his father down. I think I can convince him through the letters and when he gets back that he should give up this silly dream of being a teacher so he can be rich."

Ella Ruth rolled her eyes. "And if he doesn't?"

"Well, then, I will hopefully meet some of his wealthy friends, so my time isn't wasted."

Laura shook her head, glancing at Ella Ruth.

"And you're going to write those letters to him, Ella Ruth, pretending to be me. I wouldn't know what to say, and you know you're a much better writer than I am. You're the one who knows all of his strange references. I hardly know what he's talking about half the time. Absence makes the heart grow fonder? What does that even mean?" Amanda asked as they hurried down the hill toward the buggy parked in the shadows beneath the trees.

"It means when you are apart from someone, you miss them and become closer in spirit," Ella Ruth explained. "If I write the letters, don't you think he will figure out it wasn't you who wrote them?"

"You'll have to make them sound like me."

"That's not such a good idea," Laura said as they climbed into the buggy. "That would give it away."

"Fine. Write them to make them sound like you, but I will have to read them along with his letters so I know what you talked about," Amanda said, sitting in the back.

"It's a terrible plan," Laura whispered to Ella Ruth as they sat in the front.

"I know. But don't tell *her* that," Ella Ruth whispered back, then drove the buggy home, not realizing that she had dropped her notebook in the dark.

James hurried after Amanda to ask her what time she wanted to meet at the fair, but the crowd slowed him down. Several young women approached him, trying to get his attention, but he moved past them to follow Amanda. By the time he got outside, he saw her running through the gate with Ella Ruth and Laura. They were gone. He would just have to look up the fair schedule online and go when the pumpkin contest started. Tomorrow was Sunday, and since he would be going to church and he knew Amanda would be too, they would have to meet some time after.

Something glinted in the moonlight on the driveway, and as he walked closer, he realized it was Amanda's notebook on the ground. The glossy cover reflected the light. He picked it up, flipping through the pages, revealing her beautiful drawings and thousands of hand-written words.

She had been so hesitant to even let him read her work at the gala, and now that he had it in his hands, he longed to read the rest. He remembered she had said she had written several stories in it.

Would she be angry with him if he read them?

Her words drew him in so much that he wasn't sure he could stop himself.

Maybe I should give it back to her before I leave, he thought, but something told him not to. It was the same feeling he got when he thought about giving Amanda back the bracelet.

I should wait until I'm one-hundred percent sure she is the woman from the gala, he thought. *Then I will give both the bracelet and the notebook back.*

After Ella Ruth dropped Laura off, she and Amanda quietly entered the house.

"Well, how did it go?" Priscilla asked from where she sat on the couch, reading a book. She stood up.

Amanda gave her a summary of the evening. "He asked me to write and illustrate a story with him. I didn't expect that. I almost blew it."

"You should have expected it. He loves writing and literature, and he was probably testing you," Ella Ruth said. "You know, to see if you're me."

"Ella Ruth, can't you just teach Amanda how to draw?" Priscilla asked.

Amanda laughed. "It's hopeless. No amount of art lessons will make me less terrible at drawing."

I couldn't agree more, Ella Ruth thought.

"You're just going to have to be nearby for every date, then, Ella Ruth," Priscilla said.

"Well, that's the thing. James is leaving for an internship for a few weeks. He won't be back until next month." Amanda explained the entire situation, and Priscilla frowned.

"You can convince him to give up this silly idea of teaching, Amanda. How could he throw away the opportunity of running such a successful company? You can convince him through the letters. Actually, Ella Ruth will. Won't you, Ella Ruth?" Priscilla asked, turning to Ella Ruth.

"I'm not sure I can convince him to give up his dream," Ella Ruth replied. "Even if I tried."

"You'll have to try," Priscilla said. "Or you can kiss your laptop goodbye."

Tears pricked Ella Ruth's eyes as she let out a long breath. "I'll try, then. But I can't control what he decides."

"Well, I know, but you can do your best. So, when will you two see him again?" Priscilla asked.

"I have a date at the Common Ground Fair in a few weeks after he gets home for the silly pumpkin contest that Ella Ruth is entering," Amanda said, shooting a glare at Ella Ruth. "Could he have picked a worse place for our first date? There are so many smelly animals. I'd rather go to the mall."

"And are you going to want me to be nearby when you get engaged, too? How long do you really think you can keep this up?" Ella Ruth asked. James already seemed suspicious, and if he kept on testing Amanda, then hopefully, this entire farce would end sooner rather than later.

He hasn't given Amanda back the bracelet yet, which must mean he isn't entirely convinced, Ella Ruth realized.

So, there was still hope.

"We'll cross that bridge when we come to it," Amanda said.

"Let's get to bed. We have to feed the donkey early in the morning, remember?" Ella Ruth said sarcastically, headed for her bedroom.

"What donkey?" Priscilla asked.

Ella Ruth let out a small chuckle as she took her bag off her shoulder, opened it, then stopped walking in the hallway. She searched it frantically, but it only took her a moment to realize her notebook was gone.

Oh, no, she thought. *James Baldwin has my notebook. What if he reads all my stories over the next few weeks? And what if I don't get it back?*

CHAPTER FIFTEEN

Over the next few weeks, Ella Ruth wrote letters to James pretending to be Amanda, and he wrote back to her. They wrote to each other almost daily.

In his first letter, he had apologized for taking her notebook with him, then admitted how badly he wanted to read her stories. She couldn't help but smile when she read that, even when he begged for her forgiveness.

Honestly, it was one of the sweetest things anyone had ever said—or written—to her.

They made sure to get the mail before Irvin so he wouldn't see the envelopes from James, and every time Ella Ruth wrote a letter or received one from James, Amanda read it carefully.

"You two are so boring," she complained, reading James' latest letter. "All you talk about is books and your boring lives. This doesn't sound like me at all. You're supposed to make these letters sound like me."

"He's teaching summer classes to inner-city children," Ella Ruth said. "He's near New York City. He gets to make a real difference in those kids' lives. Don't you think that's interesting? Besides, if I wrote about things that you would write about, he would know that you aren't the woman from the gala."

Amanda tossed the letter on the bed. "Going to New York City sounds fabulous, but I wouldn't want to go to the rougher parts of the city. No, thank you."

"That's where he's needed the most," Ella Ruth said as Amanda walked out of the room.

"He asked to talk to you on the phone again. We can't keep making excuses. I already told him about our phone in the store before, so he knows we could call him."

"But then I'd have to talk to him," Amanda said, scrunching her nose. "What if you talk to him instead? Do you think he'd notice?"

"He would notice. You're going to have to talk to him. He probably would know the difference between our voices. He's talked to both of us. Besides, he would notice when he comes home."

"He's only talked to me once and talked to you twice," Amanda said. "Do you really think he would notice?"

"He might. Some people are good at remembering voices. We can't take the risk. It'll be fine. You talk to him, and I will tell you what to say if you need help."

"What day should I tell him? Sunday afternoon?"

"Whenever. Tell me when you're done writing the next one so I can read it," Amanda said, walking down the hall.

Ella Ruth sighed and picked up James' latest letter.

Dear Amanda,

I love being here. Now that I've been here for a while, I feel like I've been really bonding with these middle schoolers. There is one boy, Tyson, who is incredible at basketball, but he doesn't apply himself in writing. I know he is smart. If he just put in the same effort as he puts into basketball, he would get much better grades, but he struggles with spelling.

I have been tutoring him after the classes, and we have been playing a basketball game I made up that we use to spell words. It's really been helping him, and he has improved so much in the past week. When I see his face light up when he finally grasps how to spell a word that he has been struggling with, it makes it all so worth it. It is so rewarding!

I feel like this is what I'm meant to do with my life, but if my parents really need me to run the company, maybe I could just tutor students part-time after school or on the weekends and not teach full-time. That way, I could do both.

But would I really be happy doing it only halfway?

I miss you. I wish we could talk on the phone. What if we plan a time and I call the phone shanty phone or the store phone? Or you could call me.

I think if I could just hear your voice, it would help me so much. I have such a big decision to make, and even though I am having the best time here, it is really weighing on me.

Going to the fair with you will be so much fun. I can't wait to see you again, and I am really looking forward to it.

I can talk on the phone any weekday after 5:00 pm, any time Saturdays, or Sundays after church. Just let me know. I will list my number below.

-James

Ella Ruth smiled as she finished reading the letter. Oh, how she wished that the letter said *Dear Ella Ruth* at the beginning instead of *Dear Amanda.*

James sounded so happy and joyful to be teaching, but he also sounded so conflicted. To be honest, she truly did want to talk to him on the phone.

She sat down at her desk and began writing a letter back to him, pretending to be Amanda.

Dear James,

I am so glad to hear how much you are enjoying your time teaching in New York. And I have been thrilled every day when I have received yet another letter from you.

Ella Ruth tapped her pencil on her chin as she thought. She hated to try to talk him out of teaching full-time, but how could she do it in a subtle way?

I think your idea of tutoring students part-time after school or on the weekends is a great idea. That way, you won't let your father down, and you can still teach part-time. You could have the best of both worlds that way. Your parents need you right now, and perhaps your sister would prefer to have your help. Don't you think you should put your family first?

I can call you from our store phone when we are closed on Sunday afternoons. I hope this Sunday at 4:00 pm works for you as you will probably get the phone call before this letter arrives. We will be home from the church potluck by then and I will take a chance.

I am so looking forward to speaking with you on the phone and hearing more about your time in the city. What is it like there? Have you been able to visit Time Square or see the Statue of Liberty? I have always wanted to go to New York City and see all the different cultures, foods, and historical sites. I've read about it in books many times, and I hope one day I can see it for myself. I hope you take photos to show me.

How wonderful to hear about Tyson's progress. By using a basketball game to teach him spelling, you are using something that interests him, which is engaging him fully. It's a brilliant idea. It delights my heart each day to learn about your time with a different student and every success. I believe you will be successful in any endeavor you choose.

She began to write more about how he would make a wonderful teacher, then erased it.

Perhaps after this internship is over, you will feel like you have done your part and get the desire to teach out of your system so that you can run the company for your father. He would be so proud of you.

I am looking forward to talking with you on the phone and exchanging more letters.

Until then,

Amanda

Ella Ruth had written an 'E' while accidentally starting to sign her name, but she erased it and wrote 'Amanda' over it to cover it up. Time to give it to Amanda. She called Amanda back into the bedroom so she could read the letter.

The following Sunday afternoon, Amanda and Ella Ruth went to Irvin's store to use the phone. Ella Ruth dialed the number James had written down in his last letter. The phone rang, and James answered. Ella Ruth put it on speaker phone so she could hear what he was saying.

"Hello?"

"Hi, James. It's Amanda," Amanda said.

"Hi. It's so nice to hear from you. I have enjoyed receiving your letters."

"I've missed you so much."

Ella Ruth cringed. That was a bit forward.

"I've missed you, too," James said. "How are you?"

"I'm fine. I loved your last letter. How are you? How are your students?"

As James went on about several different students and how they were improving, Amanda made a face like she was bored, but Ella Ruth listened intently.

"There is a girl named Ramona who has improved so much with reading this week. She is very interested in dance, so like the basketball game I made up for Tyson, I made up a dance game for her where we jump onto different letters cut out from paper that we put on the floor, and we use them to spell words. She got the hang of it quickly, and now she's doing so much better in reading the past few days," James explained. "I will make up more similar games for my other students depending on what their interests are. I have a student who likes playing soccer. What do you think I should do for him?"

When James asked her the question, Amanda wasn't listening anymore by that point. Ella Ruth elbowed her.

"Oh, how interesting," Amanda said. "That is so interesting."

Ella Ruth whispered, "Tell him they could cut out letters from paper as he did for Ramona, and they could kick the ball toward the different letters."

Amanda repeated the idea back to James. "Oh, yes. That's a great idea. I'll have to think about it more to flesh it out. So, how is life at home? Are you reading any interesting books lately? Have you had any time to work on your book?"

"I try to write on my laptop when I can, and I do have other notebooks to write in for now. But I have so many chores to do, so that keeps me busy all the time. I barely have any time for myself. But my family needs my help, and they appreciate it, so I don't mind."

Ella Ruth crossed her arms.

"You must be a tremendous help to them," he said.

"Families are the most important thing in the world. That's why we need to do what's best for them and put them before ourselves," Amanda said.

Ella Ruth raised her eyebrows. She almost sounded convincing.

"I see what you're getting at."

"Have you decided yet?"

"I think so. I think I'm going to tell my father I am going to teach full-time."

"No," Amanda blurted out, then said in a softer voice, "Don't you think he will be upset? What if you regret it later on?"

"I think I would only regret my decision if I don't follow my heart," James said. "I know it sounds cliché, but it's true."

"Well, this is a huge decision. All I'm asking is that you think about it more before deciding. You did say that you would finish the internship before making any final decision. I still believe that is a good idea."

"You're right." He sighed. "I've been reading your stories in your notebook. I'm sorry that I read them... They just hooked me, and I couldn't stop reading. You're so incredibly talented, and your drawings are amazing. I hope you aren't too mad at me."

"Tell him it's okay as long as you get it back when he comes home," Ella Ruth whispered, and Amanda repeated it back to him.

"I'm not mad at all. I don't mind if you read my stories," Amanda said. "Thank you. I'm glad you like them."

"Like them? I love them. These deserve to be read by thousands of people, Amanda. I'll give it back to you when I get home. I also wanted to let you know that your stories inspired me to find my students stories that they would like to read for fun. Normally they see extra reading as torture, but I knew they would be surprised by how some books are impossible to put down. When I found myself staying up so late reading your stories, I knew I could help them find books they love. I brought in a stack of books I loved when I was younger and asked them to each choose one, and it worked! Books have become like popcorn to them. They are no longer satisfied with reading just one, but now they want another and another. In turn, their school work and reading aloud is also showing improvement. I hope reading becomes a life-long passion for them. Thank you accidentally leaving behind your stories which gave me this idea."

Tears filled Ella Ruth's eyes as she listened to James speak so passionately about how her writing connected to his students in New York and had to step away so he wouldn't hear her crying. He was doing it. He was using his gifts to make a real difference.

How she longed to do the same one day.

"Wow, that's great news!" Amanda said.

"I knew you'd think so," James said.

"Well, I have to go before anyone finds me here," Amanda said.

"Can you call again same time next week?"

"I'll try. Bye, James." Amanda hung up the phone and sighed.

Ella Ruth wiped her eyes.

"Why are you crying?" Amanda asked, bewildered.

"Did you not listen to his story just now about how he got his students to love reading?" Ella Ruth raised her hands.

"Sure, that was nice," Amanda said, shrugging. "He sounds like he's going to choose to be a teacher. I think I'm wasting my time."

"Me too. So why not quit?"

"My mother would be so disappointed in me if I gave up now. She's convinced I can change his mind, and if not, she thinks I can make connections through him. I don't want to let her down."

"Even if you know it's wrong to deceive him like this?" Ella Ruth asked. "Even if it's likely he will find out and never want to speak to you again?"

"I have to try," Amanda said. "You don't understand. I can't let my mother down. She expects so much from me."

"What she is asking you to do is wrong."

"I still have to do it."

"No, you don't. Not when it's wrong."

"Just leave me alone, Ella Ruth." Amanda waved her away. "Your mother is dead. You wouldn't understand."

Ella Ruth bit back a sharp retort she knew she would regret later as tears stung her eyes. How could Amanda say such a thing?

"Yes, she is, but she would never have asked me to lie to someone and pretend to be someone that I'm not. And even if she did, I would do the right thing and not lie." Ella Ruth marched past Amanda and walked out the door to the buggy.

CHAPTER SIXTEEN

The remainder of James' internship passed as he and Ella Ruth continued to exchange letters. Through the letters, Ella Ruth felt like she was beginning to get to know James on a much deeper level, but Amanda remained indifferent toward the letters except to let Ella Ruth know what a bother it was to have to read so many.

Finally, James returned home to Unity in time for Xavier and Esther's wedding.

At the wedding, Ella Ruth was Esther's bridesmaid along with Laura, but they wore their normal Amish attire. It wasn't against any rules in Unity, but they didn't participate in the dancing. Many people from the community attended the wedding, but they left shortly after dinner, before all of the dancing.

Some people in the community did not approve of Esther leaving to marry an *Englisher*, so they had chosen to not attend. Esther wasn't breaking any rules since she hadn't been baptized into the church yet, so she wouldn't be shunned. Still, her leaving had ruffled a few feathers, but Esther refused to be disheartened by it and was completely sure of her decision.

Ella Ruth had been looking forward to Esther's wedding as a chance to get out of the house, away from her mundane, daily chores. The wedding was held at Xavier's parents' mansion, where a large tent had been set up with twinkling lights for the reception. In the field, chairs had been set up facing a beautiful trellis where the couple would be married.

She knew James would be attending the wedding, since he was the groom's best friend, and knew he would be the best man from his letters. When she arrived at the wedding, she spotted him with Xavier outside the tent with the other groomsman, waiting for the ceremony to begin. Ella Ruth and Laura arrived with their families and walked past unnoticed—for now.

Ella Ruth went inside the mansion to congratulate Esther and help her get ready. When the ceremony was about to begin and the wedding party gathered behind the tent, James noticing her was inevitable.

"You two will walk down the aisle together," the groom's mother told James and Ella Ruth, then proceeded to tell the others who would walk down with whom.

Ella Ruth gulped, her heart racing as James came over to her to stand beside her.

"Hello, Ella Ruth. It's nice to see you. How are you?" James said as they lined up.

"Good. The ball was divine," she said, her voice shaking. "We all had a marvelous time."

"Glad to hear it."

"So glad you found your Cinderella," Ella Ruth said, and Laura raised an eyebrow at her.

"Me too. We have been writing letters for the past few weeks. I feel like I've really gotten to know her," James said.

"How was your internship?"

"It was incredible. Honestly, I hated to leave and say goodbye to all the students. I really got to know them and bond with them. They asked me to come back next summer, though as a volunteer," he explained. "I hope I can go every year."

"That's wonderful!" Ella Ruth exclaimed. "It must have been so hard to leave. I wouldn't know, though. I've never been able to travel or get to know people in other places."

"Maybe you will one day."

"I don't think it will ever happen for me. My family needs me too much. I could never just leave them for more than a few days. Besides, we aren't allowed to fly in airplanes, so I could never go to Europe."

"You want to go to Europe?" He raised his eyebrows.

"Oh, yes. There is so much history there. But I suppose all I can do is read about it in books. I'll never make it there." She froze, realizing she had said too much. She had told him something similar at the gala, and she had even told him that she couldn't leave her family.

Ugh, why did I just say all of that to him? she wondered. "Silly me. I'm sorry. I don't know why I'm telling you this."

"You never know, Ella Ruth. Maybe one day you'll make it there. What about *Rumspringa?* Does your community do that?"

"Well, yes. Not everyone goes, and I missed my chance. Ever since our mother died... Never mind." She shook her head.

"Amanda told me about that. I'm sorry."

"Thank you. Well, it's too late for me to travel now. I'll never be able to go."

"I know you aren't allowed to fly in airplanes, but why can't you leave your family for more than a few days?" he asked.

She had to give him a different reason than she had before, and she might as well tell him something truthful. With her voice barely above a whisper, she explained, "Part of it is because my two younger sisters were kidnapped by human traffickers and held in an abandoned warehouse for a few days. It was a few years ago, and they still aren't the same carefree girls they used to be. They often have nightmares at night, and when they wake up crying, I need to be there for them."

"I'm so sorry, Ella Ruth. How terrible. Your family has been through so much. I can't even imagine if something ever happened to my sister, Eliza. I'd lose my mind."

"It was very difficult for our family. It still is. Anyway, I need to be there for them."

"Well, I admire you for being so loyal to them. Even if your family has been through hard times, things can always change. You never know. Never say never." The music changed to the song Esther chose for the procession, and James stuck out his arm, smiling.

The procession began. When it was their turn, James gently led her down the grassy aisle, and for a moment, she let herself imagine it was their own wedding. Many of the people in attendance were her friends and neighbors from the community, so it was easy to let herself pretend they were there to support her. She looked up and couldn't help but smile at James, who was already smiling down at her. The sight made her heart flip in her chest, which caused her feet to trip over themselves, her foot catching in a small hole in the ground that had been covered by grass. Before she realized what was happening, she was falling forward, but two strong hands grabbed her arm to steady her, helping her regain her balance.

She blinked, her face heated fiercely with embarrassment. "Do you think anyone saw that?" Ella Ruth looked around, but everyone was still smiling as they had been.

"No." He grinned. "I don't think anyone noticed." They made their way to the front, then parted ways as they took their places. The sun was hot above them, but she barely noticed.

When Esther walked down the aisle, Ella Ruth and Laura immediately had tears running down their faces. She looked beautiful in her long, white, elegant gown and veil. Secretly, Ella Ruth hoped for a wedding dress of her own like that one someday. Esther's hair was pinned half up in a beautiful style, and the rest of her dark hair fell in curls down her back.

As Esther and Xavier said their vows, Ella Ruth continued to wipe tears from her eyes. She was so happy for her friend, and she could only hope that one day she would become just as happy if she found a person who loved her as much as Xavier clearly loved Esther. Her hopes that it could be James were suppressed too far below the surface to consider or even think about just now.

After it ended, James walked back down the aisle with Ella Ruth. "Thank you so much for catching me. You prevented me from making an utter fool of myself."

He chuckled. "Don't worry about it. Every wedding needs a good mishap. It helps make it memorable."

"Oh, really? So, are you saying people did notice me tripping? Did you only lie to me so I wouldn't feel embarrassed in front of everyone?" She put her hands on her hips.

James put up his hands defensively. "Hey, hey. So, what if they noticed? At least you didn't fall on your face in the grass. So it wasn't really a big thing, but only a little stumble. Hardly noticeable." He laughed.

"Thanks to you." She shook her head, smiling. "Come on, let's go congratulate them."

At the reception, they sat on opposite ends of the wedding party table, so she didn't get to talk to James as much as she had hoped. After the meal, all the Amish guests left.

As she drove away in the buggy with her family, Amanda whispered to her, "I just hope James doesn't dance with anyone else. I saw the way you looked at him when you two walked down the aisle. Could you be more obvious?"

"I didn't mean to," Ella Ruth said, turning away as her stomach churned.

"You have to stay away from him. Don't talk to him unless it's necessary."

"Why? Are you scared he will fall in love with me or realize I'm the one he's looking for?" Ella Ruth whispered hotly.

"Well, yes. I am. If you want what's good for Laura, you will keep your distance from him. Understand?" Amanda said in a low voice, eyes narrowed.

"Fine."

Ella Ruth wished she could have the chance to dance with James just one more time.

But she knew it wasn't meant to be.

CHAPTER SEVENTEEN

On Sunday after church and their usual potluck lunch, Amanda, Ella Ruth, Sadie, Laura, Katie, and Lilly drove to the Common Ground Fair in Laura's buggy while Irvin and Priscilla rode in their buggy with the younger children, Debra and Seth. Many communities held church services in Amish homes, but in Unity, they had built their own church that doubled as a school several years ago.

Early that morning, Irvin and Ella Ruth had driven her pumpkin on their flatbed wagon to the fairgrounds with their two horses. It had taken several of their neighbors to carefully move it onto the wagon. When the horses had pulled it to the fairgrounds, it looked almost like a pumpkin carriage in a fairytale.

Butterflies filled her belly at the thought of the contest, and she hoped more than anything that she would win the prize money so she could buy a new, better laptop one day.

In the buggy, Amanda changed into her disguise—*Englisher* clothing, complete with a hat and sunglasses. Even though they were not allowed to wear makeup, she still put it on, complete with lipstick. She wore her hair up in a bun to hide its length.

"How do I look, Sadie?" Amanda asked her sister.

"Like a true *Englisher*," Sadie said. "Truly. I don't think anyone we know will know it's you."

"We're going to have to make sure you stay away from *Daed* and anyone else who might recognize you," Ella Ruth told Amanda.

During the entire ride, Katie, Sadie, and Lilly again peppered them with questions about what the ball was like.

"Remember, four women asked me about my dress, so I handed out four of the slips of paper you gave me with your name and the store phone number on it," Ella Ruth said.

"I know, that's so incredible!" Sadie exclaimed. "And two have already called and have made appointments to meet me next month. I hope someone will actually hire me to make a dress for them. But what would I charge? How will I take their measurements? Learn about their preferences? What if they take one look at me, realize I'm Amish, and run away?"

"Nonsense," Ella Ruth said. "If they want to meet up with you, I'll go with you. Amish are known for their skilled work. I think you can use the fact that you're Amish to your advantage."

"Really?" Sadie asked.

"Of course. I'll help you however I can, Sadie."

After they arrived at the fair and parked the buggy next to several others, they walked over to where the contest would be held.

A Ferris wheel reached up to the sky, and later that evening, its twinkling lights would be seen all across the entire fairground. There was also a children's roller coaster, flying swings, and several other rides. Children walked around with cotton candy and popcorn, and food trucks lined the pathways. The smells of barbequed meats filled the air along with the scent of manure, which didn't bother Ella Ruth in the slightest.

"Ugh, that smells terrible," Amanda complained. "I can't believe you enjoy this."

"We look forward to it every year," Katie said. "We love it here. What's not to love?"

"Manure. Ugh." Amanda sidestepped a small pile of it in her high heels.

They walked to the spot where the pumpkin contest would be held, and Katie and Lilly gasped at all the enormous pumpkins. Priscilla and Irvin walked over to them with the children, and Ella Ruth shooed Amanda away.

"Quick, before my father recognizes you," she said, waving her hand. Amanda hurried away and stood in line to get popcorn.

"Your pumpkin is definitely the largest one," Irvin said, patting Ella Ruth's shoulder. "You did an excellent job growing it."

"Thank you, *Daed*," Ella Ruth said.

"They're all huge!" Debra, her younger sister, cried.

"But yours is the hugest," Seth said, and they all laughed.

"Where's Amanda?" Irvin asked, looking around.

"Getting popcorn," Lilly said, which was true. "There was a long line. She might be gone a while."

"I hope she doesn't miss the judging," Irvin said.

It's not like she cares, Ella Ruth thought. Where was James? They had agreed on their last phone call to meet here at this time.

A few moments later, she saw him walking around the corner, wearing a t-shirt that showed off his muscular arms. His dark hair was pushed to the side in an endearing way, and she ignored her pounding heart as she walked over to him. He looked...different. More confident and more joyful. She could see it in his eyes. Clearly, the internship had impacted him deeply.

"Hi, James. Amanda's in line to get popcorn," she said, gesturing. "She needs to stay away from my father and anyone else we know so they don't see her with you, wearing *Englisher* clothing."

"I understand," James said with a nod, then noticed the pumpkins. "Wow! I think those are taller than me. Which one is yours?"

"The third on the left," Ella Ruth said.

"She did a great job raising it and growing it," Laura said, stepping up behind her. "Isn't she amazing?"

James smiled at Ella Ruth tenderly, causing her heart to flip. "Yes, she is."

A man with a microphone began speaking. "They're about to announce the winner!" Ella Ruth said, hurrying over with Laura. James was not far behind them. He kept his distance, and a few moments later, Amanda joined him, holding a bag of popcorn.

"Hello, James," Amanda said coolly. "I'm so glad you're finally back from your internship. You must have been so happy to come home."

"Actually, I wanted to stay there forever. I got to know the kids, and it was so hard to leave them."

"But I thought you missed me." Amanda frowned.

"Of course, I did," he said, chuckling. "It was just hard to say goodbye to them, but I'm probably going to go back next year."

"Really?" Amanda asked, and Ella Ruth gave her a look. "I mean, that's great. Want some popcorn?"

"Oh, yes, please," James said, taking a handful. "You must be so proud of your stepsister. She must have worked really hard to grow that pumpkin. It's huge! I think it will win."

Ella Ruth smiled, overhearing their conversation.

"I'm so proud of dear Ella Ruth. Not many people are talented enough to grow such a big pumpkin," Amanda gushed with a wave of her hand, and Ella Ruth almost believed her.

She almost sounds sincere, she thought.

"Thank you, everyone, for coming to the Common Ground Fair's annual pumpkin contest!" the announcer said. "We have weighed each pumpkin. There will be two prizes today—awards will go to the heaviest one and the most beautiful pumpkin. Are you ready to hear the verdict?"

The crowd cheered, and the announcer held up two blue ribbons. Ella Ruth's heart raced, and Katie and Lilly grabbed her hands.

"For the heaviest pumpkin, third place goes to Bill Bontrager at eight hundred and ninety-two pounds. Second place goes to Fanny Montgomery at one thousand one hundred and eighteen pounds."

The crowd applauded as the two winners went up to receive their ribbons. Irvin, Katie, Lilly, and Laura turned to Ella Ruth with wide eyes.

"Fanny only got second place. That could mean—" Laura began.

"And the grand prize of one thousand dollars and the blue ribbon goes to Ella Ruth Holt with the heaviest pumpkin weighing a whopping one thousand one hundred and forty-two pounds!"

Ella Ruth covered her mouth, stifling a shriek. Her father and sisters, along with Laura, congratulated her, hugging her, and she wiped a tear from her eye as she gathered her wits and made her way to the podium. The announcer handed her an envelope of cash and a blue ribbon, which she placed on her pumpkin.

"Not only did Ella Ruth win first place for the heaviest pumpkin, but she also won the award for the most beautiful pumpkin, which is a two-hundred-and-fifty-dollar prize and another ribbon," the announcer said, handing her another envelope and ribbon. "Your pumpkin looks big and beautiful enough to be a carriage for Cinderella."

That was what her sisters had said. Ella Ruth took the prizes gratefully, stunned, as the crowd applauded. Fanny Montgomery, who usually won every year, came over to her.

"Congratulations, Ella Ruth. You earned it," she said, hugging Ella Ruth. "I hope to compete against you for many years to come. You're giving me a run for my money." She laughed, pushing her glasses higher up on her nose.

"Thank you. I plan to." Ella Ruth smiled.

After Ella Ruth made her way down from the stage, her family surrounded her, but James and Amanda kept their distance so that Irvin wouldn't see Amanda in her disguise.

"I knew you'd win," Lilly said, hugging her.

"We told you it looked like a Cinderella pumpkin!" Katie cried, also hugging her.

"She won over twelve hundred dollars for a pumpkin?" Ella Ruth overheard Priscilla ask Irvin in a low voice. For a moment, Ella Ruth stopped hearing what everyone was saying to her as she listened to Priscilla.

"Yes, and she earned it," Irvin said. "I know it was a lot of work. Well done, Ella Ruth."

"I'm so happy for you. Congratulations!" Laura said, throwing her arms around her.

"My daughter, pumpkin grower extraordinaire," Irvin said, grinning proudly.

Everyone except for James and Amanda walked around the fairgrounds, playing games, looking at farm animals, watching contests, and doing fun activities. Several of their Amish friends and neighbors were also there, and they greeted them as they passed them.

Ella Ruth made sure to stay near James and Amanda just in case Amanda needed her help. Several times Amanda ran over to Ella Ruth, asking her questions about her story when James asked her what had inspired her to write the books.

"Let's go get milkshakes. I'm buying," Ella Ruth said, and she went with Katie, Lilly, and Sadie to stand in line while Irvin and Priscilla took the two youngest children to walk around more. James and Amanda rode the Ferris wheel, and since Ella Ruth couldn't go on with them, she figured they could go somewhere else until they were done.

After waiting in line and getting their milkshakes, Amanda walked up to them. "Ugh. James is so impressed by your pumpkin, Ella Ruth. He won't stop talking about it. We shouldn't have invited him to see the judging."

Laura smiled mischievously while the others glanced at each other, smiling. This had been Laura's plan when she'd invited James here.

"That's because it *was* impressive," Sadie pointed out.

"Whose side are you on, Sadie?" Amanda snapped, causing Sadie to look at the ground.

"She doesn't have to choose a side, Amanda. Where is James, anyway?" Ella Ruth asked, putting her arm around Sadie's shoulders.

"In the bathroom. He wants to go see the Clydesdales and the rodeo." She rolled her eyes. "So boring. And yes, actually, there are sides, and Sadie needs to choose one. I found scraps of Ella Ruth's dress in your sewing kit. Did you help her sew her dress for the ball?"

"So, what if I did? I wanted to help Ella Ruth," Sadie said with a hand on her hip.

"You betrayed *Mamm* and me," Amanda proclaimed. "How dare you?"

"Let's go to the rodeo," Laura said, walking past Amanda. There were several large cords and cables on the ground for the rides, and Laura tripped over one, splashing her milkshake all over Amanda's

Englisher shirt. Some was even stuck on her hair and hat, and it dripped down into her face.

"Laura!" Amanda shrieked so loudly that several people nearby turned to look at her. "How could you?"

"Oops," Laura said innocently. "Sorry."

"Ugh!" Amanda rushed to the bathroom.

"You did that on purpose, didn't you?" Ella Ruth asked Laura. She couldn't help but smile a little, even though she knew she shouldn't be happy about what had just happened.

Laura shrugged. "Maybe."

"Either way, I have to admit that was pretty satisfying," Sadie said. "Thanks for sticking up for me, Ella Ruth."

"She shouldn't make you choose between her and me. We're all family," Ella Ruth said.

"It's not right," Lilly added.

Sadie smiled gratefully.

CHAPTER EIGHTEEN

James tapped his foot as he waited for Amanda to go to the bathroom once again. This was the fourth time in the last hour. What was going on with her? Was she not feeling well, or was she up to something?

He decided to follow her. From a distance, he saw her talking to Ella Ruth and the others. A few moments later, she ran off to the bathroom. So, maybe she truly had been going to the bathroom.

James walked up behind Ella Ruth. "Congratulations on winning the pumpkin contest. I'm very impressed. That is one incredible pumpkin. How on earth did you get it to grow that big?"

"A lot of love, determination, and patience," Laura interjected, putting her arm around Ella Ruth's shoulders.

Ella Ruth chuckled nervously. "Thank you for that, Laura."

"So, Amanda is in the bathroom again?" he asked. "Is she feeling well?"

"I accidentally spilled my milkshake on her shirt," Laura said. "I tripped on those cords on the ground."

"Oh. I'm sure she'll be out soon, then. She's been to the bathroom several times, so I was worried about her. When I asked her what the inspiration was for her novels and what her next book would be about, she clammed up and said she'd be right back. It was very strange."

Ella Ruth froze. What was going on here?

"She's fine. She was probably just fixing her hair and checking her makeup. You know how she is," Laura blurted, and Ella Ruth had to turn away to hide her shocked expression. Her friend had no filter at all.

James shifted his feet uncomfortably. "Well, I don't know her very well yet, I suppose..."

"Clearly," Laura said, chuckling. Ella Ruth shot her friend a warning look, but Laura just shrugged.

A few moments later, Amanda stomped toward them, her shirt still soaked. "Look what Laura did to me. I need to go home and change."

"I'm sure it was an accident, Amanda," James said.

"I'm not so sure it was," Amanda snapped. "This place is boring, anyway. Let's get out of here."

"I love it here," James said. "What, do you really want to leave?"

"Can we go to the mall instead?" Amanda asked. "That would be more fun."

"I still have tickets for rides I want to use up," James said, holding a strip of green tickets. "Actually, there is something I need to talk to you about, Amanda."

"You can tell me right here," Amanda said, hands on her hips.

"Okay," he said, glancing at the others. Because he suspected that Amanda was not the woman he'd met at the gala, he might as well say it in front of all of them. "Now that my internship is over and I had that amazing experience, I've decided not to take over the auto dealership. I'm going to become a full-time English teacher. I thought about tutoring part-time, but I want to give it everything I have. My sister Eliza is going to take over the company instead of me, and we are going to tell my father. Therefore, I'm turning over my inheritance to her," James said. "I'm going to live a normal life as a teacher. That doesn't affect how you feel for me, does it? I mean, it shouldn't, unless you were only after me for my money like the others were." He watched her face closely for her reaction.

This wasn't exactly true. He still had to convince his father that Eliza should run the company, but he had to know if Amanda was the one from the gala or not, and he felt that this would reveal her true intentions. Did she truly care about him, or was she only after his wealth?

"I thought maybe you'd change your mind..." Amanda turned a slight shade of green. "I... Uh..." she stammered, staring at him with wide eyes. "I need to go talk to my mother." She ran away, bits of milkshake still dripping off the hem of her shirt.

"That's what I thought," James said with a heavy sigh. So, she had only been after his money. Was that why she had tried to convince him the past few weeks over the phone and through her letters to give up his dream?

Now that he had told her he was declining the company and his inheritance, he doubted he'd ever see her again. "I guess these tickets are going to go to waste after all," he muttered.

He was certain now that Amanda was not the woman from the gala. The woman he had spent the night talking with at the gala had been kind, humble, brilliant, deep, genuine, and easy to talk to. Like the woman in the letters...when she wasn't trying to convince him not to become a teacher. Other than that, she was exactly like the woman from the gala.

How could that be possible? It was like she was two different people. Now he could see that the real Amanda was nothing like his mystery woman.

He should have noticed it immediately at the ball, but he had been so excited in thinking that he'd found the one he was looking for that he had let his emotions cloud his judgment. And the letters had completely fooled him. As they had discussed literature, writing, and his teaching experience through his letters, he felt as though he was talking to his soul mate.

It was like someone else had written those letters...not Amanda. But who? Was it possible someone other than Amanda had actually written those letters? Maybe someone who lived with Amanda?

What if one of her sisters had done it?

"Ella loves going on rides," Laura blurted, disturbing his thoughts. "Oh, girls, we were going to go see the rodeo, right? Let's go get a good seat. Have fun, you two!"

"What?" Ella Ruth whispered to Laura.

"James, you said you didn't want your tickets to go to waste, right? You should go on the Ferris wheel with Ella. I think she'd love that,"

Laura said, leaving Ella Ruth with a stunned, embarrassed expression on her face.

With that, Laura and the others scurried away, leaving Ella Ruth and James alone.

"I'm so sorry about that," Ella Ruth said. "Don't feel obligated. I should just go with them." She turned and started to walk away, but he gently took hold of her arm.

"Actually, I'd love to go on the Ferris wheel with you. Want to go with me?" he asked, not able to think about anything other than the warmth that spread through him as he touched her arm. Did she feel the same?

Now he knew that what he had felt when he'd danced with her at the ball was more than just flustered nerves. They shared a special connection, and he wanted to know why.

"I'd love to," Ella Ruth murmured, smiling. They walked to the ride, he handed over the required tickets, and they sat down.

"So, you've decided to become a teacher after all?" Ella Ruth asked. "I'm glad you're going after your dream to teach students how to write. I think it's very noble of you to follow your heart even if it means giving up your inheritance."

"Thank you," James said, tilting his head to the side.

"I'm sure it will be scary to tell your father," Ella Ruth said.

Why would she think that? "Why?"

"Well, you said you were afraid of disappointing him and that you felt like you'd never measure up to your brother."

"When did I tell you that?" he asked. He knew he'd said that to the woman he'd met at the gala, and if Amanda was not that woman, then how else would Ella Ruth know this?

"Oh, sorry. Amanda told me," she stammered. She looked away, her face reddened.

"How did you know about my brother that night at the ball?"

"Amanda told me about that, too. I'm so sorry, James. I shouldn't have even mentioned it."

"It's okay. Don't feel bad," he said. Sisters did tell each other things. It made sense.

"Ella Ruth, I don't think Amanda is the one I've been looking for. I don't think she's Cinderella from the gala," James admitted.

As the Ferris wheel began to move and they rose higher, Ella Ruth froze. "Why do you think that?"

"Every time I asked her about her novels today, she didn't know the answer. She would run off every time. At the ball, when I asked her to draw something for the story, she ran off then, too, then came back with a completed picture. She said she was nervous and couldn't draw in front of me, but what if someone drew it for her? And in her letters, she kept trying to convince me not to be a teacher, but the woman I talked to at the gala thought it was a noble calling. Other than that, in her letters, she seemed so much like the woman from the gala. How can that be possible?"

Ella Ruth nodded slowly but said nothing.

"She left the notebook behind," he said. "I admitted to her that I read the entire thing and took it with me to New York. The stories were so beautiful, so honest and complex. The illustrations were exquisite. Whoever that notebook belongs to is the woman I'm looking for, and I want to marry her one day," James said. "The thing is, I now know it's not Amanda." He felt a small amount of weight lifting off his shoulders. "How did I not see it these past few weeks? And where did she get the notebook? She must have stolen it from the real Cinderella."

"People can easily pretend to be someone else through letters," Ella Ruth said. "It's easy to hide behind words."

"You're right. But it seemed almost like two different people were writing to me. It doesn't make any sense."

"You want to marry her one day? The woman from the gala?" Ella Ruth asked, wide-eyed. "But you don't even know who she is."

"I know from the short time I spent with her and from her stories and artwork that she's a wonderful person," James said.

"Just because someone draws or writes well doesn't mean they are a good person. And what if she doesn't want to marry you?"

James sighed. "Well, I guess it wouldn't be meant to be, but I have a feeling that I'm meant for her, whoever she is. Is that crazy?"

"No," Ella Ruth murmured, and he realized just how close he was sitting next to her. He looked into her big, blue eyes that were the same color as the sky above them. Once again, he wished to see her hair without her prayer *kapp* covering it, but he didn't dare ask her to remove it. Surely, that would be considered highly offensive.

"Ella Ruth, when we danced at the ball, I felt something I've never felt with anyone else before, and I think you felt it too. I think you're amazing," he whispered, and before he even realized what he was doing, he was leaning closer to her, his eyes dropping to her lips.

A thought struck him. Amanda and Ella Ruth lived together. What if Ella Ruth had written those letters to him? But why would she do that, and why had she tried to convince him to give up teaching?

When she leaned closer to him, his heart pounded so loud he wondered if she could hear it.

The Ferris wheel suddenly lurched as the operator let on another passenger, and Ella Ruth smoothed out her skirt, turning away, a blush creeping up her neck.

"I'm so sorry. That was completely inappropriate of me," he stammered. "I don't want you to get in trouble."

"It's not that..." she began, then stopped.

"What is it then?" he asked. When she wouldn't even look at him, he asked, "Ella Ruth, are you the woman from the gala? You tried to tell me, but I rejected you because I thought Amanda was the one. Clearly, she's not. It's you, isn't it? Are you the one I've been looking for from the gala? Did you write the letters?"

Ella Ruth turned away. "I can't talk about this."

"Why?"

"I just can't. I'm sorry."

"But if you did write the letters, why did you try to convince me to give up teaching? Because other than that, they were exactly like something you would write. The way they were written is just like the way you talk. In the letters, we talked about things only you would know and love, not things Amanda would know and love. It just seems like you are the one I have been connecting with these past few weeks, not Amanda. It would explain everything."

"Don't ask me these things," Ella Ruth said, and he caught a glimpse of her face barely long enough to see that her eyes were filled with tears. He grabbed her hand, and she didn't pull away. "Why won't you tell me what's going on? I know you're hiding something."

"I can't tell you what you want to hear. I'm sorry. Please, don't ask me questions I can't answer."

By the way her face reddened and how she suddenly gripped the safety bar with her other hand with white knuckles, he could tell he had hit a nerve. He was getting close. "Ella Ruth, you are the one I feel a connection to...not Amanda."

"I need to get off this ride," Ella Ruth said, her breaths coming rapidly. Beneath his thumb, he could feel her pulse racing in her wrist.

"Ella Ruth, listen to me. I want you to know that you can tell me anything. If you don't want me to tell anyone, I won't. Your secret is safe with me," he said, squeezing her hand.

"I can't, James." She shook her head.

Now he knew for sure she was the one. Why wouldn't she just tell him? Was it because he had told them he was going to give up his inheritance?

No, that couldn't be it, could it? She wasn't after his money like all the other women.

"Is it because I'm not going to be wealthy, Ella Ruth? Is it because I told you that I declined the company and my inheritance? Is that why you're ignoring me right now?" he demanded, and she finally faced him.

"This has nothing to do with that," she said, her eyes red with unshed tears. "If you truly think that, then I'm definitely not the one you're looking for. Wealth means nothing to me."

"Then why won't you admit that you're the woman I got to know at the gala, that you're the talented artist and writer I'm falling in love with?" he asked.

"Love?" she whispered. "You've only known me for a short time."

"Amanda didn't write those letters. You did, Ella Ruth, and I've fallen in love with you more and more with each one."

She looked away.

"Am I right?"

"I never wanted to try to persuade you to give up your dream. I think you should do what you love."

"I know, Ella Ruth. But you did write those letters, didn't you?" he persisted.

"I can't say."

"I know in my heart that you're the one from the gala, Ella Ruth." He leaned a bit closer.

"You thought Amanda was the one. So, maybe your judgment is clouded."

"I was wrong. I know it was you. Why won't you just admit it?"

"There's too much at stake," she murmured. "I can't."

"What is it? What's at stake? Does this have to do with Amish rules? Could you get in trouble?"

"It's not me I'm worried about," she said softly.

"Who, then?"

"I need to get off this ride," Ella Ruth said to the ride operator, who opened the gate for her. James had been so focused on their conversation that he didn't realize the ride had come full circle and had ended. Ella Ruth stood up and got off the ride, but James was right on her heels.

"Wait!" he called, but she quickly darted away, disappearing through the crowd.

CHAPTER NINETEEN

Amanda rushed toward Priscilla, panicking. "*Mamm*, I need to talk to you." Amanda tugged on her mother's arm, who was standing in line to get lemonade with Irvin and the children.

"I'll be right back," Priscilla said to Irvin, then they moved behind a food truck to talk. "What happened to you, Amanda? You look dreadful."

"That imbecile Laura tripped and spilled her milkshake all over me. I know she did it on purpose. That's not why I'm here. James just told me he decided not to take over the company and become a teacher instead. He's giving his inheritance to his sister, who is going to run the company in his place. He's not going to be wealthy, *Mamm*!" Amanda cried, gulping in rapid breaths.

"What?" Priscilla cried, her hand flying to her chest. "I thought Ella Ruth was going to convince him not to in the letters."

"She tried, but it didn't work. He kept going on and on about how teaching English was his dream," Amanda said.

Priscilla tapped her chin. "He hasn't given you the bracelet back yet, has he?"

Amanda shook her head. "So what? I don't care about that stupid bracelet."

"That's not the point. The point is that he must not be convinced that you are the real Cinderella. Otherwise, he would have given it back to you by now. Have you done anything to make him suspicious?"

Amanda hesitated. "Well, he kept questioning me about Ella Ruth's stories and what her next book is going to be about. I didn't know, so I kept saying I had to go to the bathroom so I could ask Ella Ruth."

"That's why he's so suspicious," Priscilla snapped. "I told you to study Ella Ruth's stories."

"I did. I just didn't study what all those words mean that he was asking about."

"My point is that since he is clearly suspicious that you're an imposter, he might be testing you. Maybe he's not giving up the company and his inheritance at all. Maybe he's just seeing how you would react if you found out he wasn't going to be wealthy, and if you still want to be with him. You need to find him right now and tell him you love him no matter what, even if he has no money, because that doesn't matter to you. That's what Ella Ruth would do," Priscilla said, wrinkling her nose. "Now, go! Hurry!"

Amanda turned and hurried away.

"Ella Ruth, wait!" James called, not caring that he was shoving past people just so he could reach her in time. She didn't have a cell phone, he assumed, and even if she did, he didn't have her number. How long would it be until he could contact her again?

He caught a glimpse of her prayer *kapp* in the crowd, and she was blocked by a stroller just long enough for him to catch up to her and grab her hand.

"I need to tell you something," James said. "It's really important. Please, I only need a minute. Please."

Ella Ruth whirled around, her eyes wide, then she let out a long breath. "Fine."

He let go of her hand so no one would notice, and they walked behind a food truck where no one else could see them. A building and other food trucks surrounded them and gave them privacy.

"Ella Ruth, I know it's crazy because we don't know each other very well, but I know you're the woman from the gala, even if you deny it. I want to get to know you better. I really am falling in love with you. I fell in love with you through your letters. I'm so sorry for how I rejected you at the ball when you tried to tell me it was you. Will you forgive me? Will you give me a second chance?"

Ella Ruth's eyes were full of secrets as she gazed at him, causing his heart to race. "I want to tell you everything, but I can't."

"Why? I won't tell anyone, I promise. I'll do whatever I have to so I can see you again," he promised. "I told you your secret is safe with me."

"I can't tell you, James."

"It doesn't matter. I know it was you," James whispered. "May I kiss you, Ella Ruth?" He reached out and touched her cheek, and she smiled softly. Her eyes darted side to side to make sure no one could see them, and then she nodded ever so slightly.

She reached up and intertwined her fingers behind his neck, causing warmth to spread through him. He wanted to know everything about her—her dreams, her regrets, her best and worst memories, her favorite foods, what made her laugh. He hoped she would open up her heart to him so he could find out.

He leaned closer to her and tipped his head, brushing his lips over hers before kissing her gently. Not wanting anyone to see them, he kept it brief, but he wished more than anything that it could have lasted a few moments more.

She smiled up at him, and he couldn't help the words that spilled from his mouth. "You are the most beautiful, amazing woman I've ever met, Ella Ruth."

"Thank you," she whispered.

"And you don't care that I've given up the company and my inheritance?" he asked.

"Not at all," Ella Ruth said. "You're the one I'm falling in love with. Not your money. I think it's wonderful that you're going to become a teacher."

He grinned, elation filling his being.

"I thought maybe at first you said that to Amanda to test her and gauge her reaction," Ella Ruth admitted. "But it's true?"

"Yes, it's true. I'm gathering the courage to tell my father."

"You'll do it when the time is right."

"I have something for you," James said, pulling something from his pocket. "Your mother's charm bracelet." He set it into her palm and closed her fingers around it.

"Thank you so much. I thought I lost it after the gala. I was so devastated. I thought I'd never get it back," Ella Ruth gushed, taking it and tucking it into the pocket in her skirt.

"I didn't give the bracelet or the notebook back to Amanda because I had the feeling something wasn't right. It was strange that she didn't ask to have the bracelet back, which was supposedly such a precious, sentimental item. Well, it was precious and sentimental to you, not her. Now it makes sense."

Ella Ruth said nothing, but only stared at him intently.

He continued, "At first, I was overjoyed because I thought I had found you, but as I spent more time with her, I became more and more suspicious of her and felt more of a connection to you. I know that because you're Amish and I'm not, you could get in trouble for this. I understand if you don't want to take the risk of spending time with me."

"No, I do," Ella Ruth said. "Maybe we can meet in secret."

"I have your notebook in my car."

"Well, that's a relief."

"I will do whatever it takes to spend time with you."

"I feel the same way," she murmured.

"But how can I contact you? You don't have a secret cell phone, do you?"

Ella Ruth chuckled. "No, I don't. How about we just plan a time and place now?"

"There's a beautiful covered bridge at the edge of town. Do you know it?"

"Yes. I love that place. Can we meet there tomorrow night? I'll have to go after my family is asleep so that they won't know. How about ten o'clock? I can only stay for about an hour."

"Perfect. I'll bring the notebook and give it to you then."

"Oh, good. Thank you. I'll be glad to have that back so I can keep working on my story."

"I will wait eagerly until then, Cinderella," James said, taking her hand in his and kissing it.

Ella Ruth chuckled. "As will I, my prince."

"Prince?" James laughed.

"You don't believe her, do you?"

James whirled around to see Amanda standing behind him, crossing her arms. How long had she been standing there?

"Ella Ruth has been helping me try to win you over this entire time, James. She wrote all those letters."

"I already knew she wrote the letters," he said.

"She wrote them to help me convince you that I was her. She told me the charms on the bracelet and what they mean, and every time I had a question about her story, I ran to her, and she told me the answer," Amanda said coldly.

"So, that's where you were going," James said, then realization set in. "Wait, what?" He turned to Ella Ruth. "Is this true?"

Ella Ruth started to say something, but Amanda cut her off.

"You see, James, Ella Ruth doesn't want to leave the Amish community as I do, so she didn't see the point in pursuing a relationship with you. Instead, she helped me convince you I was her, the woman you met at the gala. I told her I'd give her a monetary reward after we were married, and she happily accepted. She's saving up for a new laptop. That's why she entered the pumpkin contest. She's just after money. Your money." Amanda shot Ella Ruth an icy stare. "So, you see, she's been playing you all along."

"But at the ball, you tried to tell me you were the one from the gala. Why would you do that?" James asked Ella Ruth, who had turned a pale shade of green. "And you just told me you don't care that I'm not going to run the company or take my inheritance."

"Because it was me from the gala," Ella Ruth cried. "And I don't care if you have an inheritance or not. I don't care about being wealthy."

"Yes, she does. She thought you were lying when you said you were declining your inheritance and the company."

Ella Ruth did just admit that she thought he'd said that to Amanda to test her.

"So, she figured that since I can't have you, she'd try to marry you for your money instead as a Plan B. And she is the one from the gala. She had a momentary lapse in judgment when she tried to tell you that. I think she was just jealous that I was getting your attention. After that, she continued to help me convince you that I was the one you were looking for. Obviously, we failed, but I thought you should know that she's just as much of an imposter as I am," Amanda said.

"Is this true?" James asked Ella Ruth.

"Well, yes, part of it is true, but Amanda didn't promise me—"

"Remember Laura, Ella Ruth," Amanda interjected, hands on her hips.

"What about Laura?" James asked.

Ella Ruth froze and clamped her mouth shut.

"Laura was in on it too. That's why she was with us at the ball," Amanda said. "They were sitting behind that big plant when we were writing the story together. Ella Ruth was whispering information about the story to me from behind the plant, and she was the one who drew the pictures. She played you, James. We both did. But now it appears that neither one of us will end up with you."

"James, wait. I can explain everything," Ella Ruth said. "Not everything she's saying is true. There's so much more to it." She reached for his arm, but he jerked away.

"I've heard enough," James said, his heart aching. Had she been playing him like a fool this entire time? "I bet you two got some good laughs out of this at my expense."

"No. It wasn't like that at all. I had no choice, James," Ella Ruth cried, but James was already walking away.

"You always have a choice," he said, his heart breaking with each step he took. "And you chose to deceive me."

All he felt was shock of further betrayal and deceit. He could not think clearly or even demand an explanation. He was wounded, and had to get out of there before they saw him cry.

With that, he turned and walked away.

CHAPTER TWENTY

"Why did you do that, Amanda? He already knew you were lying about who you were," Ella Ruth demanded. "You probably figured if you couldn't have him, then I couldn't either. Is that right?"

"Yes, you're right. I don't see why you should end up with him and be happy when I'm the one who is heartbroken here," Amanda said, adjusting her *Englisher* hat.

"You're the one who is heartbroken? You made me sound like a liar to him. You told him I was after his money, but that was you. I did what you asked me to, but he saw through it. That's not my fault. Why are you doing this?" Ella Ruth cried. "And how long were you standing there?"

"I told my mother about how James told me he wasn't going to be wealthy after all, but she also thought he might be testing me, so I came back here to try to win him back. When I saw you two together, I followed you and listened to your conversation. I saw you kiss him, and I heard everything you said."

"He confirmed that he really is giving up the money. So why can't you just leave us alone?" Ella Ruth asked. "What did I ever do to make you hate me so much, Amanda?"

"I don't hate you," Amanda said. "I wasn't born Amish. I'm not like you, so I'm not afraid of revenge. You let him believe you're Cinderella, so you broke our agreement, so I'm going to tell your secret. I'm going to tell your father about your laptop. And if you ever see James again, I'll tell everyone about Laura's secret."

"No! What if I tell everyone you dressed up as an *Englisher* and tried to win James over?"

"You did the same thing," Amanda said. "So, I'd just tell everyone you did it too."

"But you're wearing *Englisher* clothing," Ella Ruth pointed out.

"I have to change first. My dress is in my purse." She patted the purse at her hip. "But mark my words, I will tell him by the end of the day," Amanda shot back.

"Please don't!" Ella Ruth cried, but Amanda was already walking into the crowd, and Ella Ruth hurried after her. By the time she got through the crowd, she had seen Amanda going into the bathroom. A moment later, she came out dressed in her Amish dress and prayer *kapp,* walking over to their family and Laura. She walked right up to Irvin and began talking to him, pulling him aside.

She's doing it, Ella Ruth thought as she hurried across the fairgrounds, avoiding strollers and small children holding cotton candy. By the time she reached them, her father had a stunned look on his face.

He turned to her. "Ella Ruth, is this true? You write stories on a secret laptop you keep hidden in the barn?"

Laura, Katie, and Lilly frowned sympathetically but said nothing. They were probably just as shocked as she was. Debra and Seth's eyes went wide. Priscilla and Amanda smiled smugly, and all Ella Ruth could do was stare at the ground.

"Yes, *Daed*. It's true. I love to write, and I can write so much faster when I type on the laptop. I'm sorry if I've disappointed you," Ella Ruth said, her heart physically aching. First, James rejected her, and now she'd let down her father.

Laura crossed her arms, glaring at Amanda.

"I'm sorry, but I have to take it away when we get home," Irvin said solemnly. "You know it's forbidden."

"I know," Ella Ruth said, hanging her head.

"It's getting late. We should go. We will continue this discussion at home," Irvin said, guiding the children toward the exit with Amanda and Priscilla.

"I'm so sorry she just did that," Laura said. "How could she?"

Ella Ruth explained everything that had just happened. "I have to meet with James and tell him my side of the story, but I'm not sure he'd believe me. Amanda mixed in so much truth in her lies that it sounded so convincing."

"Well, how can you contact him?" Katie asked.

"We were supposed to meet at the covered bridge tomorrow night at ten until Amanda came in and ruined everything," Ella Ruth said.

"Do you think he'll still go?" Lilly asked.

"I don't think so. You should have seen the look in his eyes. He truly believes I am just as much of an imposter as Amanda is."

"Still, you have to tell James the truth somehow," Katie said.

"Maybe we should just let things be," Ella Ruth said, but her heart broke at the mere thought.

"You care too much about him to just let things be. You two share a special connection, and I'm going to help you win him back," Laura said, tapping her chin thoughtfully. "Somehow. We'll figure it out."

"For now, we have to go home," Ella Ruth said as Irvin beckoned to them to follow. She turned and began to walk away. "But we'll figure something out."

James walked through the door of the mansion, a myriad of emotions swirling through him—anger, hurt, regret, and sorrow. How did he not realize that not only one but both of them were deceiving him? They were just like all the other women he'd invited to the ball who had clamored for his attention. They were only after his money.

But it still didn't make sense... Why had Ella Ruth tried to convince him to not be a teacher in the letters when she had encouraged him to in person?

Eliza saw him in the hall and hurried over to him. "What's wrong, James?"

"I just realized that the woman I thought was Cinderella was an imposter, and the real Cinderella was also actually an imposter," he spat out.

"I'm so sorry," his younger sister murmured. "That's horrible. But are you sure you aren't just jumping to conclusions again like you often do?"

James hesitated for a moment. "No. They probably had the whole thing planned out. I am such an idiot."

"Don't blame yourself."

"Thanks. That makes me feel a lot better," he said sarcastically.

"Want to go play ping pong? That always makes you feel better."

"Actually, I'm going to talk to Dad right now." He marched down the hallway to his father's office with determination, his chin held high.

"Right now? Don't you think you should take some time to get over what just happened first?" Eliza asked. "Don't you want to plan what you're going to say?"

"I've been mulling it over in my head for weeks. I might as well just get it over with. I'm as ready now as I'll ever be." He walked right up to the office door and knocked. When his father said to come in, he opened the door.

"Dad, I need to talk to you about something really important," James said, striding in.

"Have a seat, both of you," Richard, his father, said, ending a phone call. He set the phone on his desk and folded his hands as James and Eliza sat down. "What's on your mind?"

"I'm going to get right to the point. I think Eliza would be much better at running the company than I would," James said. His heart was racing, but he wouldn't let it show. "I'm going to apply for a teaching job, and you're right. I can't do both. She's been preparing for this her whole life, and she loves this company. Let her run it, Dad. If that means that I have to give up my inheritance, so be it. I'm willing to pay that price."

"You would give up your entire inheritance to become a teacher? Don't get me wrong, it is an honorable profession, but it doesn't pay much," his father said.

"I know. I don't care about the salary. It's my passion to teach writing, and that's what I'm going to do. My mind is made up."

"I can't force you to run the company, James," Richard said. "So, if you are sure you want to refuse, I will indeed have you run it, Eliza."

"Thank you, Dad," Eliza said, unsuccessfully trying to hide her excitement as her feet tapped the floor and she clasped her hands together. "I won't let you down."

Richard nodded to her, smiling, then turned to James. "But you should know, son, that I'm very disappointed in you. As my oldest son, I thought you would be the one to take it over."

"Brett would have never done this, right? Is that what you're thinking right now, Dad? I'm sorry I don't measure up to my brother. I'll never be good enough in your eyes," James said, a tear coursing down his cheek. Combined with what had happened at the fair, this was hitting him hard.

"I never said that," Richard said, standing up.

"You didn't have to." James abruptly stood up and stormed out of the room, wiping a tear from his eye.

CHAPTER TWENTY-ONE

The buggy ride home was shrouded in uncomfortable silence. When they arrived home, Irvin climbed down and said, "Where is it, Ella Ruth?"

Ella Ruth climbed down. "I keep it hidden in the barn. I'll go get it." She turned and trudged toward the barn, walked inside, and pulled her laptop and case out of its hiding spot in the wall behind a loose board. When she walked outside, she couldn't help but notice Amanda smiling smugly at her, crossing her arms.

Ignoring her, Ella Ruth handed the laptop case to her father. "I'm sorry, *Daed*."

"Everyone but Ella Ruth, please go inside," Irvin said as the sun was beginning to set behind the fields. Amanda reluctantly turned and walked into the house with everyone else.

Once they were alone, Ella Ruth said, "You know how much I love writing books. When I write on this, I can write so much faster than when I write by hand, and my hand doesn't cramp up. I can copy and paste sections and move them around if I have to, and I can save several copies to be safe..."

"I understand why you did it, Ella Ruth, but laptops are forbidden in our community. I don't make the rules, but you could be tempted by the internet on this computer."

"I don't even use it for the internet," Ella Ruth said. "We don't have internet here, so when I'm here, I can only use it for writing, anyway. When I charge it at the café, I keep it hidden so no one would see me with it."

"You charged it at the café?" her father asked.

"I had to. We don't have outlets here," Ella Ruth said.

"What if someone saw you? I don't want people to think ill of you," Irvin said, rubbing his temple. "I don't want you to get in trouble with the elders, Ella Ruth. This family has been through enough."

"I know, I know. The last thing I wanted to do was hurt you and disappoint you," Ella Ruth cried, covering her face with her hands. The emotions of everything that had happened that day came crashing down on her, and she began to sob, her shoulders wracking.

"Oh, my dear," Irvin said, taking her into his arms. "You could never be a disappointment. I have to admit I was shocked at first, but I'm also glad you're pursuing your dream. I just hope that it doesn't take you away from us."

Ella Ruth nodded, unable to speak for a few moments until she choked out, "I just love to write."

"I know. And you're a wonderful, talented writer. I hate to take this away from you, but I have to in order to protect you. Do you understand?" he asked gently.

She nodded again. Would she ever get her laptop back? Not only was that gone, but James still had her notebook, and she doubted he'd ever want to see her again.

As the realization set in, she cried even harder as her father tried in vain to console her.

James was angry with her; both of her writing tools were gone, and she'd let down her father. She'd have to get a new notebook and start her story all over again.

"That went well," Eliza said sarcastically as she hurried down the hallway to keep up with James' long strides.

"It went about as well as I thought," James said. "Actually, it went better than I thought because he agreed and didn't blow up."

"That's true," Eliza said. "Thank you, James. I know you're upset about your girlfriend—"

"She's not my girlfriend," James said, approaching the door. "She lied to me."

"I know. I really appreciate you talking to Dad even though you're sad about what happened," Eliza said, causing James to finally slow down.

"You're welcome. I'm glad he agreed to let you take over the company. You're the perfect person for the job. You'll be amazing."

"Thanks. Where are you going?"

"The bookstore. I need a distraction, and the best place to find distraction is a store full of books. I'm going to get lost in a world of time travel and fighting dragons."

Eliza chuckled. "Sounds wonderful. Mind if I join you?"

"I'd love that."

"First, we're going out to dinner at Molly's Diner. I know you love their burgers. Then we'll go bowling downtown, and then we'll go to the bookstore. Okay?"

He gave a small smile at her effort to try to make him feel better. "Sounds like a plan."

"How could you?" Priscilla asked once Ella Ruth got inside. She'd pulled her aside to talk to her in the hallway while the others were in the kitchen. "Why did you go and ruin everything?"

"James had already figured out that I was the one from the gala, not Amanda," Ella Ruth said. "I didn't ruin everything."

"You could have tried harder so he wouldn't figure it out." Priscilla put her hands on her hips.

"It's not my fault that Amanda didn't convince him. He was suspicious from the start once he got over the shock of finding her and thinking she was the one he was looking for. There's nothing I could have done differently. You can't blame me for this. I warned her he would figure it out," Ella Ruth said. "She didn't have to go tell my father about the laptop."

"I'm glad she did," Priscilla said. "You have been breaking the rules. You know we don't allow technology here."

"You, Sadie, and Amanda weren't always Amish. Do you ever struggle with using modern conveniences and technology?" Ella Ruth blurted.

Priscilla hesitated. "That's none of your business."

Ella Ruth sighed. "Just trying to make conversation."

"Because of you, my daughter's future has been ruined."

"He gave up his inheritance. That's not my fault either."

"Ugh." Priscilla threw her hands up. "Maybe he wouldn't have if you hadn't told him he should go after his dream of becoming a teacher. All I know is our plan failed. I don't want you to see him ever again."

"That's not fair," Ella Ruth said. "But it doesn't matter. I'm sure he never wants to see me again."

"And for good reason. Now go make dinner." Priscilla pointed to the kitchen.

Ella Ruth trudged to the kitchen with a heavy heart.

"What happened?" Katie whispered to Ella Ruth at the woodstove.

"Priscilla blames me for everything," Ella Ruth whispered.

"That's not fair," Lilly said. "None of this was your fault."

"She doesn't see it that way."

"Are you going to sneak out and meet him tonight?" Katie whispered.

"I don't think he wants to see me." Ella Ruth sighed.

"You still need to try," Katie said.

"I do need my notebook back," Ella Ruth said. "But I don't think he'll go. Priscilla told me I'm not allowed to see him again."

"We'll help you," Katie said.

"I don't want you to get in trouble, too," Ella Ruth said. "I guess I have to cut my losses. I'm never going to see James again, and I'm never getting my notebook back. At least I got my bracelet back." She turned and started peeling potatoes for dinner.

Chapter Twenty-two

The next few days passed at a sloth's pace, and all Ella Ruth could think about was the look on James' face right before he had turned and walked away from her at the fair. What did he think of her? Would he ever speak to her again? How could she ever explain her side of the story to him?

One evening after the dishes were washed from dinner, Katie and Lilly asked their father if they could go to the bookstore. It closed at eight o'clock, so if they hurried, they would still have time.

"Take Ella Ruth with you," Irvin said as he read a book in his favorite chair. Ella Ruth noticed Priscilla's lips tighten into a thin line, but she said nothing to counter her husband.

"We'll be back soon," Ella Ruth said, grateful to get out of the house. "Anyone else want to come?"

"I will," Sadie said. "Amanda?"

"No, thanks," she said glumly, turning to face the window. "I don't feel like going anywhere right now."

"Suit yourself," Sadie said, and they all went outside and climbed into the buggy.

"Let's swing by Laura's house and see if she wants to come," Ella Ruth said. "It's on the way."

They all agreed, and a few moments later, Laura was driving with them to the bookstore. "Thanks for picking me up. I've been wanting to get another mystery novel."

Ella Ruth told Laura everything that had happened since they had seen each other.

"He was so hurt when Amanda said all those things to him," Ella Ruth said. "What if he never speaks to me again?"

"Not if I have anything to do with it," Laura said.

"I'm sorry about my mother and Amanda," Sadie said to Ella Ruth. "It's not right how they're treating you. I'd like to blame our past, but that still gives them no excuse."

"Do you mind if I ask what happened to the three of you before you came here?" Ella Ruth asked as she drove the buggy. "I know none of you have wanted to talk about it before, so I understand if you don't want to answer."

"That's okay," Sadie said. "I suppose I wasn't ready to talk about it before, but I am now. You're right about those things. Amanda and I weren't always Amish, but the three of us were born Amish. Our biological father was a kind Amish man, but he died when we were very young children. We had a happy Amish childhood here in Unity until then, from what I can remember. We ran out of money after he died, and my mother was too proud to ask anyone for help, so she married the first man who proposed to her, an *Englisher* man. He charmed her so much that we left the Amish so she could marry him. It was nice for a while, but after a few years, he lost his job and started drinking when he couldn't find another one. As time passed, he drank more and more, and he became an abusive drunk. Now that I look back, there were red flags. My mother worked as a waitress but didn't make very much, so we lived in poverty. I remember our roof leaked every time it rained, and we barely ever had enough food for all of us, but the worst part was how terribly he treated us. I think he felt like a failure, so he took it out on us. He died of a heart attack a few years ago."

"I'm so sorry," Ella Ruth said, and Katie and Lilly echoed her words. "No wonder Amanda and Priscilla are so bitter."

"Our mother took the brunt of his abuse, but Amanda is so outspoken that she often butted heads with him, and she paid for it dearly. I just kept my head down and avoided him as much as I could. She was abused a lot more than I was. Still, that shouldn't give her and my mother an excuse to take their pain out on you."

"That's terrible. They're hurting," Katie said, frowning.

"Yes, they are," Sadie said. "So, I know they're unkind to you, and it's not right, but what they really need is love."

Laura's eyes were wide as she listened.

"I had no idea." Ella Ruth's heart ached for them. She was blessed with a kind, loving father who had never once mistreated her or her siblings. What must it have been like for Amanda, Priscilla, and Sadie to have someone abusive in their family?

"After he died, my mother decided to rejoin the Amish. That's when she met Irvin, and you know the rest of the story," Sadie said.

"I think that when my mother rejoined the Amish, her heart wasn't in it. She just didn't know what else to do. I, on the other hand, love being Amish. I don't think Amanda feels the same way as I do, though. She always says that she wants to marry someone wealthy and live a luxurious life, and she has so much bitterness in her heart."

"This place heals people," Ella Ruth said. "The Lord will heal her heart if she lets Him. She's built so many walls and won't let anyone in. Now I understand why."

"I pray that with time the Lord will help Amanda and my mother forgive my stepfather and let go of the past, but that could take years. I just want them to be happy again. They weren't always like this. They used to be so lively, so joyful," Sadie said.

"Joyful?" Lilly's eyes widened. "I can hardly imagine it."

"I think the people they used to be are still there somewhere deep in their hearts. They might need our help to find themselves again," Sadie said.

"Thank you for telling us," Ella Ruth said. "I'll try to be more compassionate toward them. I have to admit I haven't been giving it my best effort. I think I've let bitterness grow in my own heart toward them."

"Who could blame you?" Lilly asked.

"Still, it's wrong. I need to be more understanding and loving toward them and make them feel wanted," Ella Ruth said. "Not just tolerated."

Katie and Lilly fell silent.

"I suppose you're right," Katie said. "But it won't be easy."

"It definitely won't be easy," Ella Ruth said. "But it's the right thing to do."

For the rest of the ride to the bookstore, all that could be heard was the *clip-clop* of the horse's hooves on the road.

Please help me forgive Amanda and Priscilla and be more loving and compassionate toward them, Ella Ruth prayed. *Even if it seems almost impossible.*

When they arrived, she parked the buggy in front of the bookstore, and they all went inside. Ella Ruth walked immediately toward the fantasy and science fiction section. The bell on the door rang, and someone came into the store. Through the shelves, she saw a mop of wavy, dark hair. Was that...?

"James," she whispered, then pivoted and walked toward her sisters and Laura.

"What's wrong?" Katie asked when she saw Ella Ruth's expression.

"James is here," Ella Ruth said. "I can't face him right now. We need to go."

"Why? Now is your chance to talk to him. It's not like he has a way to reach you," Laura said.

"Why not see if you can explain things to him?" Sadie asked.

"I tried that at the fair, and he didn't want to listen," Ella Ruth said, shaking her head. "Let's just go."

"Why not at least see if he has your notebook so you can get it back?" Lilly asked.

"I've already accepted that I'm not getting that back. I'll just rewrite my stories."

"Fine. First, let me just pay for my book. Then we'll go," Lilly said. "Just wait here for a minute. Come on, Katie."

"I want to look around for a few minutes. You go ahead," Katie said.

"Come on, Katie. Just come with me," Lilly insisted, looping her arm through Katie's.

"Fine," Katie said, huffing as she followed her sister. Laura followed them.

"Sadie, come with us," Lilly said, and Sadie trailed behind them.

They walked to the cash register and talked to Debbie, the owner, while Ella Ruth busied herself with browsing the true crime section. After several moments, Ella Ruth wondered what was taking so long. She looked through the shelves at the checkout, but no one was there. Did they leave without her? What were they up to?

Ella Ruth looked toward the fantasy and science fiction section where James was and realized that Katie, Sadie, Laura, and Lilly were talking to him. What were they doing? She marched over to them, and just before she reached them, they darted away and hurried out the door along with James' sister, Eliza, and Debbie, the store owner. There were no other customers in the store at the moment, so she and James were left alone.

Debbie locked the door from the outside and waved, smiling apologetically, while her sisters, Laura, and Eliza grinned mischievously.

"You've got to be kidding me." Ella Ruth sighed.

"That was very clever," James said from behind the bookshelf. He walked out from behind it, his hands in his pockets. His dark eyes searched hers, and her heart fluttered at the mere sight of him. "Your sisters and Laura explained everything to me."

"We're not letting you out until you make things right," Laura said from outside, her voice muffled. Debbie nodded, holding up the key.

"Great. Now we're stuck here," Ella Ruth said. "I know you're angry with me, and I don't blame you."

"I'm not angry with you," James said. "I was hurt. I didn't realize Amanda was forcing you to help her deceive me."

"She told me that if I told you that I was the one from the gala, she would tell everyone not only that I secretly write books on a laptop but that Laura sneaks out to the movies. Laura has been baptized into the church, unlike me, so she could be shunned if that happened. That's why I couldn't tell you before," Ella Ruth said in a rush.

"They did say that," James said, frowning as he took a step toward her. "That was incredibly wrong of her."

"Amanda lied when she said she offered me money. That's not true. You know I don't care about money or wealth," Ella Ruth said, taking a step toward him.

"You did say that you didn't care if I gave up my inheritance," James said.

"She mixed in so much truth in her lies that it was convincing," Ella Ruth said. "So, I don't blame you for believing her."

"I should have realized she was trying to deceive me even more," James said. "Your sisters told me that Amanda told your father about the laptop anyway and that he took it away. I'm so sorry to hear that."

Ella Ruth sighed. "I should have known it would come to that."

"I'm so sorry for not believing you, Ella Ruth," James said, coming even closer to her. "I believed Amanda instead of you. I was a fool. You were only trying to protect your friend. That's noble of you. I admire your courage."

"Thank you," Ella Ruth said, smiling as her eyes darted to the floor. He was so handsome that when she looked into his eyes, her heart raced wildly in her chest.

"I have a terrible habit of jumping to conclusions. My sister often points it out to me. I assumed you were deceitful and that you were only after my money, but I couldn't have been more wrong. I'm so sorry."

"You were hurt, confused, and upset."

"That was no excuse for how I behaved. It should have been a dead giveaway from the start that you were the one I fell in love with at the ball." He was now close enough to gently touch her chin, causing her to finally look into his eyes. "Will you forgive me, Ella Ruth, for how I reacted at the fair?" he whispered.

His touch sent a surge of warmth straight to her heart. "Of course, I do. Will you forgive me for deceiving you?"

"Yes, as long as you kiss me right now." He smiled, his gaze dropping to her lips.

"Deal." She grinned and wrapped her arms around him, standing on her tip toes and briefly pressing her lips to his.

CHAPTER TWENTY-THREE

A loud applause came from outside the bookstore, and they both looked up to see a crowd had gathered on the sidewalk to watch their conversation. Ella Ruth's sisters jumped up and down, clapping and laughing along with Eliza and Laura.

Ella Ruth laughed. "I knew they were up to something."

"And my sister was their accomplice," James said, still holding Ella Ruth in his arms. "We might as well give them more to talk and cheer about." He kissed her again, and joy overflowed from Ella Ruth's heart into the form of tears spilling from her eyes.

Debbie finally opened the door and came inside with the others, along with several people who had been watching from the sidewalk. "Thank you for bringing more customers to my store today," Debbie said cheerfully, then wagged a finger at them. "You two are too stubborn for your own good."

"I guess we needed some nudging," Ella Ruth said. "Thank you all. I'm not sure I would have had the courage to face James otherwise."

"You would have eventually," James said, smiling down at her. "As I said, you are courageous."

She smiled, a blush creeping up her neck. Her sisters hugged her, grinning as Eliza slapped her brother playfully on the back.

"Finally, you came to your senses, big brother. Ella Ruth is one incredible woman," she said, then turned to Ella Ruth. "He talks about you nonstop. He has ever since the gala. I can see why."

"I'm so glad you two made things right," Katie said. "But what does this mean? Are you going to start courting?"

"If you'll have me," James said to Ella Ruth. "But I have to ask you properly first."

Ella Ruth smiled at the thought, then a shadow crossed her face.

"Would you get in trouble?" he asked.

"I might," she said. "Half the street just saw us kiss, so I suppose the word will get out sooner rather than later." Maybe it had been risky to kiss him like that in front of all those people, but she didn't care, and she didn't regret it.

"But you haven't been baptized into the church yet, right? So, you won't get shunned, at least?" he asked. "Forgive me. I'm not familiar with all the rules."

"You're right," Ella Ruth said. "I wouldn't be shunned, but I could still get in trouble if I don't do things according to the rules. I'm going to have to speak to my father about this and pray."

"I understand," James said. "Take all the time you need. I will be waiting. We'll have to talk about it later."

"No, you can go talk right now," Laura said. "We'll pay for our books and go to the coffee shop while you two talk. Want to come, Eliza?"

"I'd love to. Take your time, you two," she said, and the four young women paid for their books and left the store.

"Let's take a walk," James said, smiling.

Ella Ruth nodded, gave Debbie a hug, and they left the store. Behind the shops, there was a path that led to the woods, and they slowly meandered down it hand in hand.

"I guess I'll get straight to the point. I don't know if you love me, but I'm falling in love with you, and I knew it from that night we talked at the gala. You're unlike any woman I've ever met," he said.

"I'm falling in love with you, too, James," she said as the sun set behind them, casting a pink and orange glow across the trees and long shadows across the grass.

"I don't want to ask you to leave the Amish to be with me. If you want me to join, then I will," he said. "Would I still be allowed to be a teacher in public schools?"

"I don't think so," Ella Ruth said. "But I have to be honest. I'm not sure I will always be Amish."

"Really? Because of your love of writing?" he asked.

She nodded. "I want to get my books published. There was a man in our community who published his book years ago, but that was before the publishing industry evolved. Now I would need the internet, which isn't allowed, and I would need a computer to type my books so I can submit them for publication, either traditionally or independently. I have so many book ideas that I think I would prefer to independently publish so I can release them without having to wait three years for each book with traditional publishing."

"It sounds like you've thought a lot about this, but I hope you take your time deciding."

"I have thought a lot about this," she agreed. "At least I could still see my family often if I left. I even wonder if I might like to become an English teacher as well. It could take several years for me to publish enough books to make a solid income, and I would love to share my passion for writing with students."

"You would make a wonderful teacher, Ella Ruth," James said. "Speaking of teaching, I applied for a teaching position at the local middle school."

"Really? Did you talk to your father?"

James nodded. "I told him I'd made up my mind about teaching, so he told Eliza she could run the company, but he's disappointed in me."

"I think if he ever saw you teach, he wouldn't be disappointed anymore," Ella Ruth said.

He sighed. "That would never happen. I've accepted it. I don't think I'd ever make him happy no matter what I do."

"I'm sorry." She squeezed his hand.

He shrugged. "It is what it is. Eliza is excited, so I'm happy for her. You're both about to experience so many new things. If you leave, that is."

She nodded. "Also, if I left the church, I could see the world," Ella Ruth said. "I've always wanted to travel to Europe and somewhere tropical like Hawaii."

"I've been to Hawaii," James said. "I would love to take you there some day, and Europe too."

"Sounds like a dream come true." Her smile faded. "I would be able to do the things I love if I left, but I would miss my family."

"Well, you could live nearby and visit them whenever you'd like, right?" he asked. "They would understand, I hope."

"Yes, they would. Every young Amish person has the choice of staying Amish or leaving. My friend Esther left to marry your friend Xavier, who hosted the gala."

"Yes, of course," James said. "I just don't want you to get into any trouble because of me. I feel terrible about you losing your laptop."

"That's not your fault. That reminds me, do you still have my notebook?"

"Yes, I do. It's in my car. We can walk over and get it."

They walked back down the path and reached the sidewalk, where James unlocked his car and retrieved the notebook. He handed it to her, and she hugged it to her chest.

"I thought I'd never get this back. I thought you might never want to see me again."

"I have to admit I was angry at first, but then I realized how much I wanted to be with you. I'm glad our sisters locked us inside that bookstore." He smiled at her, causing her heart to flutter. Down the street, Ella Ruth's sisters and Eliza came out of the coffee shop.

"Can we make plans to meet tomorrow night at ten o'clock at the covered bridge?" he asked.

"That sounds like a great plan."

"So, can you call me on the phone in your father's store again? You still have my number?"

"Yes to both questions," Ella Ruth said with a chuckle, then heard laughing from down the street. "Let's go join them."

An hour later, Ella Ruth drove the buggy home.

"He couldn't take his eyes off you," Sadie said. "He's in love."

Katie, Laura, and Lilly giggled.

"Thank you so much for locking us in that bookstore together," Ella Ruth said, then chuckled. "It's funny when you think about it."

"See? I told you she'd thank us," Laura said mischievously.

After they dropped off Laura at her house, they continued on home.

"I really like Eliza," Katie said.

"Me too. She's a firecracker," Ella Ruth said as she climbed down and unhitched the horse once they arrived.

"So, are you going to meet James tomorrow night?" Lilly asked.

"Yes, absolutely. I'll go put Pumpkin in her stall for the night." Ella Ruth led her horse across the driveway to the barn. "I can't believe it," she said to Pumpkin. "He forgave me, and he's falling in love with me. Me! It just seems too good to be true."

Pumpkin neighed, tossing her head.

"Maybe it is too good to be true," Ella Ruth said as she led the horse into her stall and filled her water bucket. "If word got out, I could get in trouble, and so could Laura." She filled the feed bucket and patted the horse's side. "Tomorrow night, I'll come to get you, and we'll ride out to the covered bridge to see him. Goodnight, girl."

Ella Ruth closed the stall door and went inside. Now that she had her notebook back, she wanted to pick up on her story where she had left off.

Chapter Twenty-four

The next day passed painfully slow as Ella Ruth waited for night to come. Priscilla gave her a long list of chores to do, and then she left to run errands with Amanda. Katie and Lilly went to work with Irvin at the Unity Community Store down the lane, and Debra and Seth went to play at their friend's house, so Ella Ruth was left to take care of the animals, clean the house, cook dinner—and on top of all of that, it was laundry day. Laundry took much longer with a Maytag washer rather than an electric washing machine, and she hung each piece of clothing out on the clothesline with wooden pins.

By the time she'd cooked and cleaned up dinner, she was exhausted, so she snuck up to her room to take a nap. When she woke up, her sisters had gone to bed, but she hadn't heard them come in. She glanced at the battery-operated clock and realized it was nine-thirty, so she jumped up and walked to the door. When she tried to open it, it didn't budge. She tried again and again, but it was as though someone had locked it from the outside. This was an old house, so the locks were old as well.

Had Amanda or Priscilla done this to her? But neither of them knew about her secret date with James tonight. She wanted to call for someone to come unlock the door, but everyone was in bed by now, and she didn't want to wake everyone up.

Ella Ruth hurried to the window, but she was two stories up, and there was no way she could climb down. She had no way of contacting James, so he would be waiting there alone in the dark. Defeated, she sat down at the chair beside the window, letting her head drop in her hands.

No, she wouldn't cry. She didn't want to wake her sisters.

Why was Amanda or Priscilla doing this to her? Yes, she knew they'd suffered in the past, but why couldn't they just let her be happy?

Ella Ruth trudged back to her bed, pulled a book off the night stand, and turned on her battery-operated light. She tried to distract herself with a time travel novel, but she could barely get past the first page before tears fell from her eyes.

The next morning when Ella Ruth tried to open the door, it opened easily.

"Well, that's strange," she muttered.

"What?" Lilly asked, yawning as she sat up in bed.

Ella Ruth shut the door. "When I tried to leave last night, the door was locked from the outside."

"Do you think Amanda did it?" Katie asked.

Ella Ruth nodded. "James already chose me. Why is she still trying to keep me from him?"

"I think she doesn't want to see you happy," Lilly said. "Maybe it makes her feel better about herself."

"I know we should be more loving and compassionate toward her, but this makes it hard." Ella Ruth turned from the door and began brushing out her long hair.

"I know, but God never said it would be easy to follow His commandments," Katie said.

"You're right." Ella Ruth sighed. "I'll walk to the phone shanty or the store later to call him and apologize for not going."

"If she sees you walk to the phone shanty, she'll be suspicious. Let's ask *Daed* if you can come to the store today with us for the morning," Katie said.

"Who will do the chores here?" Ella Ruth asked.

"You can come to help us stock shelves this morning and come back in time to make lunch and dinner, and we'll help you clean up tonight as always," Lilly said. "Come on. We just got in a big shipment. It might even be fun."

"Okay," Ella Ruth said with a smile. "Let's ask him at breakfast."

Less than an hour later, after they all shared a silent prayer over the food at the table, Lilly asked, "*Daed*, can Ella Ruth come to the store today to help us unload that shipment we got yesterday? We could really use the help."

"What about the chores here? We need her here," Amanda huffed.

"What about the animals and the cooking and cleaning?" Priscilla asked.

"We could use her help at the store. Priscilla, you wouldn't mind cooking lunch today, would you? Amanda and Sadie, you can do the cleaning," Irvin said as he poured a glass of milk for Debra and Seth.

Amanda and Priscilla blinked, glancing at each other.

"We're glad to help. Right?" Sadie asked, giving her mother and sister a questioning look.

"Thank you. It would give Ella Ruth a break. We would all appreciate it," Irvin said as he continued to eat his scrambled eggs. Either he didn't notice Amanda's and Priscilla's shocked expressions, or he was politely ignoring their stunned reactions.

Ella Ruth saw Katie and Lilly smiling out of the corner of her eye, and she couldn't help but smile for a moment as well.

A half-hour later, Ella Ruth was walking out the door with her father, Katie, Lilly, Debra, and Seth, and they all climbed in the buggy. Irvin hitched up his horse, Clarence, then drove down the lane.

Before going to work, they dropped off Debra and Seth at a friend's house to play.

"I wish I could come to work with you all more often," Ella Ruth said. "It's nice to be out of the house and doing something other than cooking and cleaning."

"I know, Ella Ruth, but we do need you to take care of things at home," Irvin said. "Believe me, I would love your help at the store."

"Why not ask Amanda and *Mamm* to do more?" Ella Ruth asked. She'd almost slipped up and referred to her stepmother by her first name. "At least Sadie has been helping me more lately."

Irvin sighed. "I'm going to try again, but I know they've been through a lot, and they say it makes them emotionally exhausted. I feel guilty for asking them to do more."

But were they telling the truth?

They arrived at the store, and the morning flew by as the three sisters stocked shelves while Irvin helped customers. When there was finally a lull, and Irvin went out back to take inventory, Ella Ruth hurried over to the phone and dialed James' number, which she'd memorized.

"Hello?"

"James, it's Ella Ruth."

"Oh, I'm so glad to hear from you. What happened? Are you okay?"

"I'm fine. Someone locked me in my room last night."

"Do you mean..."

"I think so," Ella Ruth said. "I'm so sorry I couldn't make it. Did you wait long?"

"Oh, no. I'm really sorry that happened to you, Ella Ruth. Don't worry about me. I waited about an hour and a half. I had a book to read. We can try again tonight if you want."

"Yes, same time, same place?"

"Sure."

"I have to go. I'm working at my father's store."

"See you tonight," he said, his voice hopeful.

"Bye." She hung up, turned, and got back to work stocking the shelves.

Just before noon, the door flew open, the bell above it chiming loudly as someone ran inside. Ella Ruth turned to see Sadie barreling toward them, arms flailing.

"My mother... She..." Sadie paused to catch her breath, hands on her knees. "I ran here as fast as I could. My mother sold your horse, Ella Ruth."

Chapter Twenty-five

"What? Pumpkin? No!" Ella Ruth screamed, not caring that a customer was staring at her with wide eyes. She bolted out the door, quickly followed by her father, Katie, and Lilly. "We have to go stop her right now!"

"I'll go with you. Katie, Lilly, mind the store with Sadie," Irvin said, climbing into the driver's seat of the buggy. Ella Ruth sat beside him.

"Hurry!" Sadie called, waving her hand.

Irvin drove the buggy as quickly as he could down the lane, gravel flying up behind them.

"How could she do this?" Ella Ruth cried, her heart racing as her palms began to sweat. "She is so cruel to me, *Daed*. This has to stop."

"Cruel?" her father asked. "She is not cruel to you."

"There is so much you don't know. I have to tell you everything," Ella Ruth said. She told her father everything from how she'd sneaked out to the gala, how she'd met James, and how she'd helped Amanda deceive James because she'd forced her to. She told him about the letters, too, and how she had written them pretending to be Amanda. "I only did it because she threatened to tell everyone that Laura sneaks out to the movie theaters at night, but I've done that too. Now that *Mamm* has sold my horse, I feel so hopeless. James has chosen me over Amanda, so I fear they may tell everyone Laura's secret anyway, out of spite." She paused, giving her father a sidelong glance. "I should have told you all of this sooner. I'm so sorry I hid it from you. I was afraid you'd take my laptop, but that already happened, and I've been so afraid they will tell people about Laura. Are you angry with me?"

"Angry with you?" Irvin chuckled. "Why would I be angry? None of this was your fault. Amanda and Priscilla should not have asked you to deceive James."

"I mean, are you angry with me for the other things, like sneaking out and becoming friends with an *Englisher* man?"

Irvin chuckled. "No, my dear. You never even got to go on your *Rumspringa* because of your mother's death. I always expected you to want to experience the outside world at some point, and I know you love to write, so I suspected that was why you haven't been baptized into the church yet. I expected you to sneak out or meet a young man at some point. You have such an adventurous spirit. If you have feelings for this James, then I just hope he is a good man. And I would like to meet him."

"Really?" Ella Ruth asked as tears burned in her eyes and a lump grew in her throat.

"*Ja.* I always had a feeling you might not stay Amish, Ella Ruth, so if you are considering that option, just know I will support your decision either way, but I do hope you will stay. You don't have to hide things from me, my daughter. I love you exactly the way you are."

"I love you, too, *Daed*." She looped her arm through his, leaning her head on his shoulder.

"I am shocked by how Amanda and Priscilla have been treating you, and I am so sorry," Irvin apologized. "I wish I had seen it sooner. Now I see why they don't help you with the chores. Why are they doing this to you?"

"I don't know," Ella Ruth said. "I know they suffered terribly before they met us, and they left the Amish for several years so they weren't always Amish, but still..."

"It gives them no excuse to be so cruel to you," Irvin said firmly. "This stops today, starting with getting your horse back."

"Thank you, *Daed*," Ella Ruth said, tears streaming down her face. "But what about Laura? What if they tell everyone her secret? She has been baptized, so she could be shunned. I would hate for that to happen because of me."

"It's not your fault," Irvin said. "I will let them know that if they begin to slander your friend, I will be speaking to the bishop about their actions. This behavior is unacceptable. This is not the Amish way."

The buggy rolled into the driveway, and Ella Ruth jumped out before it had fully stopped. "Where is Pumpkin?" she asked, hot tears rolling down her cheeks. "How could you do this?"

"I see Sadie ran off to tell you," Priscilla said, standing in the driveway with her arms crossed. Amanda stood next to her in a similar manner.

"And I'm glad she did, Priscilla," Irvin said. "Stop. This must stop right now. Today. Ella Ruth told me everything."

Priscilla's eyes widened, and her face paled slightly.

"Pumpkin was my late wife's horse. She gave her to Ella Ruth before she died. You had no right to sell her. Where is she? Who bought her?" Irvin asked.

"Joseph's employee came by to pick her up," Priscilla said. "I thought we could use the money. He made a good offer."

"She was not your horse to sell," Irvin said. "We have a great deal to talk about, but first, we need to get Pumpkin back."

A car drove down the lane, and everyone turned to look because it was a rare occurrence. Was that James' car?

He pulled into their driveway and got out. "Your sisters called me from the phone in the store, Ella Ruth. I'm sorry about your horse."

"James?" Amanda shrieked, throwing her hands up. "You've got to be kidding me."

Priscilla only stared at him, her jaw dropping. "What is he doing here?" she whispered to Amanda.

"Is this James?" Irvin asked, walking up to him. He stuck out his hand. "I'm Irvin Holt, Ella Ruth's father. Glad to meet you."

A stunned look flashed across James' face, then he grinned. "Nice to meet you. I'm James Baldwin."

At the sight of her father greeting him so warmly, Ella Ruth smiled, forgetting about her horse for only a moment.

"I would love to sit down and talk with you about your intentions with my daughter, but we are pressed for time right now," Irvin said.

"That's why I'm here. I want to help you find your horse. Let me drive you," James offered.

"Thank you," Ella Ruth said. "Joseph bought her. We have to go to his stables right away and buy her back."

"Where is the money?" Irvin asked Priscilla.

She pressed her lips into a thin line.

"This horse means so much to my daughter, Priscilla," Irvin said. "I know you weren't Amish for your entire life, and I know you suffered a great deal before you came here, but this is not the Amish way, and you have been Amish long enough to know that. God calls us to love one another, not betray one another. Please give us the money so we can go buy back Ella Ruth's horse." He held out his hand.

Priscilla sighed and handed him the cash with a frown.

"Thank you," Ella Ruth said.

"You might be too late. Joseph sells horses very quickly," Amanda said.

"Well, we must pray that we will get there in time," Ella Ruth said, then got into the car with James and her father before they sped down the lane.

God, please let us get there in time, she prayed. *Please help us get her back.*

A few minutes later, they arrived at Joseph's horse stable. Ella Ruth scanned the pasture for her horse but didn't see her.

As James pulled into the driveway, they approached a large trailer. As the car stopped, Ella Ruth saw Pumpkin behind the trailer as a man was leading her inside.

"No!" Ella Ruth cried, throwing open the door and scrambling out. "Stop! That's my horse!"

Joseph, the owner of the horse stables, held up a hand. "Hello, Ella Ruth. Your stepmother just sold my employee this horse."

"My wife sold the horse without telling us," Irvin said, right on Ella Ruth's heels. "Pumpkin is Ella Ruth's horse. I'm sorry, but there's been a big misunderstanding, Joseph."

James walked up behind Ella Ruth. "Can we buy her back?"

"I just bought this horse," the *Englisher* man said as he led Pumpkin into the trailer. "It's done."

"I have the money right here," Irvin said, holding up the cash. "I can pay you back what you paid to Priscilla."

"I sold Pumpkin to Mr. Garrison for more than what I paid," Joseph said to Irvin in a low voice. "You know how this works. I have no say in the matter now, Irvin. It's all up to Mr. Garrison. I'm sorry."

"Mr. Garrison, Pumpkin was my late wife's horse, and now she's my daughter's horse. She's like a part of our family. Won't you please let me buy her back from you?" Irvin pleaded.

The man scratched his short white beard thoughtfully. "You can have her for double what I paid Joseph."

"Double?" Ella Ruth gasped.

Irvin shook his head and slowly turned to Ella Ruth. "I don't have the money, Ella Ruth. I'm so sorry."

"Well, then, I'll be going now," Mr. Garrison said, tugging Pumpkin toward the trailer, but she snorted and stomped her feet, resisting.

"No! Pumpkin, it's okay, I'm here," Ella Ruth said soothingly, walking toward her horse, and Pumpkin stomped her feet again.

"Back up, girl. You're spooking her," Mr. Garrison said, waving his hand.

"She doesn't like strangers or trailers," Ella Ruth said. "You're making her nervous."

"Don't tell me what to do with my horse," the man snapped.

"Excuse me, sir, please be respectful to this young woman," James interjected firmly. "And please let me buy Pumpkin from you for double what you paid." He put his hands on his hips.

"Double?" The man froze. "In cash?"

"Yes. I obviously don't have thousands of dollars in cash on me here right now, but I can get it to you later today."

"I don't want to wait around," Mr. Garrison said.

"We can't let you do this," Irvin said, and Ella Ruth knew he was right. It was too much to accept.

"I want to do this, sir," James said to Irvin, then he turned to Ella Ruth. "Please. Consider it a gift."

Ella Ruth didn't know what to say. She wanted to accept, but she wasn't sure if Irvin would allow it. Besides, she wasn't even officially dating or courting James yet. This was quite a grand gesture, but she desperately wanted Pumpkin back.

"Let me make this simple for all of you," Mr. Garrison announced. "Either I get triple in cash right now, or I'm out of here."

"Will you take this cash as a deposit? I can get the rest to you this afternoon," James asked, gesturing to the cash Irvin held.

"How do I know you won't go back on your word?"

"How do we know you won't just take the cash and walk?" James asked.

"I want all the cash now or I *will* walk." Mr. Garrison narrowed his eyes.

James' eyes darted to Irvin and Ella Ruth. "I'm sorry."

"You tried," Irvin said, but Ella Ruth couldn't speak. Tears coursed down her face as Pumpkin disappeared into the trailer and the doors slammed shut. Her heart physically ached in her chest, feeling as though it was literally cracking into two as she ran toward the trailer.

It began to move away, but Ella Ruth called, "I love you, Pumpkin. I'll try to get you back!"

As the trailer drove down the driveway and turned onto the road, Ella Ruth fell to her knees, devastation sinking in as she wrapped her arms around herself.

CHAPTER TWENTY-SIX

Irvin was right—Pumpkin was part of the family. Just like that, she was gone, hauled away in an *Englisher's* trailer. Would he take care of her well?

No one could take care of Pumpkin as well as Ella Ruth. She knew everything Pumpkin liked—how she liked to be brushed, what she liked to eat, and how she even enjoyed bedtime stories.

"Come here," Irvin said, pulling her into his arms. "I'm so sorry, my dear."

"I'm going to try to get her back," James said, gently putting a hand on her shoulder and helping her stand.

"How? Do you know his name?" Ella Ruth asked.

"The trailer said Garrison Stables. I'm sure I can search for it online and find it," James said.

"It doesn't matter, James. We don't have the money to buy her back, not triple the amount she was sold for," Irvin said, patting him on the shoulder. "We tried."

"I have the money," James said. "Let me buy her back."

"We couldn't accept that," Ella Ruth said, slowly shaking her head. She wanted to accept, but it wouldn't be right to let him use his money to buy Pumpkin back, and she knew her father would never agree to it.

"She's right," Irvin said. "But thank you for the offer."

"I'm sorry," Joseph said, walking up to them. "I'm so terribly sorry. If I had known, I never would have sold Pumpkin to him. He was already here when my employee arrived with Pumpkin, and he bought her immediately. I feel terrible. I didn't realize that you didn't know."

"It's not your fault," Irvin said. "My wife sold her without telling anyone." He sighed. "We'll get going now."

Irvin and Ella Ruth turned and started walking down the driveway.

"Let me give you a ride back," James said, catching up to them.

"I'd rather just walk home, but thank you, James," she said, wiping away a tear. "It's not that far. Thank you for trying."

James could see the devastation and defeat in her eyes. This time, her stepmother had truly crushed Ella Ruth's spirit, and it broke James' heart to see her this way. She should be loved and cherished every day, not threatened and mistreated.

"I understand," James said, realizing she needed some time. He could leave right now for the bank to get cash and then go straight to Garrison Stables to buy Pumpkin back. James knew that if he told Ella Ruth or Irvin about his plans that they would never agree to it, so he was just going to do it. "I'm so sorry this happened, Ella Ruth."

James got in his car and drove away, headed for the bank. He couldn't wait to see the look on Ella Ruth's face when he brought Pumpkin back to her.

⁂

"Priscilla has crossed the line again," Irvin said solemnly to Ella Ruth as they walked home. "I'm so terribly sorry. I don't know how she could have done this."

"I think it's because James chose me over Amanda," Ella Ruth said. "But I think that even if I stopped seeing him, she would still find a reason to do things like this to me." She looked up at her father, whose lips were drawn into a thin line of worry. "What are you going to do?" She hated seeing him so troubled, especially after he had gone through so much when her mother had died and when her sisters had been kidnapped. She had hoped that her father wouldn't have to endure so much sorrow ever again.

"I'm not sure what to do," Irvin said. "I will talk to her, but I fear she won't stop. If she does something like this again, I may need to go to the bishop. Hopefully, my conversation with her today will get through to her, and it won't come to that. Our family has suffered enough already. It's time to put all of this behind us."

Ella Ruth nodded.

"James was very helpful. I see why you like him," Irvin said, and she smiled.

"He is a good man."

"Is he a believer?"

"Yes," Ella Ruth said. "He goes to the little church down the road and studies the Bible earnestly."

"That is good to hear," Irvin said. "He was so kind to offer to buy Pumpkin back. I was surprised when you turned him down."

"Well, first of all, I knew you wouldn't accept it."

Irvin nodded. "It's a great deal of money."

"Second of all, I don't want to feel like I owe him anything. If I accepted such a large gift from him, he might expect me to court or even marry him. To be honest, even though I'd like to accept his proposal more than anything if he did ask me, I don't think I could leave all of you right now. I know you all need my help at home with the chores, and I fear that if I left..."

"That Priscilla would begin to mistreat one of your siblings in your place," Irvin said with a sigh, shaking his head.

"Exactly. I let her mistreat me because I don't want Katie and Lilly to have to endure it. They've been through so much already. And Debra and Seth are so young. If she's going to take her pain out on anyone, it should be me," Ella Ruth said. "Because I can take it."

Irvin stopped and faced his daughter. "You are brave, and you have such a loving heart," he said. "I am so proud that you are my daughter."

Tears sprang up in her eyes as he hugged her.

"But you shouldn't have to bear this," Irvin said. "I will do everything I can to make sure Amanda and Priscilla stop mistreating you, my dear, and that they don't do it to anyone else."

"Thank you," she said.

As they approached the house, Irvin gestured to the store down the lane. "You can go on ahead to the store. I'm sure they need your help. I'll go talk to Priscilla and Amanda, and I will meet you there afterward."

Ella Ruth nodded and walked down the lane toward the store. As she did, she glanced over her shoulder to see Irvin walking into the house.

"Lord, give him the words to say," Ella Ruth prayed, "and please give Priscilla an open heart."

When she reached the store, Katie, Lilly, and Sadie all ran over to her.

"What happened?" Katie asked.

"Did you get Pumpkin back?" Lilly asked.

"I'm so sorry my mother did this," Sadie said, her eyes filling with tears. "I feel terrible about it."

"I know you had nothing to do with it, Sadie," Ella Ruth said, hugging her. "But no, we didn't get her back." She explained what happened with the new buyer, and they all tried to comfort her, but their kind words and hugs did nothing to stop the tears from spilling down her cheeks. "I love Pumpkin so much. She was *Mamm's* horse, and she's been like part of the family since I was young when we first got her. I feel like a part of me was taken away when she got in that trailer. And how will her new owner treat her? Will she be sold again? What if she goes to...the slaughter house?"

The mere thought sent her into another round of sobs, and her sisters patted her back and tried in vain to console her.

"I just have to accept the fact that I'll never see Pumpkin again," she whispered.

"Well, I'm glad we had this talk," Irvin said. "So, you admit that selling Pumpkin and the way you've been treating Ella Ruth is wrong?"

"Yes," Priscilla said as they sat at the kitchen table. Amanda sat beside her, squirming.

She's lying, Amanda thought. She knew her mother well enough to tell when she was lying.

"And we are very sorry, aren't we, Amanda?" Priscilla glanced at her daughter.

"Yes, I am sorry," Amanda said, and she meant it. Tears suddenly sprang up in her eyes as guilt gripped her like a giant fist, squeezing her until she couldn't breathe. Maybe her mother wasn't sorry, but she certainly was. The sight of Ella Ruth's distraught expression as tears rolled down her cheeks was burned into Amanda's memory.

She would never forget the look of despair in Ella Ruth's eyes. It reminded her of the heartbreak she had endured while living with her abusive stepfather.

"Good," Irvin said. "You can both apologize to her later. I'm going back to the store." He walked out the door, leaving Amanda and Priscilla alone.

"Wow. You were so convincing, I almost believed you," Priscilla said with a chuckle, turning to her daughter.

"This isn't funny, Mom. What we have done is wrong," Amanda cried. "Why don't you feel guilty about this? Why do you dislike Ella Ruth so much?"

"Every time I see her with Irvin and how much he loves her, all I can think about is how much I regret how your stepfather abused you. I wish you had always had a father who loved you that much all along. I just want her to leave so that Irvin will love you and Sadie more, plus she deserves to pay for ruining your future with James. She has already talked about leaving the Amish, so we just need to give her a nudge by making her miserable," Priscilla said with a sinister grin.

"What?" Amanda threw her hands up. "I thought this was about sabotaging her relationship with James so I could have a chance with him."

"It started that way, but it's changed now that we know you have no shot with James," Priscilla said.

"She didn't ruin my chance with James. That was all because of me and how I lied to him. Besides, he didn't even like me. This is wrong, Mom. We shouldn't have sold Pumpkin. We shouldn't have done any of this!" Amanda stood up so quickly that she almost knocked her chair over.

"You don't want payback?"

"No!" Amanda cried. "She was right. If I had married him for his money, it would have been a sham of a marriage. She did me a favor. Don't you feel guilty at all?" Amanda asked.

Priscilla hesitated. "But she ruined your future. We have to make her pay."

"She doesn't deserve any of this."

"I don't care. Now, you are my daughter, so listen to me. We are going to get our revenge, and we are going to get her to leave for good. Are you on my side or not, Amanda?" Priscilla demanded.

Amanda hesitated. This was wrong. How could she make her mother see that? She saw the desperation in her mother's eyes.

I can't disappoint her, Amanda thought.

"I'm on your side, Mom," she said begrudgingly.

"Good girl." Priscilla smiled with satisfaction.

Chapter Twenty-seven

James felt like a king as he handed Mr. Garrison the amount of cash he had asked for, and one of the stable hands loaded Pumpkin into a trailer to deliver to Ella Ruth's house. He drove in his car ahead of the trailer, smiling the entire way.

Then a thought struck him. What if she still didn't accept his gift of returning Pumpkin even after he arrived? What would he do? Hopefully, even if she refused at first, he could persuade her and her father to accept his gesture.

As he drove down her driveway with Mr. Garrison's trailer not far behind him, anxiety struck him. Was this too bold of a move? He hadn't known Ella Ruth long, but he knew he was falling in love with her.

If he was honest with himself, he wanted to marry her one day. He had never felt like this about anyone before. He would do anything for her. To him, this was not too grand of a gesture, but she might think it was. And what would her father say?

When he arrived, Irvin Holt walked out of the house, his eyes wide with surprise. "Hello again, James. What do we have here?"

"I bought Pumpkin back," James said as he got out of the car. He held up his hands. "I know Ella Ruth said she couldn't accept me buying back Pumpkin for her, but she was so devastated, I had to do this for her. I sincerely hope you will both accept."

"This is a very generous thing you have done for my daughter," Irvin said, nodding toward the trailer as the driver exited the truck that had been pulling it. "You must truly care about her."

"I do, sir. I am falling in love with your daughter. We couldn't talk about it earlier, but you said you wanted to know my intentions, and to be frank, I want to marry her one day. I would like to court her first, if she will have me. I'm not expecting anything from her by giving her back her horse. I'm not trying to show off. I'm only doing this because I want her to be happy again. When I saw how broken-hearted she was, it was devastating, and I want to bring her as much joy as she has brought me."

Irvin furrowed his brows and crossed his arms. "I see. So, you want to marry my daughter one day. Do you realize she would have to leave the Amish church if she married you?"

"Yes, sir, and if she doesn't want to leave, I would be willing to join the church to marry her," he said bluntly. "I'd leave everything behind."

Irvin raised his eyebrows. "So, you do love her."

"Yes, sir." James' heart pounded as he watched Irvin's expression soften.

"Not many people join the Amish and stay permanently. Do you think you could do it?"

"I have no doubt. I'm planning on giving up the company and my inheritance, anyway. It's my dream to become an English teacher, but I'd give that up too if I had to. Being with Ella Ruth is more important to me."

"And you are a Christian, correct?"

"Yes, sir. I'm a born-again follower of Jesus," James said. "I go to the church down the road, but I would be happy to convert to the Amish faith for your daughter."

Ella Ruth's father let out a long breath, then stuck out his hand. "She never got to go on her *Rumspringa* because her mother passed away at the time when she would have gone. She hasn't been baptized into the church yet, so she wouldn't be shunned if she courted you or married you, but it would be frowned upon by some. However, if you both have the intention of marriage, you have my blessing to court."

"I understand," James said, shaking his hand firmly. "Thank you, sir. I appreciate it greatly. I am waiting for the right time to ask her. I won't disappoint you."

Irvin chuckled. "Don't make promises you can't keep. Everyone makes mistakes."

"I suppose. But I do promise to do everything I can to make your daughter happy every day for the rest of our lives if she will have me. Lord knows I don't deserve her."

"Ah. You are a man after my own heart, James. I like you." Irvin grinned, and a huge blanket of relief and gratitude fell over James. "I wouldn't trust just anyone with one of my daughters."

"I am sure I will be the same way if I ever have a daughter of my own," James said, smiling.

"Yes, one day you will understand." Irvin nodded toward the direction of the road where the Unity Community Store was located. "Ella Ruth is at the store with her sisters. I am on my way there now. Shall I go with you to tell her the news? We can put Pumpkin in the pasture first."

"Yes, sir. That would be great," James said, grinning.

"Please call me Irvin," Irvin said, walking with him toward the gate of the trailer. They led Pumpkin out, who immediately seemed happy to be home once she saw her familiar surroundings. She scampered off into the pasture to join their other horse, Clarence.

"Thank you, James. I sincerely thank you. You are about to make my daughter very happy. I don't know how I can ever repay you," Irvin said, clapping him on the back.

"I don't want you to repay me. This is my gift to her."

"Let's go tell her the good news," Irvin said with a childlike smile.

Ella Ruth wiped away a tear as she stacked jars of local honey on the store shelf. All she could see was the image of Pumpkin fearfully entering the trailer in her mind, playing over and over again. The store was painfully silent as her sisters tried to come up with words that might comfort her, but nothing eased the ache in her chest.

"Please, Lord, let her new owner take good care of her," she whispered, her hands shaking as she stacked another jar.

Suddenly the door opened, and she whirled around to see her father.

"Ella Ruth, come outside," Irvin said, waving her over. "Quickly!"

The four young women dropped everything and ran out the door to see James standing by his car.

"James has something to tell you," Irvin said, trying in vain to hide a grin.

"What's going on?" Ella Ruth asked. She felt a seed of hope blooming in her belly, but she quickly squashed it. They couldn't have bought Pumpkin back.

Could they have?

"I bought Pumpkin back for you," James said, walking toward her, palms upward. "Please don't be angry, but I brought the money to Mr. Garrison, and he accepted. She's in the pasture at your house right now."

"And she is clearly happy to be home," Irvin said, giving her an expectant look. Her sisters stood by her, clasping their hands and smiling.

Ella Ruth blinked in surprise as several emotions swirled through her. She was ecstatic to have her beloved horse home, but James had gone behind her back to accomplish it. That was a huge amount of money he had just spent on her. Should she stubbornly refuse?

"Are you angry?" he murmured.

"Say thank you," Katie whispered beside her.

Ella Ruth let out a long breath, letting go of any negative feelings. This man loved her, and he had done a wonderful, generous thing for her. "Thank you, James. Thank you!" Not caring that her family was watching, she ran forward and threw her arms around him.

"I'm just glad to see you happy," he whispered into her ear. "I couldn't bear to see you so sad. I know you love your horse."

"I just can't believe you got her back! Thank you," she cried, then pulled away, tears of joy in her eyes. She turned to her father. "May I go see her?"

"It's almost time to close, anyway. Let's close the store and go home," Irvin said.

After the store was closed, James offered all of them a ride in his car. When they all said they would rather walk, he left his car there and walked the short distance down the lane with them to their house. Debra and Seth were playing outside when the group arrived. They had been at a neighbor's house playing with their friends when Pumpkin had been sold, so they didn't even know what had happened until they got home.

Ella Ruth ran to the pasture, climbed over the wooden fence, and threw her arms around Pumpkin's neck. "I'm so glad you're back, girl. I thought I'd never see you again!"

The horse whinnied in reply, her nose twitching. Ella Ruth pulled away to pat her face, laughing when Pumpkin nuzzled her.

"Aww. I love you, too, Pumpkin."

As she talked softly to her horse, she couldn't help but notice a commotion in the yard.

"Will you stay for dinner, James?" Irvin asked. "It's the least we can do to thank you."

Priscilla and Amanda stood on the porch, their arms crossed.

"I don't want to intrude," James said, glancing at them.

"Please, stay! We'd love to have you," Lilly cried, and the others agreed.

"Thank you. I'd love to," he said.

"Come on inside," Katie said, beckoning from the porch, then they led him inside, leaving Ella Ruth and Irvin outside.

"He's a very kind and thoughtful young man, from what I can tell. Although, we did just meet," Irvin said, approaching the pasture.

Ella Ruth walked toward the fence to meet him. "He is, *Daed*. He truly is."

"He told me his intentions. I know you two must share a deep connection if he feels that way about you," Irvin said. "I can tell he loves you very much."

"We haven't known each other very long, but yes. We do share a deep connection," Ella Ruth agreed. "I love him, *Daed*." Just saying the very words thrilled her, and a smile spread across her face.

"I know. I could see it in your eyes when you looked at him," Irvin said, sighing. "I always had a feeling you wouldn't stay Amish forever. Are you thinking of leaving?"

"I've been giving it a lot of thought and prayer," Ella Ruth said. "I just hate to leave you all."

"We would be fine. We would miss you, of course, but you do have the freedom to leave if you want to. You haven't been baptized. We would still be able to talk to you and see you, but we would miss you."

She nodded. "I would miss you all too."

"I just hope you give this a great amount of thought and prayer before you make your decision," he said earnestly.

"I am. I will," she said. "I'm not taking this decision lightly."

"Word might get out about this. I wouldn't be surprised if the bishop spoke to you about it. He won't reprimand you, but he might ask you to reconsider," Irvin explained.

"I expected that. Word travels quickly here."

"I want you to know that if you do decide to leave the community, I will support your decision either way, and I want you to feel free to leave, if that's what you wish. I don't want you to worry about us."

"But what about the chores?" she asked. "Who will make Debra and Seth's lunches for school? Who will stay with Katie and Lilly when they wake up from nightmares in the middle of the night?"

"No one could ever replace you, Ella Ruth. You do so much for our family. But we would get by. I will take care of them, and they will take care of each other."

"And what about Priscilla and Amanda? Do you think they will ever have a change of heart?" Ella Ruth asked.

"I hope one day they will," Irvin said. "Maybe with time, God will change them, but there is no way to know for sure. God brought them into our lives for a reason. We have to be forgiving and under-standing. Most of all, we need to love them. They've suffered, too."

Ella Ruth sighed. She knew in her head that she should forgive and love them, and she thought she had, but every now and then, resentment toward them would creep up in her heart.

Would she ever be able to truly forgive them and put all this behind her?

"Come on. Let's go inside and see how James is doing," Irvin said.

Chapter Twenty-eight

James let the Holts lead him into their house. He had never been inside an Amish home before, but it was surprisingly cozy and inviting. The woodstove made the house warmer than it was outside, even on a summer evening with the windows open, because they had no air conditioning or fans. The walls were a pleasant blue in the kitchen and yellow in the living room, which also surprised him. He'd expected all white walls. A couch and sofa sat in the living room next to a tall bookshelf filled with books, puzzles, and games like Scrabble and Dutch Blitz.

Sadie, Katie, and Lilly made small talk with him in the kitchen for a bit while Amanda and Priscilla stayed in the living room. A few moments later, Irvin and Ella Ruth came inside.

"Your home is lovely," he said.

"Thank you," Irvin replied.

"I'm going to make dinner," Ella Ruth said. "Please make yourself at home."

"Do you want to play Scrabble with us?" Debra asked, and Seth nodded.

"Sounds like fun," James said.

"I'll play too," Irvin said.

Katie, Sadie, and Lilly joined Ella Ruth in the kitchen as Priscilla and Amanda continued to sit awkwardly in the living room.

"I'm sure they could use help making dinner," Irvin said, nodding his head toward the kitchen.

Priscilla sighed and walked into the kitchen with Amanda walking right behind her. "Can we help?" Priscilla asked.

Ella Ruth whirled around in surprise, almost dropping the potato she was peeling. "Sure." This had never happened before, so she was at a loss for words.

"Here, you can peel these carrots, Amanda," Sadie said, coming to her rescue.

"And you can shell these peas, *Mamm*, while we make the dumplings and cook the chicken," Lilly added.

Wordlessly, the two women began their tasks. Ella Ruth could feel the tension in the air as they worked, and to make it worse, there was little conversation to break up the awkwardness. The only conversation came from the living room, where the others were playing a game. No one wanted to bring up the elephant—or the horse—in the room since Priscilla had not apologized to Ella Ruth yet.

Would she ever apologize to her? What if she didn't feel like she had even done anything wrong?

"I'm sorry if having James here makes you uncomfortable, Amanda," Ella Ruth said.

Amanda shrugged, keeping her eyes on the carrot she was peeling.

"She's fine," Pricilla interjected.

Ella Ruth turned back toward the counter, where she began chopping the potatoes. She had so many thoughts swirling through her mind, so many things she wanted to say and ask them, like why they seemed to hate her so much. What had she ever done to them?

But she kept silent, not wanting to make matters worse. Perhaps, if she gave them time, they would apologize to her. And if not, she would have to accept that, though she hoped it would not make her heart even more bitter than it already was.

Lord, help me forgive them no matter what, she prayed.

Sadie briefly placed her hand on her arm as if to silently encourage her, and Ella Ruth gave her a grateful, small smile.

When dinner was ready, everyone sat down, and Ella Ruth sat beside James.

"We do a silent prayer," she whispered to him, and he nodded. Everyone closed their eyes for about thirty seconds, then Irvin began stirring and scooping food onto the children's plates to signal that the prayer was over.

"Wow, this is delicious," James said, taking a bite of the chicken and dumplings.

"It was our mother's recipe," Ella Ruth said. "She was an amazing cook."

"It's incredible," James said. "So, Debra beat me at Scrabble. Twice."

Debra grinned. "I'm a good speller."

"You certainly are," James said.

Seth only smiled since he still spoke only German. He hadn't started going to school yet, which was when the Amish children in Unity began to learn English.

"I think Seth will be winning by this time next year," James added.

For the rest of the meal, Amanda and Priscilla remained silent, awkwardly picking at their food while everyone else made conversation. When everyone was finished, James played another round of Scrabble with Irvin and the children as the ladies washed the dishes. When they were finished, Amanda and Priscilla excused themselves and each went to their own room.

"I take it their conversation with *Daed* didn't go very well," Sadie murmured after they'd left.

"I don't know how it went yet," Ella Ruth said. "I'm not sure if they're angry or remorseful."

"They haven't said a word since we got home," Lilly said, and Katie frowned.

"I think they're bitter," Sadie said with a sigh. "I know them better than anyone, and I can tell. They don't seem apologetic or as if they regret their actions. I'm sorry, Ella Ruth, but I don't think they are going to apologize to you. To me, it seems as if they don't believe they did anything wrong. That's what I'm sensing. I'm so sorry." She gently patted Ella Ruth's back.

"Thank you, Sadie. I suppose all we can do is pray and be kind to them. Only God can change their hearts."

Katie and Lilly nodded.

"Ella Ruth, may I speak to you outside?" James said as their Scrabble game ended. "Debra beat me again!"

Ella Ruth chuckled. "Let's go on the front porch."

"Good evening, everyone," James said. "Thank you so much for inviting me to stay for dinner. It was delicious."

Everyone said goodbye, then Ella Ruth and James walked out the door.

Outside, the sun was just starting to brush the tips of the trees in the forest beyond the Amish homes, casting long shadows over the farm fields. Tangerine and rosy hues colored the sky, turning the edges of the clouds pink.

James and Ella Ruth sat on the sturdy porch swing that Irvin had made before she was born. When James looked at her, her heart flipped.

"Do you think you would ever leave the Amish, Ella Ruth?" James asked softly.

"I haven't decided yet," Ella Ruth said with a sigh. "To be honest, I have always dreamed of leaving, but I feel responsible for my family. I feel like I need to stay to take care of everyone." Her voice dropped to a whisper. "I'm afraid to leave them with Priscilla and Amanda. Sadly, I'm afraid if I leave, they might start picking on one of my siblings. I hope that's not the case, but that's what I'm afraid of. My father assures me he will take care of everyone, and I know he has talked to them about it, but I still worry about it."

"I know they've deeply hurt you," James said. "I noticed they didn't say anything this evening."

"I'm not sure why," Ella Ruth said. "I don't know how my father's conversation with them today went, but Sadie said she doesn't think they are sorry."

"I'm sorry to hear that," James said. "Are you still going to forgive them?"

"Yes," Ella Ruth said, then stared at her lap. "I have to try."

"I know it must be hard," James said. "But the Lord calls us to forgive so we don't carry bitterness in our hearts. We're hurting ourselves if we don't forgive."

Ella Ruth knew that, but her heart didn't want to cooperate. "It's not fair what they've done to me. They hurt me over and over for no reason, and I'm just supposed to forgive them just like that?" she blurted, then covered her mouth.

Her words had revealed her heart's true thoughts.

"I suppose I'm not ready to forgive them yet," she added quietly.

"I understand it might take some time," James said, patting her hand. "But I hope one day soon you can, even if they don't apologize. I fear we might not be able to truly move on in our relationship until that happens."

"I suppose you're right. You probably don't want to court someone with a bitter heart."

"You don't have a bitter heart, Ella Ruth. You have a kind heart." He squeezed her hand.

But I do have bitterness in my heart, she thought glumly.

"I just don't want you to become even more hurt than you already are. Also, maybe if you forgive them, you might feel at ease about leaving if that is what you truly want to do, as long as you know for sure. I hope you take all the time you need to decide. Then we can talk about our relationship."

She looked up at him with questions in her eyes. "Is that why you asked me if I had ever thought of leaving?"

"I asked you because I want to be with you, but I also don't want you to get in trouble. And I certainly don't want you to leave just to be with me. It should be for the right reasons."

"Absolutely." She nodded slowly, a myriad of emotions and thoughts circling through her. "It's a lot to consider."

He nodded, then kissed her on the cheek. "I should get going. Thank you so much for dinner. It was scrumptious."

She smiled. "Thank you. I did have help. I'm glad you stayed. And thank you so much for returning Pumpkin to me."

"It was my absolute pleasure. Just seeing the smile on your face was priceless." He waved, then walked down the lane toward his car.

Amanda and Priscilla watched from the window upstairs as James and Ella Ruth talked quietly on the front porch swing.

"So, she's going to find it in her heart to *forgive* us," Priscilla said, waving her hand mockingly. "I couldn't care less."

"So, they're courting now," Amanda said, shaking her head. "Ugh. Why does he want to marry her? She's getting *my* happy ending! That should have been me. I worked so hard trying to make him like me."

"I know, my dear," Priscilla said. "She stole your prince, and she's going to pay for it."

"Why didn't he fall in love with *me*? What's so great about her?" Amanda frowned, jealousy burning inside her along with sadness. All her life, she'd felt unworthy, and she had hoped that maybe if James—or any young man—wanted to date her, that she would feel better about herself. "Apparently I'm not good enough for him," she muttered.

"You are perfect just the way you are, Amanda. You're beautiful and ambitious, so I don't see any reason why he would choose her over you unless she persuaded him to. If it wasn't for her, you would be dating him by now. We need to do something to keep her from him once and for all. Maybe then he will realize just how wonderful you are."

"What do you have in mind?" Amanda asked hesitantly.

"Her laptop is stowed away in our bedroom closet. Irvin hid it there. We can plug it in somewhere downtown and delete the books she wrote," Priscilla said. "She will spend all her spare time rewriting the books, so she will have no more time for him. I tried giving her lists of chores to do, but that didn't work. Irvin just insisted that we help her."

"If we delete her books, won't that devastate her?" Amanda asked, having a moment of doubt as guilt crept in. "Her writing means everything to her. It will crush her."

"My dear, sometimes getting what you want means taking drastic measures and hurting someone in the process," Priscilla said, putting a hand on her daughter's shoulder. "I never want you to have to wonder how you're going to pay the bills or buy food. I don't want you to live in a house with mold in a leaking roof like where we used to live. I made terrible choices in the past, and I had to live with them, but the worst part was seeing you girls pay for my mistakes. Especially you, Amanda. I know he abused you much more than Sadie."

"I'm outspoken. He hated me for it," Amanda said, crossing her arms. A shiver crawled down her spine at the memories of her stepfather's abuse.

"Irvin is a kind man, and I am blessed to have him as a husband, but you and Sadie don't have to stay here. You could have a much better, more luxurious life. I want you to date James, get your foot in the door, and marry wealthy, even if it isn't him. You could meet so many people in high society through him. I will do anything to make sure you girls have a better life than this. You don't want to be Amish your whole life, do you? You weren't raised Amish, so why stay Amish when you can have the luxuries of the outside world? Do you really want to wash dishes by hand and go without electricity every day for the rest of your life?" Priscilla asked. She walked to her bedroom closet with Amanda close behind her, then opened the door and pulled out the laptop.

Amanda nodded. "I do want to be wealthy and not have to worry about money. But won't you come with us?"

"No. I married Irvin, so I'm staying. He may not be wealthy, but he is a very good and kind husband and father. Finally, I've met someone who loves me, and I love him, but I want a better life for you. We must do this, Amanda. We must delete her books and show her once and for all that she shouldn't have stolen James from you. She shouldn't have stolen your happy ending." Priscilla opened the laptop. "It has a dead battery. We'll have to charge it downtown at the coffee shop tomorrow."

"How long do you think it will take her to realize the book files are gone? She doesn't have access to the laptop anymore."

"Hmm." Priscilla tapped her chin. "Maybe I can tell her it fell out of the closet, and she should make sure it's not broken and that she should make sure her files are all still there."

"You think she'll believe that and check the files?"

"Maybe."

Amanda turned and walked out of the room, leaving Priscilla alone in the bedroom. She sat down on the bed, wrapping her arms around herself as memories assailed her.

Priscilla remembered coming home from the grocery store with her daughters to the small house where they had lived with Marvin, Priscilla's second husband. They opened the door to see him sitting in his usual chair in the living room, watching television.

"Oh, good, you're back. I'm hungry," he grumbled, nodding briefly in their direction. "Are you going to make dinner?"

"Of course," Priscilla said as her daughters helped her carry the bags inside.

"What are you making?"

"Potato soup." Priscilla set two bags down on the table gingerly.

"You made that the other day," Marvin snapped.

"Well, potatoes were on sale, and I'm trying to save money."

Marvin had been fired for drinking on the job a few months ago and had previously gambled away his savings. Priscilla could only find work as a waitress at the local diner, so they could hardly buy enough groceries to feed the four of them after the bills were paid.

Not to mention Marvin's expensive habits.

"Did you get my beer and cigarettes?" he demanded, getting up out of his chair and stumbling into the kitchen.

Priscilla let out a slow breath, noticing her daughters' wide, frightened eyes. She nodded toward their bedroom door. "Go," she whispered to them, and they scurried down the hall. She turned to Marvin. "I told you before that we can't afford it. I used the money to buy food."

No warning. No reason. No chance for Priscilla to evade him. He swung his open hand toward her face, the blow a sharp sting on her cheek.

"Go get it. Right now, Priscilla." Marvin's face reddened as he seethed, he then ambled back to his chair and sat down. If she did as he said, he would leave her daughters alone.

Priscilla hurried out the door and headed back to the grocery store.

Chapter Twenty-nine

Down the hall of their home in Unity, Amanda was struggling with her own memories.

She also remembered that day as she hid in the bedroom she shared with Sadie in that tiny house. Tears had streamed down her face as she'd witnessed her stepfather hit her mother, and she held back a strangled cry along with the urge to lunge at him and fight back.

"This will all be over soon when we leave him," Sadie whispered, rubbing her sister's back.

"I'm not sure I can wait until then," Amanda whispered back. "What are we waiting for?"

"Mom says we're waiting for the right time," Sadie said. "Like when he leaves the house for a while."

"He hasn't left the house in days. He hasn't even showered in days."

"He'll leave eventually."

Once they left him, they would no longer have to endure his violent outbursts. They had plans to go back home to their mother's relatives in Unity, Maine—an Amish community. Amanda didn't mind. She just wanted to be anywhere but here. Amanda's bag had been packed for over a week, hidden in her closet beside Sadie's.

From her vantage point, where she peeked through the crack of her slightly open door, Amanda could see her stepfather in his chair. To her, he was no longer her stepfather or even a relative. A stranger sat in the living room. He was not the kind, charming man that their mother had married. He was not the man who had showered them with compliments, gifts, and fun outings as he won them over.

Once the wedding was over, he had become a completely different person. He had hidden his alcohol addiction from them.

Marvin yawned from the living room. This was usually about the time he would fall asleep again while watching television.

Priscilla returned from the store. Amanda wasn't sure where her mother had found the money, and she wasn't sure she wanted to know. Earlier, at the store, they couldn't even afford to buy enough food for the week.

"Next time, do as I ask," Marvin said, walking into the kitchen and taking a beer. He then proceeded to call Priscilla something that made Amanda's blood boil. "You're completely worthless."

Amanda began to open the door, but Sadie held her back. "Mom said to stay here."

"I can't let him talk to her like that." Amanda wrenched out of her grip.

Priscilla frowned and turned away from him, opening a cabinet to put the groceries away.

"Look at me when I'm talking to you!" he roared, then backhanded her again.

"That's it. I can't stay here," Amanda said, flinging open the door and marching down the hall. "Don't hit my mother! And don't talk to her that way!"

"Don't tell me what to do, Amanda," Marvin said, slapping her across the face, then shoving her hard. Amanda fell backward onto the kitchen floor, watching in horror as her stepfather turned to her mother. "Control your daughters!" he yelled, then shoved her as well, so they were now both on the floor. As Marvin walked over to Priscilla, his fury was at a level Amanda had never seen before. He would hurt Priscilla badly—she didn't stand a chance at deflecting his blows.

Amanda scrambled to her feet. She pulled at his arms, but he shoved her away. She fell on the floor again but quickly got back up. Frantic, she searched for something to stop him with. Anything...

The set of knives on the kitchen counter.

Too dangerous. But her stepfather was out of control, so intoxicated and angry that he might actually kill her mother as he wrapped his hands around her throat.

Amanda refused to let that happen.

She didn't know if she should call the police or go find help. That might take too long.

As Priscilla fought for air, Amanda quickly realized she was running out of time. She had to stop her stepfather *now*.

She grabbed the umbrella by the door.

Sadie was now in the hallway, watching with wide eyes. "Amanda, don't!"

Ignoring her, Amanda gripped the umbrella tightly in her hands as Marvin began to violently attack Priscilla. Would he stop? Would he kill her? Amanda couldn't let him hurt her mother anymore.

She swung the umbrella until the wooden handle struck Marvin's skull, sending him reeling. He tried to balance himself, arms flailing, but he was too drunk. He fell sideways as Priscilla scrambled to get out of the way. On his way toward the floor, he hit his head on the corner of the open cabinet, which caused his head to then slam into the countertop, and he finally landed on the floor in a heap, his head slamming against the linoleum.

His eyes went blank as blood pooled rapidly around his head.

Priscilla screamed. "Is he...dead?"

Frantic, Amanda bent down and checked him over. He wasn't breathing. She felt for his pulse—no heartbeat.

She had killed him!

She choked on fear as she stared at him. How long she stood there, immobile, was a mystery. Seconds? Hours? Time lost all meaning.

Then she remembered her mother and sister.

She struggled to her feet and made her way to her mother, who lay still on the floor. Sadie burst into tears and ran over to them, throwing her arms around them.

"He's dead!" Sadie cried.

"Maybe this is for the best," Amanda said solemnly. "I know that sounds terrible, but now he can't hurt us anymore."

Sadie stared at her with wide eyes, considering her words.

"You're right, Amanda," Priscilla said. "You've saved us. You saved our lives. I think he might have killed me. If not today, he would have eventually, and then you would have been left alone with him. I'm so sorry I let him deceive me into marrying him. I'm so sorry he hurt you both. I thought by marrying him, I was making our future secure, but instead, our lives became miserable. I'm so sorry. I'm so, so sorry." Priscilla wept as her daughters held her on the cold, linoleum floor.

Finally, Priscilla paused long enough to whisper, "We should call an ambulance and the police."

Wiping away tears, Amanda pulled herself up to the counter, reached for the phone, and made the call.

"What is your emergency?" asked the phone operator.

"My father attacked my mother. He tried to choke her," Amanda cried. "I thought he was going to kill her. I hit him in the back of the head, and he...he's dead. I killed him. I didn't mean to. I was just trying to protect my mother from him, trying to distract him, but he hit his head on the cabinet door, the counter, and the floor. It was just self-defense."

Saying it aloud made everything real. Amanda gave the phone operator all the information necessary as she sank onto the cold tiles. She collapsed beside her feeble mother and terrified sister, and they held each other until the police and ambulance arrived.

A bird singing outside her window brought Amanda back to the present. She was safe here at her home in Unity with her family. Her stepfather would never hurt her again.

Even though she knew she was safe, she wondered if these horrible memories would ever leave her alone.

CHAPTER THIRTY

The next day, Ella Ruth went to work with Irvin, Katie, and Lilly. They also brought along Sadie, Debra, and Seth so that Priscilla could run errands with Amanda.

Amanda put the laptop in a cloth bag to disguise it, then she and her mother ordered coffee and sat down at one of the tables to charge the laptop. Amanda plugged it in under the table, and they sat for several minutes, reading books and sipping their drinks while they waited. They didn't need it to be on for long, only enough to delete the manuscript files, so after about twenty minutes, they got up and returned to their buggy.

"Oh no," Amanda said as she opened it. "There's a password."

"Try writing," Priscilla suggested. "Or James." When those didn't work, they tried the name of each family member, including Ella Ruth's mother's name, but none of them worked.

"What was the name of her silly giant pumpkin?" Priscilla asked.

"Gertrude!" Amanda cried, but that wasn't it either. "Oh! Her horse. Her horse's name is Pumpkin." She typed in the letters, then clapped her hands. It had worked. They were in.

Amanda opened her files and found the most recent manuscript that Ella Ruth had been working on. "Wow. It's eighty-five thousand words."

"Delete it, dear. She stole your happiness. She has to pay for what she's done," Priscilla said coldly.

As Amanda right-clicked the file and hovered over the delete button, a twinge of guilt rose up within her.

"Delete it, Amanda," her mother urged.

"What if this isn't the answer?" Amanda asked.

Priscilla sighed, took the laptop from Amanda, and deleted the file. She turned to Amanda, the iciness of revenge in her hard stare. "Do you remember how our life used to be? You had a chance to change your life for the better, to marry into a life of luxury and wealth. You could have taken Sadie with you. I want only the best for you two, and she ripped it right out of your hands. This is what she gets for ruining my daughters' future." Priscilla scrolled through the files. "What are the titles of the other two manuscripts? Do you remember when you read them in preparation for the ball? There are so many files here."

"I...don't remember," Amanda lied. She did remember, but she didn't want her mother to delete them.

Was she going soft? Why was she suddenly doubting their plan? Confusion and guilt whirled together within her.

"Well, then, I suppose I should just delete all of these," Priscilla said, highlighting all the files.

"No!" Amanda shouted, grabbing Priscilla's arm. "Don't do that. It would be too obvious that it was us. If you only do one file, it's more believable that it was a computer error." Amanda was no computer expert, but she had used computers for school during their time in the *Englisher* world. Hopefully, she sounded convincing.

"Hmm." Priscilla tapped her nails on the keyboard. "I suppose you're right. Rewriting this one manuscript will keep her busy enough."

"Right," Amanda said, nodding. "Now, let's put the laptop back in the bag and finish our errands before someone sees us."

Amanda hoped that was the end of it, but then her mother said, "Oh wait, I have to open the trash folder and delete it from there first."

Amanda's heart sank.

That evening, Ella Ruth walked through the door of their home with her sisters after a productive day of working at the store.

"Ella Ruth, please begin making dinner," Priscilla called out from where she sat in the living room. Irvin was outside checking on the animals, so she didn't hesitate to order Ella Ruth around. "Also, your laptop fell off the top shelf of our closet. I think it might be broken," she added casually, inspecting her nails.

"What?" Ella Ruth cried, dashing down the hallway to the master bedroom. Panic surged through her from her chest to the tips of her fingers as she barreled into the bedroom and flung open the closet door. Her laptop was still in its case on the top shelf, and she carefully pulled it down as she sat on the bed. She opened it, looked it over for damage, then tried turning it on even though she hadn't charged it in days. To her surprise, it turned on and had some battery life.

How was this possible? This laptop had terrible battery life. There was no way it could still have some charge left. Unless...

"Oh, no," she whispered, realization slamming into her like a galloping horse. Did her stepmother and Amanda charge the laptop to tamper with it? What if they had deleted something? What if...

Sickness filled her belly, and her hands trembled as she opened her files as she looked through the folder containing her manuscripts she had been working on for the past several years.

Sadie, Lilly, and Katie ran down the hall and joined her in the bedroom.

"What happened? Is it broken?" Sadie asked.

"No, but it's worse than that," Ella Ruth choked out, her heart pounding as she realized the most recent manuscript she had been writing for over a year was missing. "Where is it?"

"Where's what?" Katie asked, coming closer. Lilly sat on the bed beside her.

"My book is gone," Ella Ruth said. "My most recent one isn't here. I know it was here in this folder."

"Check the trash bin," Sadie murmured, a grave expression on her face.

Ella Ruth slowly nodded, opening the trash bin application on her computer. "It's not there. They must have permanently deleted it." Panic filled her voice as her whole body shook. "Will I have to rewrite it? That took me years to write, and I wasn't even done!"

"Can you restore it?" Katie asked, grabbing her arm.

"I don't know," Ella Ruth said, tears slipping down her cheeks.

"Do you have a software that backs up your files?" Sadie asked.

"Oh...yes. I think I still have it. I don't know how to use it. I've never lost a file before," Ella Ruth said. "I remember I got it when I bought the laptop, just in case."

"Well, then, there's hope. Maybe the company can restore it for you if you call them," Sadie said.

"The laptop has battery life since I last used it days ago, so it had to have been charged within the past day or so. The battery doesn't last long, even when it's sleeping." She turned it toward them so they could see.

"They must have gone somewhere downtown to charge it," Sadie said, her face burning red with fury. "We need to go tell your father."

Katie and Lilly nodded.

"They've crossed the line many times, but this is so cruel," Katie added.

"I think we should tell the bishop," Lilly suggested.

"Tell the bishop?" Ella Ruth asked in surprise, checking Sadie's reaction.

Sadie slowly nodded. "I have to agree. This has to stop. Let's go tell Irvin first." She whirled around and marched out of the room.

Ella Ruth hesitated. She hated confrontation.

"Come on, Ella Ruth. She's right. This needs to stop. *Daed* asked them to stop, and they didn't listen. Now we need to go to the elders," Katie said, gently tugging on her arm and coaxing her off the bed. Lilly took her other arm, and together they walked her out of the room.

Ever since they had been kidnapped, Ella Ruth had always been there for them, singing them back to sleep after they woke up from nightmares and encouraging them when they felt as though they couldn't get through the day. Now they were literally supporting her, holding her up and helping her walk down the hall to confront her stepmother and stepsister for betraying her so horribly.

Irvin came through the front door and pulled off his boots. Debra and Seth, who had been outside with their father, scampered into the house and also removed their shoes.

"*Daed,* there is something we need to tell you," Sadie said as Katie and Lilly helped Ella Ruth walk into the kitchen. Ella Ruth felt a knot forming in her stomach, growing and tangling even more with each passing second. She could feel Priscilla and Amanda's eyes on her.

Irvin's eyes also fell on Ella Ruth as he noticed her pale, shocked expression. "What's wrong, Ella Ruth?"

Debra and Seth, who were about to set up a game in the living room, ran over to their sister. "What's wrong?"

Ella Ruth's mouth went dry as she tried to swallow. "My manuscript has been deleted from my laptop." She looked down at her younger siblings. "The book I wrote is all gone. I worked really hard on it."

"Gone? Why?" Seth asked. Debra gasped, placing her small hands over her mouth.

"Deleted?" Irvin asked. "Was it just moved? I'm not sure how it works, but there must be some explanation."

"It's gone," Ella Ruth said. "It was deliberately, permanently deleted."

"We believe that either *Mamm* or Amanda or both of them did this," Sadie interjected.

"Sadie!" Priscilla cried, a hand on her heart. "How dare you accuse us of such a thing?"

"Why do you think that?" Irvin asked.

"The laptop was charged today while we were at work. The battery doesn't last more than a few hours. Amanda and Priscilla were the only ones who knew the laptop was in your closet," Ella Ruth began.

"This is preposterous!" Priscilla cut in, standing up. "That is a serious accusation. What proof do you have?"

Amanda's face went pale as her hands fidgeted in her lap.

"I would like to hear your side of the story, Ella Ruth. Please proceed," Irvin said, holding up a hand. He turned to his wife and Amanda. "Please let her speak."

Amanda and Priscilla frowned and sat back down.

Ella Ruth sat down at the table. "When we came home, *Mamm* told me the laptop had fallen down from the closet and might be broken. It wasn't broken, but I believe she said that so I would check it and realize the file was gone. That's when I noticed it had some battery life left, and the battery only lasts a few hours. It was charged earlier today while we were at work. Who else would have charged it, deleted a file, then put it back where they found it? The children don't know how to use a laptop, and no one else knew where it was."

Irvin took in a deep breath and turned to Priscilla and Amanda. "What do you have to say to this?"

"This is ridiculous. I don't have to defend myself because I didn't do it," Priscilla said, shaking her head and crossing her arms. "You shouldn't accuse people of serious things like this, Ella Ruth."

Irvin turned to Amanda. "Amanda, what do you have to say?"

Amanda hesitated, her eyes darting between Irvin, Ella Ruth, and her mother, who gave her a warning look.

"I..." she stammered.

"Well?" Priscilla prodded. "We didn't do it. Tell him, Amanda."

Amanda squirmed in her seat, her hands wringing in her lap as her eyes became glassy with unshed tears.

"Amanda?" Ella Ruth asked. "Are you okay?"

Amanda shook her head, squeezing her eyes shut.

Ella Ruth stood and walked over to Amanda, kneeling in front of her, filled with concern for her stepsister, who was clearly holding back tears. "Amanda, what's wrong?"

"Tell them, Amanda," Priscilla urged her. "Tell them we didn't do this."

"But we did!" Amanda blurted out, jolting out of her seat.

CHAPTER THIRTY-ONE

Ella Ruth's heart lurched into her throat as she stood. She could barely believe her ears. The blood drained from her face as she gripped the edge of the handcrafted chair with white knuckles.

Amanda continued, "At first, I wanted to get back at you, Ella Ruth, and *Mamm* wanted me to do it, so I did. But it's my own fault. I made that choice. I helped my mother delete that file."

"Amanda!" Priscilla cried, also jumping to her feet, wide-eyed as though someone had thrown ice water on her face. "How could you do this to me? To us?"

"*Mamm*—Mom—it's time we admit how wrong we are—how wrong we have been." She turned to Ella Ruth. "The letters, the horse, locking you in your room, lying to James, deleting your book... We've been treating you horribly, and I don't know about my mother, but I am sorry." She briefly touched Ella Ruth's arm, then pulled away as if she was afraid of getting shocked.

"So, you did lock me in my room?" Ella Ruth asked.

Amanda nodded. "I heard you talking to Pumpkin in the barn about your date with James." She hung her head.

"Why did you do all of this? Why have you both been treating me so cruelly?" Ella Ruth asked, her voice barely above a whisper.

"Amanda, you don't have to answer her. This is preposterous. Let's go," Priscilla said, tugging on Amanda's arm.

"No," Amanda said, pulling away. She turned to Ella Ruth. "You're right, Ella Ruth. We have been treating you cruelly. Sadie, Mom, and I have been through so much, but it isn't fair that we have been taking it out on you. Well, Sadie hasn't. Only my mother and I."

Priscilla sighed and shook her head.

"My stepfather was abusive to us, and it hardened my heart." She sighed as her lip trembled. "When I came here and saw how much *Daed* loves all of you, I suppose it made me jealous. You're the oldest of the children still living at home, and I guess you remind me of how I used to be when my father loved me."

Ella Ruth's heart wrenched. What hardships had Amanda, Priscilla, and Sadie endured?

Amanda is jealous of me? she thought.

"But I love all of you," Irvin insisted.

"Still, I felt like I would never belong, like I would never truly be a part of this family. You are so kind and good, Ella Ruth. Even though we were harsh to you and did horrible, mean things to you, you never took revenge on us. You continued to be kind to us. It made me realize over time how wrong we were, even though I didn't want to admit it," Amanda said. "So, I ignored that voice in my heart telling me to stop."

"Don't you want to be with James and have a better life?" Priscilla asked Amanda. "I thought you wanted to be wealthy. To live a life of luxury after living in a small house with a leaky roof and no food on the table."

"James doesn't love me. He obviously loves Ella Ruth, and there's nothing I can do about that. Besides, those things don't matter, Mom," Amanda said, reverting to what she had always called her mother growing up. She made a sweeping motion with her hand. "This is what matters. Family. And we have hurt them terribly. We've hurt Ella Ruth terribly." She peered into Ella Ruth's face with tear-filled eyes. "How were you able to be kind to us even though we did all those things to you? And how could you ever forgive me? Us?"

"The Lord calls us to forgive seventy times seven," Ella Ruth said, touching Amanda's arm. Amanda flinched at first, then her eyes softened.

"Seventy times seven?" she asked, perplexed.

"It means we are called to forgive every time someone wrongs us, no matter how many times that may be."

"But why not just hold a grudge or get revenge?"

"That only hurts the person who was wronged," Ella Ruth said. "If I refused to forgive you, my heart would grow bitter, and I would be cold to you in return, then our relationship would crumble. What good could come of that? That's why the Lord calls us to forgive, so we can move forward."

Amanda slowly nodded, then stared at Ella Ruth curiously.

"The only reason I'm able to forgive you is because Jesus is in my heart and helps me to forgive. I could never do it on my own," Ella Ruth explained.

"In your heart?" Amanda asked. "What do you mean?"

"That means that I have accepted Jesus as my savior and live to serve Him," Ella Ruth explained. "Now He lives within me."

"I went to Sunday School as a child, but I don't remember much. And I have to admit that I don't listen very well in church." Amanda chuckled. "But I want to learn more about God."

"I'll help you," Ella Ruth said, looping her arm through Amanda's.

"We'll all help you," Sadie said, walking over and giving Amanda a hug, followed by Katie and Lilly.

Tears streamed down Irvin's face.

"Thank you. There is one more thing..." Amanda said in a trembling voice. Her body shook as she began to weep bitterly. "I killed him."

Shock ricocheted through Ella Ruth's chest. "Who, Amanda? What do you mean?"

Sadie threw her arms around her sister, crying with her. What on earth had happened to them?

"Amanda," Priscilla whispered. "It was an accident. You were only trying to protect me." She came closer, wrapping her arms around both of her daughters.

Irvin glanced at Debra and Seth, who had been quietly listening to the conversation. "Children, go play outside for a few moments." They scampered outside.

"What does she mean, Priscilla?" Irvin asked, approaching the group hug.

"I killed my stepfather," Amanda cried between sobs. She looked up, eyes red. "I didn't mean to. I was just trying to protect my mother from him. I only wanted to slow him down so we could get away. I hit him on the head with an umbrella handle. He hit his head on the cabinet door, then the counter, and then the floor."

"It was self-defense," Priscilla said, tears coursing down her cheeks. "She was protecting me. He was attacking me."

Ella Ruth stared at them in shock along with Irvin, Katie, and Lilly.

"Priscilla, I didn't know about any of this," Irvin said. "Why didn't you ever tell me?"

"I asked her not to," Amanda said. "I made her and Sadie promise to never tell anyone. I wasn't charged, so it's not on my record, but still. I don't want anyone to know. I guess by not talking about it, I've let myself become even more bitter and disheartened."

Irving put his arms around Amanda, then Sadie and Priscilla. "I'm sorry the three of you went through something so terrible."

No wonder Amanda was so bitter. She had been taking out her pain on Ella Ruth.

"It's no excuse for how I've been treating you, Ella Ruth, but for some reason, putting you down and letting you do all the chores made me feel better. But it only lasted for a moment until the shame and guilt of what I was doing to you crept in. It made me feel even worse. I thought if I married James, I could live a life of wealth and forget about my past. But now I see I was a fool. I'm so sorry, Ella

Ruth." Amanda could barely get the words out between sobs, and she had to take deep breaths to calm herself.

"I want you to live a better life," Priscilla said. "I only want what is best for you and Sadie. I'm the one who deleted the file. I have been telling her what to do this entire time."

"But I could have refused because I knew it was wrong. Part of me wanted to justify what we were doing, but deep down, I knew it was all wrong. I didn't want to let you down, Mom. That was also part of it. I have already disappointed you enough." Amanda frowned, her lip trembling once more as a new round of sobs washed over her. Sadie held her, gently patting her back.

"You have never been a disappointment to me, Amanda," Priscilla said as Sadie released her sister. "Both of you."

"Really?" Amanda asked, sniffling. "I thought you wouldn't be proud of me unless I married someone wealthy."

"No, no, no." Priscilla shook her head. "I just thought that was best for you. But I was wrong. You're a better woman than I am, Amanda, to admit when you're wrong. And Sadie, you tried to tell us before that we were wrong and we didn't listen to you. I see how wrong I was now." Priscilla's voice cracked. "My daughters are wiser than I am. I am so proud of you both." She threw her arms around them once more.

Ella Ruth caught her father's eye, and they exchanged a small smile.

"It's not too late, Mom," Sadie said into her mother's shoulder, her voice muffled.

"For what?" Priscilla asked.

"To admit you were wrong," Amanda said.

Priscilla pulled away, wiping her eyes. Her eyebrows knit together, and she shifted her weight uncomfortably. "I know. My daughters, you are an inspiration to me. When we were living in that house, living that horrible life, you were the only things that kept me going. You made life worth living when I wanted to give up. You were the only sunshine in my life. And now you have shown me what repentance is. This is not easy for me to do." She stared at the floor. "Like Amanda, I think I took my pain out on you as well, Ella Ruth, after being physically and verbally abused. The bitterness built up in my heart. I suppose I took it out on you in particular because..." Priscilla slowly shook her head. "To be honest, I'm not really sure why. When James started showing an interest in you instead of Amanda, I was willing to do anything to put a stop to it, so I sabotaged your chances with him. I was also wrong not to help you with any of the chores for all this time. It was so wrong of me to sell your horse and to delete your book. Just the thought of what I did makes me sick. I hope you'll be able to recover it. You must be heartbroken." Her voice trembled. "I thought I wouldn't be able to find the words, but that all tumbled out so quickly. What I'm trying to say is I'm so sorry, Ella Ruth."

Ella Ruth reached out and touched her stepmother's shoulder. Something inside her broke loose, lifting a burden from her chest as she realized she finally truly forgave her stepmother and stepsister.

Now she was truly free. "I forgive you, *Mamm*."

CHAPTER THIRTY-TWO

Priscilla let out a strangled cry and threw her arms around Ella Ruth, sobbing into her shoulder. Behind her, Ella Ruth could hear her father crying as well, which only caused her own eyes to sting with tears. Any time her father cried, she instantly began to cry as well.

"I have a confession, too," Ella Ruth said, finally pulling away. "I have to admit that forgiving you was difficult for me. Bitterness grew inside my heart toward both of you, Amanda and *Mamm*. I wanted to be kinder to you, make you feel more welcome, and treat you more like family, but I was bitter."

"It's understandable," Amanda said.

"That doesn't make it right. What I felt in my heart was wrong. I'm sorry."

"Oh, we forgive you, right, Mom?" Amanda looked at her mother.

"Yes, we do," Priscilla said, smiling.

Irvin sniffled, and they all turned to him. He was wiping the tears from his face with a handkerchief. Katie and Lilly stood beside him, their eyes also filled with tears.

"*Daed*, Katie, Lilly, are you okay?" Ella Ruth asked.

"I'm just so glad to see all of you finally making amends," Irvin said, his voice cracking. "It makes my heart happy."

Katie and Lilly nodded in agreement.

"It's about time," Lilly said, causing them all to chuckle.

"Now we are all truly one big happy family. Can you imagine how much better life will be now that you will be getting along?" Katie asked. "It's going to be wonderful."

"Yes, it will," Ella Ruth said with a grin.

"There is one more thing we need to do," Amanda said, turning to her mother. "We need to apologize to James."

Priscilla nodded. "It won't be easy, but you're right. We do."

"What if we invite him over for dinner?" Amanda asked.

"That's a great idea. And from now on, we are going to help with the cooking. And the cleaning. We will do our share," Priscilla said. "It was wrong of us not to help."

"This is a new beginning for all of us," Ella Ruth said. "Let's make the most of it."

"I agree," Amanda said, "but right now, you should find out if you can get your book file back."

"I don't know how," Ella Ruth said. "I need someone who is better with computers, and I would need to use the internet and a phone. Maybe James can help me."

"Go on and see him now," Irvin said as Lilly ran to the bedroom to retrieve the laptop. She handed the bag to Ella Ruth.

"Thank you," Ella Ruth said, but doubt crept in. What if she couldn't get the file back? What if she had to rewrite the entire book all over again? It had taken her months and months of hard work, and the thought of rewriting the book seemed too daunting to think about.

Priscilla frowned. "Do you really think you can get it back? I hope so."

"I think so…but I'm not sure." Ella Ruth's stomach tightened, and she bit her lip to keep from crying once more.

Amanda noticed her distress and touched her arm, her face pale. "I feel sick just thinking about it. I hope with all my heart that you can get the file back. If not… I don't think I'd be able to stand the guilt. I feel guilty about it enough now. I will do everything I can to help you rewrite it, if that's what it takes."

Katie and Lilly rushed to her side. "We will help, too."

"Me too," Priscilla added. "Though I'm not a very good writer."

"Thank you all. I appreciate it. But that would be something I would need to do on my own. Let's just pray James can help me get the file back. I have heard of people accidentally deleting files on their computers and recovering them. There is hope." Even as she said the words, fear knotted her stomach, but she ignored the feeling as she walked out the door to the buggy.

With her laptop bag slung over her shoulder, Ella Ruth drove to James' house. She drove up to the gate, which was closed, and rang the buzzer.

A voice sounded, "Hello, do you have an appointment?"

"No," Ella Ruth said. "I'm James' friend, Ella Ruth. He will want to see me."

"Please hold." A few moments later, the voice said, "Please enter."

The gate slowly opened inward, and Ella Ruth drove her buggy through and parked it in the driveway. James rushed out the door to greet her.

"Ella Ruth!" he called, jogging over. "What a surprise. To what do I owe the pleasure of this visit?"

Ella Ruth frowned, even though she wanted to smile and forget about the anxiety and fear clawing at her chest. What if her book was gone forever? Yes, she had forgiven Amanda and Priscilla, and it was only through the strength that had come from the Lord that she had prayed for.

But the fear still remained. At the thought of all her hard work lost and the concern in James' eyes, she felt her eyes well up with tears and began to weep. Finally, the realization of her book file being unrecoverable slammed into her like a runaway horse.

"What's wrong?" James asked, wrapping his arms around Ella Ruth. "What happened?"

Ella Ruth couldn't get a word out between sobs, so she just cried on his shoulder for several minutes until she could calm herself long enough to explain.

"Priscilla and Amanda deleted my book from my computer," she said, sniffling.

"What?" James jumped back, his face red. "How could they do such a horrible thing? How could anyone be so heartless?"

"It's a long story, but I have forgiven her," Ella Ruth said, then explained everything as they sat down on a bench near the garden.

The fountain bubbled in the distance, and the scents of the flowers soothed her, but not as much as how James held her hand and put his arm around her.

"I can't believe you forgave them just like that after everything they did to you," James said, the anger clear on his face. "It was so wrong of them."

"It wasn't easy to forgive them," Ella Ruth said. "I asked the Lord to help me forgive them, and He did. That was the only way I could do it. I know you're angry, but I hope you can forgive them too. They are sincerely sorry."

"I don't care what they did to me, but I'm not sure I can forgive them for how deeply they've hurt you. I mean, Amanda pretended to be you and threatened you so you would help her convince me that she was you. Who does that? Then they sold your horse and deleted your novel. They seem completely heartless to me. I thought the Amish were supposed to be kind, good people."

"Well, we are human just like everyone else," Ella Ruth said. "But they weren't always Amish. They aren't as familiar with our way of life."

"Really?" James' eyebrows shot up.

"Priscilla grew up Amish and married an Amish man, but after she was widowed with two children, she left to marry an *Englisher*. After her second husband also died, she rejoined the Amish and married my father. Her second husband ended up being abusive. It was very hard on them. Amanda must have been so deeply hurt."

"That gives her no excuse to take it out on you," James said. "Though, what they went through was horrible. It must have been hard on them."

"I know, and she took it out on me. They both did, but I've forgiven them."

James sighed and stared into her eyes, causing her heart to flutter. "You're amazing, Ella Ruth. I don't know how you can forgive two people who hurt you so deeply. You put me to shame. I know the Lord calls us to forgive, so I'm going to pray for the strength to forgive them as you did."

"The Lord will help you. I know it's hard, but it will help all of us heal and put this behind us."

James nodded. "In my head, I know you're right, but my heart is being stubborn."

Ella Ruth laughed. "I know the feeling."

James touched her chin and gently brought his lips down to meet hers. "My heart also just wants to sit here and keep holding you, but I see you brought your laptop. Want me to try to get the file back? I can't make any promises, but I'll sure try."

"Yes, thank you," Ella Ruth said, handing him the bag. "It has a terrible battery life, so we probably have to charge it. I also subscribed to a company that stores and backs up my files digitally, so we can call them."

"Oh, that's great! Then we can get it back, no problem. Let's go inside and call them," James said.

They went inside and sat at a table near a window, plugged in the laptop, and called the company. After being on hold for a while and speaking with someone, Ella Ruth's heart plummeted.

"I'm sorry, Miss Holt, but the debit card you had on file expired just over a month ago. We tried to bill you, but it didn't go through. We emailed you to notify you."

Debit cards were allowed in Unity, but she didn't use hers very often. "I didn't realize it expired. I hardly use my debit card except to pay for this. I don't have internet at my house, so I rarely check my email," Ella Ruth said as her chest constricted. "I must have not seen the email. Does this mean my files aren't backed up anymore?"

"Unfortunately, yes. After a grace period of thirty days with no payment, the account goes inactive and is no longer backed up. I'm very sorry."

Ella Ruth froze for a moment as sheer panic, realization and dread washed over her. The impact was so overwhelming that she let her head drop onto her folded arms on the table. Sobs wracked her body as the full realization hit.

She would have to rewrite her entire novel. This wasn't supposed to happen. She thought her files had been protected.

I already forgave Amanda and Priscilla, God, Ella Ruth thought. *That was when it was easier because I thought I'd be able to get my book file back. But it's gone. I don't want to be bitter toward them. I already forgave them. I can't un-forgive them now that things have changed...*

Have I truly forgiven them?

Her body shook so hard that she didn't realize for several moments that James was right beside her with his arm around her, rubbing small circles on her back comfortingly. She barely felt his touch because the pain inside her was so excruciating.

When her mother died, she felt as though her heart had shattered beyond repair. She had loved her mother with all her heart, and when she realized she would never see her again, this was how she had felt. Yes, this was only a book. It wasn't as though she had lost someone she loved, but this book was a part of her that she had poured her heart into for months. Years, really. And now it was gone forever.

Her mind reeled with a thousand thoughts as her mind fought with itself. She knew what she had to do, but she didn't want to do it.

"I don't even know what to say," James whispered. "I'm so sorry. I checked, and there's no way to recover it from your hard drive. It was erased permanently."

Anger welled up inside her all over again. "How could they do this to me?"

Have you truly forgiven them? a voice inside her whispered. *You must truly forgive them.*

"It's too hard," she whispered.

"What?"

She finally lifted her head. "I thought I forgave them, but... I'm not sure I have."

"That's understandable, Ella Ruth. You're clearly heartbroken."

Forgive others as I have forgiven you...

She shook her head as her thoughts warred within her. "But the Lord told me to forgive them."

"We need to pray, Ella Ruth." James took her hands and bowed his head. She closed her eyes, letting his voice wash over her. "Dear Lord, please help Ella Ruth. I know she is so deeply hurt, but we both know you want her to forgive her stepmother and stepsister. You did it once before, so please help her again. Help her love them and forgive them so they can be reunited as a family."

Ella Ruth's lip trembled as she felt something break inside her. No, it wasn't her heart—that was already broken. It was the anger she had been clinging to. It was gone.

"I want our family to be reunited, like you said, James. The only way that will happen is if I put aside my anger. I forgive them. I wrote the book once, and I can write it again. Earlier, when we forgave each other and everyone was so joyful, we were truly a family. My father was so happy. I haven't seen him that happy in so long. Everyone was happy. I don't want to lose that. I forgive them," she whispered, then felt a peace like nothing she had ever known wash over her. She fell into James' arms, tears streaming down her cheeks.

Did that really just happen? she wondered. *I'm free.*

CHAPTER THIRTY-THREE

James pulled back and held her face in his hands. "Ella Ruth, you are the most amazing woman I've ever met. I love you."

She blinked in surprise. "I love you too," she whispered.

He was about to lean in and kiss her, then he jumped back, eyes wide. "Wait. Did you ever email my aunt your book? Remember how I told you about her at the gala, and I said she might be able to give you some pointers if you send her your book?"

Ella Ruth nodded. "Yes, I sent it to her that week."

"The whole book?"

"Yes, the whole thing, like you said."

"If you emailed her the whole book, then you can download it from the email!" James cried.

Ella Ruth's hands flew to her face. "Really? I've never done that before. I'm still new to all of this. And I completely forgot about that email."

"Let's check." James pushed the laptop toward her on the table. "Can you pull up your email and log in?"

Ella Ruth's hands trembled as she pulled up her email Sent folder and searched for James' aunt's name. She located the email, opened it, and there was the file. She downloaded it, opened it, and shouted for joy when she saw the full word count.

"Oh, thank the Lord. There it is!" Ella Ruth cried as tears of joy streamed down her cheeks. "I think I wrote a few scenes since then, but I've been so busy that it wasn't much. I can easily rewrite those. Oh, thank you, James!" She reached out and grabbed his hands.

"I'm just glad you sent her the book. This is wonderful, Ella Ruth. I'm so glad you got it back. What a relief." He sighed.

"It's an incredible relief." She felt a weight lift off her shoulders. Finally, the knot of anxiety in her stomach vanished.

"Did my aunt ever reply to your email?" James asked, gesturing to the computer. "I know she would love your work."

Ella Ruth shook her head. "No. Maybe she is just really busy."

"I wonder if she didn't see the email. She did mention once that she gets several emails a day. I will ask her for you."

"I don't want to bother her."

James waved his hand. "No, no. Trust me. She will want to read your book. You deserve a chance, Ella Ruth. I'll text her and ask her if she saw your email. I know once she gets the chance to read it, she will love it as much as I do."

She smiled.

"I can't even imagine how you must feel to have it back."

"God has been faithful to me," Ella Ruth said. "I wasn't sure I could let go of the past, but once I did, this blessing came to me.

I'm so thankful." She paused. "When I thought the file was gone forever but still decided to forgive my stepmother and stepsister, I felt this...peace. Freedom. It was unlike anything I've ever experienced before."

James smiled. "I'm glad you've made things right with them and in your heart. Maybe now that all of this is behind us, we can talk about our future. I know you said you wouldn't even consider leaving the Amish before."

"That was when my family was divided," Ella Ruth said. "Now that we are unified, I feel at peace about it. I have known for a long time now that I wasn't going to stay Amish forever, and my father knows it too. He has given me his blessing and will support my decision either way. Now the fear of leaving my family is gone. I know that they will get along now and take care of each other."

"That's wonderful. I don't want to rush you, though. You should take your time and think and pray about it," James said, squeezing her hand.

"I will," Ella Ruth said. "Oh, that reminds me. My stepmother and stepsister want to have you over for dinner tomorrow night."

James hesitated. "Really?"

"They want to apologize to you in person. Will you come?"

"Absolutely. I'll be there."

"Oh, good. I can't wait."

The next afternoon, Ella Ruth prepared dinner with her stepmother and stepsisters while Katie and Lilly were working at the store with Irvin and the children played outside.

"What can I do to help?" Amanda asked eagerly. Even though she expected this, Ella Ruth still blinked in surprise.

"Here, you can mash the potatoes," Ella Ruth said.

Amanda grabbed the potato masher and began vigorously smashing the potatoes in a pot.

"And what can I do?" Priscilla asked. "I'm not a very good cook, to be honest. I wasn't able to teach my daughters how to cook. I'm sorry if we aren't very good at this."

"Oh, Mom, you taught us the best you could," Sadie said, touching her mother's shoulder.

"You're making an effort to help, and that's all that matters. You're all doing a great job. Here, do you want to slice the bread and then peel and slice the carrots?" Ella Ruth asked.

Priscilla nodded, smiled, and set to work.

Ella Ruth smiled at her stepmother. Even though it had been a while since Priscilla and Irvin had married, now they felt like a true family. The wall of ice that had been between her and her stepmother and Amanda had finally shattered.

A few hours later, James arrived. Ella Ruth hurried to the door to greet him.

"Hello," she said, smiling up at him.

"Hi," he said. "I'm so glad to be here."

Amanda, Priscilla, and Sadie peeked into the entryway.

"Thank you all for inviting me over," James said to them, waving.

"Thank you for coming," Priscilla said, glancing at the floor. "Please come in. We can sit in the living room before dinner."

"We have a lot to talk about," Amanda added. "I mean, we have something to say to you. Something important."

James removed his shoes and followed them into the living room, and they all sat down. James sat on the sofa beside Ella Ruth, and Amanda, Sadie, and Priscilla sat on the couch across from them.

Sadie gave them an encouraging look, and Priscilla and Amanda glanced at each other nervously.

Amanda's hands fidgeted in her lap. "I'm going to get straight to the point, James. We have acted horribly toward you and Ella Ruth. She has forgiven us. I don't know how, but she has."

"We never should have tried to sabotage your relationship, and we shouldn't have lied to you, sold Ella Ruth's horse, or deleted her book," Priscilla said. "I'm so glad you were able to help her with both of those things. There were so many things that we shouldn't have done to both of you. We weren't always Amish. I don't know any other Amish person who would behave the way we did. I thought the best thing for Amanda would be if she married someone wealthy like you, but still, that's no excuse. I see now that you love Ella Ruth. Anyway, we are very sorry."

"We are so sorry. I never should have deceived you and forced Ella Ruth to help me pretend to be her. I hope you can forgive my mother and me," Amanda added. "Though, I wouldn't blame you if you didn't."

"I forgive you both," James said graciously. "I have to admit that I was angry at first when I found out that you lied to me about the gala, sold Ella Ruth's horse, and when she told me you deleted her book. I am protective of Ella Ruth, and I feel compelled to do something when I see anyone treated unfairly."

"That's why you will make such a good teacher," Ella Ruth murmured with a smile.

"Thank you." He nodded to Ella Ruth, then turned to Priscilla and Amanda. "But now that I have had time to pray about it, I asked God to give me the strength to forgive you, and He has. So yes, I forgive you. Ella Ruth has been an inspiration to me through all of this." He turned and smiled at her, and warmth flooded through her like warm honey as his gaze met hers.

"She has been an inspiration to us too," Priscilla said. "Even after everything we did to her, she still remained kind and gracious to us. She never retaliated. I am so honored to call you my stepdaughter—I mean, my daughter, Ella Ruth." Tears filled Priscilla's eyes as she smiled at Ella Ruth, who felt her own eyes sting with tears.

"Thank you, *Mamm*," Ella Ruth murmured, her heart nearly bursting with gratitude and joy.

Irvin came into the house, followed by Katie, Lilly, Debra, and Seth.

"Hello, James." Irvin noticed the smiles on everyone's faces and asked, "What did I miss?"

Priscilla smiled. "James has graciously forgiven us. All is well now."

"That's wonderful news," Irvin exclaimed. "We have a fun evening ahead of us. Dinner smells delicious. Let's go eat before it gets cold."

"That's a great idea," James said, then Debra tugged on his sleeve.

"Will you play Scrabble with me again after dinner?" Debra asked shyly, tugging on the white ribbon of her prayer *kapp*.

"Absolutely, dear one," James said with a grin. "And you'll probably win again."

Debra giggled and scampered away to her seat at the table.

They shared a meal filled with boisterous conversation and laughter. Ella Ruth finally felt as though they had put the pain of the past behind them once and for all. There was not even a trace of awkwardness between them that she could detect. Priscilla and Amanda were truly coming out of their shells, making jokes, and laughing along with everyone at the table.

"This is absolutely delicious," James said, gesturing to the food.

"Priscilla, Sadie, and Amanda made it," Ella Ruth said.

"Oh, you did most of the work," Amanda said.

"No, really, I didn't. I was mostly delegating the work to all of you because you were so eager to help." Ella Ruth chuckled. "You all did a great job."

Amanda, Sadie, and Priscilla graciously thanked them, and once dinner was over, they played games in the living room, talking and laughing into the evening.

When it was time for James to leave, she joined him on the porch, and they sat down on the swing that her father had made.

"That was a great dinner," James said.

Ella Ruth nodded. "I'm so glad they made amends with you."

"Me too, which brings me to this next part. I already spoke to your father," he said, his hands fidgeting in his lap. "I told him my intentions, and he gave us his blessing."

"What are your intentions?" she asked, just above a whisper, her heart pounding.

CHAPTER THIRTY-FOUR

"I want to marry you one day, Ella Ruth. You're the most amazing woman I've ever met. I want to spend the rest of my life getting to know you more and more," James said. "I know we haven't known each other very long, but I feel like I've known you forever. Remember when I asked if you ever thought about leaving the Amish?"

She nodded. "I still want to, and now that my family has made amends, I feel peace in my heart at the thought of leaving. I know that if I leave, I won't be leaving them in turmoil. In my heart, I know that Priscilla and Amanda want to change for the better, so I'm no longer worried about leaving my siblings. Besides, I'll visit them all the time, and I plan on living close by."

"I'm so glad to hear that," James said, peering deep into her eyes. "So, I've been waiting for the right time to ask you this. Now it feels right. Ella Ruth, may I court you?"

"Yes," Ella Ruth said. "Yes!"

He reached for her hand and wrapped his fingers around hers warmly, and his tender touch sent flutters to her heart. She smiled up at him, and he grinned back at her.

"I'm so happy," he whispered.

"Me too. For now, I'm going to keep it a secret, since you're not Amish. I wouldn't be shunned, but still, I don't want anyone to know. I could get in trouble with the elders and bishop of the church."

"You could get in trouble? Are you sure you still want to court, then?" he asked, his eyes full of concern.

"Absolutely." She squeezed his hand. "I don't care if I get in trouble."

"But I don't want you to get in trouble. And I don't want you to feel like you'd have to leave the Amish to be with me, so I want you to know I've decided that I will join if you don't want to leave. If the church will let me," he said.

"No, no. I couldn't ask you to give up your dream of teaching. In my heart, I know that leaving is the right choice for me. I have for a long time, but I was afraid. I want to pursue my dream and become an author, and I want to see the world. I do plan on leaving the Amish soon, but I have to figure out where I'm going to live, and I'll need to find a full-time job first. It's going to be bittersweet to leave, but I know my family and friends will welcome me back whenever I visit, which will be often."

"That's a relief," James said. "Are you nervous about leaving?"

Ella Ruth hesitated. "A little. I'm not sure how people will react to me leaving. I'm not sure everyone will be supportive."

"Don't worry about them," James said. "All that matters is what you think of yourself."

"I'm worried that when I leave, I won't fit in out there. At least, not at first. It might take me a while to get used to how the *Englisher* world works. I'll need to learn how to drive, too. It might take some time for me to get settled, but it will be worth it."

"You're so talented, Ella Ruth, and you're a hard worker. I'm sure you'll have no problem finding a job. Maybe you can work at a library or a bookstore, where you can learn even more about writing."

"Oh, I'd love that." Ella Ruth clasped her hands together.

"Speaking of writing, I texted my aunt about your email. She said she never saw it because she gets so many, but she promised to read your story this week, or at least part of it," James said. "And she'll tell you what she thinks."

Ella Ruth's heart somersaulted in her chest. "Really? She's a best-selling author. I'm a bit nervous to hear what she thinks of my work."

"You have nothing to worry about. You're incredibly talented. Maybe she might point out something that could be improved, but that's a good thing, right?"

Ella Ruth nodded.

"And who knows? Maybe she will recommend you to her agent or an agent that her agent knows. I hear that's a good way to find an agent. It's good to have connections in the industry."

"But I don't want to get an agent only because I knew someone who helped me." She frowned. "I want to earn it."

"You don't have to worry about that either. Agents only take on authors when they are confident they can sell their book to a publisher. They won't take you on unless your work is exactly what they're looking for. And some might turn you down not because your book isn't good enough but only because it's not what publishers are looking for at the time. It can take a lot of queries and a lot of rejections, but eventually, I am sure you will find an agent if that's the way you want to go. I do remember you saying that you want to self-publish, though. Do you think you want to self-publish instead?"

"I do like the idea of doing everything myself and having control over my work, but I'm still new to using computers, so the thought of learning how to do online ads, build an email list, and publish all my books on my own seems daunting. Yet, at the same time, I want to learn everything about it," Ella Ruth said, the speed of her words picking up with each passing second as excitement grew within her.

"Well, once you're no longer Amish, you'll have access to the internet, and a whole new world of opportunities and possibilities will open up for you. There are online courses and videos online that can teach you what you need to know. I will help you, if you want."

"Really? That would be great."

"That sounds interesting to me," James said. "Speaking of learning, I have some news. I got a teaching job at the middle school in town."

"You did? Wow, James, that's amazing!" Ella Ruth cried, throwing her arms around him. "Congratulations."

"Thank you. I'm really excited to start in the fall. Everything is falling into place for us, Ella Ruth."

"What about your father? Is he still upset?"

"Well, yes, but I think he will realize this is better for everyone. Eventually. It doesn't matter." He squeezed her hand. "I have you, and we are going to have so many adventures together. It might take time, and it might be slow-going at first to get your writing career going, but I know, without a doubt, you will succeed in whatever you choose to do. And I can't wait to watch you do it."

He grinned at her as joy and peace washed over her, then leaned closer and gently brushed his lips against hers, sending warm tingles from the top of her head to the tips of her toes.

The door creaked open, and they both looked up to see Amanda stepping outside onto the porch.

"I'm sorry to interrupt," she said, wringing her hands. "I just wanted to say I am so happy for you, and I wish you the best."

"Thank you, Amanda," Ella Ruth said, standing up to give her a hug.

"That means a lot," James added. "Thank you."

Priscilla also stepped out onto the porch. "I wish the best for you both. You two make such a cute couple. It's obvious you adore each other."

Irvin stepped out onto the porch. "Is there a party out here?" Katie, Lilly, Debra, and Seth followed closely behind.

"I guess now is a good time to let everyone know that James and I are courting," Ella Ruth announced, and everyone congratulated them.

"I figured you'd ask her sooner than later," Irvin said to James. "Since you already asked my permission."

"But does this mean...you are going to leave us?" Katie asked. "Are you going to become an *Englisher*?"

"You're leaving?" Lilly demanded. She frowned. "I guess I shouldn't be surprised. You've been talking about it for years."

"Yes," Ella Ruth said. "I have decided to leave the Amish church. I've known in my heart for years that I wouldn't stay forever, but I will always hold onto the Amish teachings about the Lord in my heart. I want to be with James. I want to pursue my dream of writing, and in order to pursue publishing, I'm going to need to use a computer and the internet. There is a whole world out there, and I want to explore it, but I'm going to miss you all so much."

Tears filled Irvin's eyes. "I always knew that you would fly away, but I knew I would never be ready for it."

Ella Ruth threw her arms around her father. "I'm not leaving just yet. I have things to sort out first. But I will visit all the time after I leave. I promise. And if you ever need me, I'll come home right away."

"Your mother always told me you would go one day," Irvin said, wiping a tear that had tracked down her cheek. "She said your imagination and your ambition would take you far. And she was right. She would be proud of you, Ella Ruth."

Ella Ruth choked on a sob, and soon her sisters were crying, and everyone huddled together in one group hug. Irvin even pulled James in beside him.

When they broke apart, James cleared his throat. "I want to thank you, Priscilla and Amanda, for inviting me here tonight and for your apology. It means so much to me. I am astounded by your change of heart and your sincerity." He turned to Ella Ruth. "Ella Ruth, your family is amazing. I look forward to getting to know all of you better."

"Well, if you two get married, you'll get to know us really well," Katie blurted, and everyone chuckled.

"You're right, Katie," James agreed, and Ella Ruth's heart fluttered when he smiled at her warmly. "And I will introduce you to my family."

"I've always wanted to go to an *Englisher* wedding," Lilly said with a sigh, clasping her hands together.

"I think that might be sooner than later," Amanda said, looping her arm through Ella Ruth's with a grin.

CHAPTER THIRTY-FIVE

The following Sunday at church, Ella Ruth grabbed Laura's arm after the service ended and told her everything that had happened since they had last seen each other.

"What?" Laura whispered after Ella Ruth explained everything. "They did what?"

"But we have all forgiven each other," Ella Ruth said, "So I can finally move on."

"And you're really going to leave?" Laura asked, wide-eyed.

Ella Ruth nodded. "I know in my heart it's the right decision for me."

Laura threw her arms around her friend. "I'm going to miss you so much."

"I'm going to miss you too."

"Excuse me. Sorry to interrupt." Someone cleared their throat behind Ella Ruth, and she turned to see Bishop Byler. "Good morning, Ella Ruth. May we speak outside for a moment?"

"Good morning, Bishop Byler." Ella Ruth nodded. "Of course, we can."

Laura blinked and backed away. "See you later, Ella."

Ella Ruth walked outside with the bishop, noticing several people giving her suspicious glances, including a group of women in the corner of the room who were talking in hushed tones.

"I heard she is going to leave the Amish to marry an *Englisher* man, just like her friend Esther recently did," Margaret Miller whispered, shaking her head. "Perhaps her friend had a bad influence on her."

"We need to be careful about who we let our children spend time with," another woman added. "No matter who they are. Even members of the church can turn astray."

Ella Ruth was barely able to make out what they were saying so quietly, but she ignored them and walked outside with the bishop. She had known that not everyone would approve of her decision to leave the Amish church.

"Well, I guess I'll get straight to the point. Word has spread, and I hear you have become good friends with a young *Englisher* man and are planning to leave the church," the bishop said, clasping his hands together with concern in his voice.

"That is true, yes." She nodded calmly. "I might as well be straightforward and let you know that we are courting with the intention of marriage."

The bishop nodded. "I see. Well, do you plan on leaving before you are engaged?"

"Yes," Ella Ruth said. "If that's a problem, I can leave sooner. I don't want to cause any trouble."

"I know, I know. Well, it's not exactly forbidden because you haven't been baptized into the church yet, but it is frowned upon, and some will disapprove. In many other Amish communities, it would be forbidden. I know you will need some time to make arrangements for finding a new place to live. However, I do implore you to reconsider leaving, Ella Ruth. I can't stop you from leaving. No one can. But you will be greatly missed, and I worry that if you leave, you might let go of the values you were raised with," the bishop said, removing his black hat from his head and wringing it in his hands.

"I appreciate your concern, Bishop Byler, but I will always keep the values I was raised with in my heart and as the center of my life. I will always obey God and study His word, go to church, and be a Christian. James is a Christian as well, and if we have children, we will raise them with those same Christian values. I assure you that even if I leave the Amish church, I will still be the same person, Bishop Byler. That will never change," Ella Ruth assured him.

The bishop nodded, his long white beard bobbing. "Well, I see you have made up your mind, and your father told me that you have already spoken about it with him and your family, so I supposed there is nothing I can say to change your mind. I had to try, though."

"I appreciate you trying, Bishop Byler. It shows you care."

"Well, Esther recently left, and now you, so it is sad to see you go. But I pray you find happiness in your new life, and if you marry James, I hope you have a long and happy marriage." The bishop smiled warmly.

"Thank you very much. That means a lot to me."

The bishop nodded and returned to the church. Ella Ruth turned around to see the same group of women standing outside the church door. Clearly, they had been listening to their conversation. Ella Ruth smiled, waved at them, and walked away.

Her older sisters Leah and Charlotte walked over with their husbands and children. When Ella Ruth gave them the news, they were all happy for her, smiling and hugging her, even though they all said they would miss her. However, she assured them she'd visit quite often. Laura joined in along with the rest of Ella Ruth's sisters, then several other of her friends came over to share the joy.

The ones she loved most were happy for her and supported her decision, and that was all that mattered to her.

Two months later...

James stood in front of his middle school English class of seventh graders.

"For homework tonight, I want you to write an essay on your favorite childhood memory," he said, pacing. "It can be anything from when you lost your first tooth to when you overcame a fear or when you did something fun with your friends or parents."

A young boy's hand went up. His name was Aiden, and he often seemed sad at school. James had talked to him about it before, but the boy wouldn't say much. "What if we can't think of anything?" he asked with a frown.

James' heart constricted. "I'm sure you can think of something. I could help you after class, if you want."

"What about when we went to the park, and you found that lost cat?" a girl beside him asked.

"What about when we had a sleepover, and you got a candy stuck in your nose?" a boy beside him asked, and the classroom erupted in laughter.

Aiden chuckled. "That was pretty funny."

"See? I'm sure you have plenty of good memories to choose from," James said as the bell rang. Everyone stood up, gathered their things, and walked out, except for Aiden, who approached James' desk.

"How are you doing, Aiden?" James asked.

Aiden shrugged.

"Last time, you said your dad was working a lot and not spending much time with you," James said. "Has he been able to spend more time with you?"

Aiden shook his head. "Not really. My mom says we need the money, so he's been working overtime, whatever that is. When he gets home, he's too tired to go outside and play soccer or catch with me. He's even too tired to play checkers with me. He just falls asleep in his chair."

"You know, my dad worked a lot when I was a kid, too, and sometimes he didn't spend much time with me or do fun things with my sister and me. But that doesn't mean he doesn't care about you or want to do those things with you. I bet he wants to, but he's just too tired from working so much. He's working a lot because he loves you. Even if he doesn't say it, he loves you, Aiden. Sometimes people just forget to say it, but that doesn't mean it isn't true. Even if my dad couldn't spend a lot of time with me growing up and he often forgot to say it, I knew he loved me and still does."

Tears pooled in Aiden's eyes, but he swiped them away. "Really?"

"Yeah. Maybe this won't last too much longer, and your dad will be able to spend more time with you again. If you want, we could hang out. We could play soccer or catch in the parking lot after school with some of the other kids."

"Really?" he repeated, his eyes wide and hopeful.

"Absolutely," James said with a grin. "I can meet you out there after school today, actually."

"Okay! I'll see you then. Thanks, Mr. Baldwin." Aiden grinned and hurried out of the classroom as James turned to his desk with a smile on his face. He was about to sit down and grade papers when he heard the classroom door open. "Did you forget something, Aiden?" he asked, then froze when he saw his father standing there with tears in his eyes. "Dad?"

"I'm so sorry, James," Richard said, slowly approaching him. "I'm sorry I worked all the time and didn't spend much time doing things with you and Eliza all these years. I'm sorry if I made you feel like I blamed you for Brett's death. I did at first, but not anymore. I avoided you because you look so much like him, and you reminded me of him. I'm sorry I was disappointed in you when you chose to teach over running the company. Most of all, I'm sorry I haven't said I love you every day of your life because I do love you, James. And I'm so proud of you."

A sob burst out of James' mouth as he ran toward his father and embraced him. For the first time in years, James' father hugged him tightly. James couldn't remember the last time he'd done that.

"I know I'm not the most affectionate person," Richard said. "But I should say I love you more. We know how short life is, and you can lose someone you love in the blink of an eye. When I saw you talking to that boy, I realized how wrong I was. I've been standing there listening for a while, and you're an incredible teacher, James. I'm sorry. I was so wrong."

"I forgive you, Dad," James choked out in disbelief. Was his father actually admitting he was wrong?

Richard pulled away, wiping his eyes. "I shouldn't have made you feel bad for doing what you love. Eliza is so excited about taking over the company, and she will be great at it. I should have been more understanding."

"Yes, she will. We've both found our way. I know you just want what's best for us."

"I do, and now I know what that is. You're going to marry Ella Ruth, aren't you? She's a wonderful young lady."

James nodded. "Yes, she is, and yes. I already have the ring. I'm just waiting for the right time to propose after she leaves the Amish."

"I'm so happy for you both. I am looking forward to getting to know her better."

"That can be arranged," James said with a smile.

Four months later...

Ella Ruth stood outside her house as her family followed her out the door.

"This is not goodbye," she said to all of them. "I can come visit any time. I'll be back whenever you need me."

Irvin's eyes were already filling with tears. All of her siblings surrounded her, hugging her one by one. A few months ago, she had started working at the local bookstore she loved so much, and she now had an apartment. James was helping her move in today, but she didn't have very many belongings. It would all fit in his car, but she planned to buy new *Englisher* clothing and furniture once she settled in. Most of all, she planned on using the money she had won from the pumpkin contest to buy a new laptop with a better battery life.

"Call us and let us know once you're settled in," Priscilla said.

"Don't forget," Amanda reminded her.

"I won't forget," Ella Ruth said, chuckling. "I'm moving downtown, not across the country!"

"It just feels like you're going to be so far away," Katie said.

"We're going to miss you so much," Lilly added.

"I'm going to miss you all too, but I'll be back to visit before you know it. And now that I have a cell phone, I'll call you on the store phone all the time," Ella Ruth said.

Debra and Seth hugged her waist, and Sadie put her arms around Ella Ruth's shoulders.

"You're going to do big things, Ella Ruth. We're all excited to see where your dreams take you." Sadie grinned.

"Thanks." Ella Ruth smiled and turned when she heard the sound of a car rumbling down the driveway. "There's James."

James stopped the car in the driveway. "Hi, everyone."

They all greeted him. Her family had already helped her take her packed bags outside, and they helped load her few belongings into the car.

Ella Ruth turned to her father, whose eyes were red with tears. "I always knew this day would come, Ella Ruth. I'm happy you've found your path, but I'm still sad to see you go."

Ella Ruth threw her arms around him. "You're the best father I could have ever hoped for."

Irvin patted her back. "I'm so proud of you. I love you."

"I love you too."

"Thank you, James, for helping her move," Irvin said. "You be good to her, you hear?"

James smiled. "I will. In fact, I have something I want to ask you, Ella Ruth." He got down on one knee and pulled a small black box out of his pocket.

Ella Ruth's vision swam with tears as her heart pounded wildly in her chest. Was he about to...?

"Ella Ruth Holt, you are the most incredible woman I've ever met. I love you with all of my heart, and I want to spend every day of the rest of my life with you, making you happy. Will you marry me?" James asked, opening the box to reveal a sparkling garnet engagement ring. Ella Ruth threw her arms around his neck.

"Yes! Yes!" she shouted, and everyone started crying all over again, congratulating them and hugging them.

"I am so happy for you both," Irvin cried, hugging her once more. "He is a good man, Ella Ruth."

She smiled. "I know, *Daed*. You don't have to worry about me."

"I'm your father. It's my job to worry." He took her hand and placed it in James' hand, then they walked toward the car.

Ella Ruth waved and climbed in the car with James, both sorrow and excitement filling her all at once.

"Are you ready?" James asked.

"Yes," Ella Ruth said with a nod. "Let's go start our adventure."

She waved out the window as they drove down the lane, kicking up dust behind them. They drove past their neighbors' house, where Mr. and Mrs. Muller were pulling weeds in their garden. Ella Ruth was about to wave to them, but they both frowned in disapproval at her, slowly shaking their heads.

The same thing happened when she had told a group of women she knew at a quilting party a few months ago that she was planning to leave the Amish and become an *Englisher* and pursue her dream of writing books. Most of them were genuinely happy for her, but a few of them had given her looks of downright disapproval.

And it hurt as much then as it did now.

"Are you okay?" James asked as he drove, glancing at her.

"Clearly, some people don't agree with my choice to leave," Ella Ruth said with a heavy heart. "It makes me sad, but I don't need their approval."

"That's right," James said. "You can't make everyone happy. That's what my dad says. All that matters is what you think of your choices."

"I know in my heart I made the right choice. I am at peace with God. I prayed long and hard about it. I know this is the right thing for me to do," she said with finality.

"I suppose not everyone we invite from your community will come to the wedding," James pointed out.

"And that's okay," Ella Ruth said. "If they don't approve of my decision, they don't have to come. All I know is my family and friends will be there, and you and your family will be there, so that's all we need for it to be the happiest day of our lives."

EPILOGUE

Six Months Later...

The Baptist church's bell rang overhead on the warm summer day of James and Ella Ruth's wedding. Her heart soared at the sight of dozens of buggies in the parking lot along with several cars that belonged to James' friends and family.

Because Ella Ruth had not been baptized into the Amish faith, she was not shunned when she left, so many of her friends and neighbors came to her wedding ceremony, but she guessed that they would leave after dinner was served at the reception, since there would be music and dancing after eating. That was the way it had been at her friend Esther's wedding when she had married an *Englisher*.

Ella Ruth was just glad they had come to support her, even if it meant attending the ceremony at an *Englisher* church. Most people might be surprised that her Amish friends and neighbors would come, but there was no rule against them going to an *Englisher* wedding or stepping foot inside an *Englisher* church.

And some of them chose not to come...but Ella Ruth didn't hold it against them.

"You look beautiful, Ella," Laura said, clasping her hands together and sighing. Ella Ruth's sisters nodded in agreement as she got ready in a small room downstairs.

"Thank you again, Sadie, for making such a beautiful wedding gown for me," Ella Ruth said, smiling at Sadie in the mirror.

Sadie grinned. "It was my honor. You know, one of the women from the ball left a message on the store phone. She got my number from the slip of paper you gave her. She ordered a dress for her engagement party three months from now. It's going to be a huge event."

"That's great news!" Ella Ruth cried.

"Once everyone sees Ella Ruth's wedding dress, you'll definitely get more orders," Amanda said.

"I hope so," Sadie said, clasping her hands together. "I'm nervous. This will be my first order for a client."

"Look at this gown!" Laura cried. "You're so talented."

"You'll do great. You have nothing to worry about." Ella Ruth put her arm around Sadie's shoulders.

"*Daed* is going to cry when he sees you, Ella Ruth," Katie added.

"So will James!" Amanda cried, causing them all to giggle.

"It's time to go," Priscilla said, holding Ella Ruth's veil in her hands. "I know your mother would have done this, but... May I?"

"Of course, *Mamm*," Ella Ruth said. "Thank you." She turned around so Priscilla could pin the veil into her hair, which was curled and pinned up in an elegant updo. Her hair had been down to her knees when she was Amish. After leaving, she had cut off two feet and had donated it to a wig-making organization for those affected by cancer, but her hair was still long. It felt good to help someone in need.

Priscilla carefully placed the comb of the veil into Ella Ruth's updo, and Ella Ruth turned around. "There," Priscilla said. "Perfect. You are a stunning bride, Ella Ruth. You and James make a wonderful couple. I am so happy for you." Tears filled Priscilla's eyes.

"Oh, no," Amanda said, fanning her face. "Don't cry. Then I'll cry."

"We'll all cry," Lilly said.

They each took turns giving Ella Ruth a hug. "Thank you, all of you, for being so supportive."

The pastor's wife poked her head in and said, "It's time." This was the church where James attended, and now it was Ella Ruth's church as well.

Everyone left the room, and Ella Ruth walked out last. She stepped out and saw her father waiting for her. To her surprise, he had agreed to walk her down the aisle, even though it was an *Englisher* wedding.

At the sight of her, his eyes immediately reddened with tears. "Oh, Ella Ruth, I know we aren't supposed to comment on outward appearances, but you look beautiful. I am so proud of you, and your mother would be too."

Ella Ruth choked back a sob. "Thank you, *Daed*. I can feel her here with us."

"Me too." He smiled through his tears. "Let's go. James is waiting for you." He held out his elbow, and Ella Ruth looped her arm through his and waited for the doors to open. Once they did, her breath caught in her throat as the music began and they moved down the aisle.

At the sight of all her Amish friends and neighbors there to support her, she smiled, overwhelmed with gratitude as her heart swelled. She just wished everyone from her community had come, but some disapproved and chose to stay home. But she couldn't think about that now. The ones she loved most were here, and that was all that mattered.

And she knew her mother was watching from heaven. Ella Ruth could feel it in her heart.

Thank you, Lord, she prayed when she saw James standing at the front of the church, who was wiping tears from his eyes.

Irvin kissed Ella Ruth's forehead as he gave her away, and she joined hands with James, who was radiantly beaming with obvious joy. Throughout the short ceremony, he wiped tears from his eyes. Beside Ella Ruth stood her bridesmaids: Katie, Sadie, Amanda, Lilly, and Laura. In Unity, they had no rules against the Amish being in *Englisher* weddings, and the bishop had no objections as long as they left before the dancing began.

Because Amish weddings didn't have flowers, a cake, a white dress, music, or decorations, planning an *Englisher* wedding had been an entirely new concept to Ella Ruth. She had chosen simple decorations—just a few vases of flowers on the altar.

Also out of consideration for their Amish guests, after the vows, Ella Ruth and James decided to only share a very brief kiss. At Amish weddings, the bride and groom do not kiss. Ella Ruth didn't want any of them to feel uncomfortable, but she did also want to share a kiss with her new husband on their wedding day at the altar to signify the beginning of their new life together.

After the ceremony, they went downstairs for the meal, and their guests continuously approached them to congratulate them. She thanked each person for coming.

"I pray that you have a long and happy life together," Bishop Byler said, shaking James' hand. Then he turned to Ella Ruth. "We will miss you, but I'm glad you have found your path."

"Thank you, Bishop Byler," Ella Ruth said with a smile.

Ella Ruth's friend Esther and her husband Xavier approached them. Xavier's gala had been where Ella Ruth had first met James.

"My best friend is married," Xavier said, hugging James. "Congratulations."

"We're so happy for you," Esther said, hugging Ella Ruth.

"Thank you," Ella Ruth said. "And thank you so much for helping me when I left the Amish. I think it was because of you helping me study that I got my driver's license. I couldn't parallel park for the life of me until you helped me practice."

Esther chuckled. "You did that all on your own. Any updates on your second book?"

"Yes. It's in the final editing stages, but it will be released just before Thanksgiving. I'm so glad I chose to self-publish my first one. James' aunt has been helping me by reading it and giving me feedback, just like she did for the first book. She's helped me improve my writing so much. I feel honored to even email her."

"Are you kidding? Aunt Adeline loves your work," James said, then chuckled.

"Are you talking about me?" Aunt Adeline sauntered up to them. "I thought I heard my name. You know, James, it's a good thing that you asked me if I had received Ella Ruth's email last summer. I get so many emails, and it just slipped through the cracks. Once he told me about it, I opened the email and read her entire book that night. I stayed up all night reading!"

"It really is an incredible book," Esther agreed. "I couldn't stop reading it either. I can't wait to read the second one."

"It's going to be fabulous," Aunt Adeline said with a wave of her hand. "And these two are a dynamic duo in the self-publishing world."

"I love learning the advertising, and James has been helping me. He found my cover designer, and we've been learning how to create online ads together," Ella Ruth said.

"Well done," Xavier said. "Your cover is fantastic."

"She's also built up quite the large social media following," James added. "Everyone wants to know more about the author who left the Amish."

All of Ella Ruth's sisters, Eliza, and Laura joined them. Charlotte and Leah, Ella Ruth's two older married sisters, came over to her and hugged her.

"Congratulations," Charlotte said, squeezing her tight.

"We are so happy for you," Leah added.

"They make a great team, don't they?" Esther asked. "Have you heard about her book?"

"Oh, yes. I think that was clear when your first book was such a huge success. Congratulations, Miss Bestselling Author. I can't believe you were on the news and everything," Charlotte said.

"That's right," Laura said, twirling her prayer *kapp* ribbon. "My best friend is famous."

"I am not," Ella Ruth said with a laugh.

"You are," Amanda said.

"We are all so proud of you," Sadie said, and Katie and Lilly agreed.

"Congratulations!" Eliza said. "I'm so happy for you guys." She playfully punched James in the arm, and he laughed at her.

"Oh, thank you," Ella Ruth said, her cheeks burning. "It's been quite a ride. James has been the mastermind behind the book launch."

"It was a lot of work setting up the launch, and we still have a lot to learn, but I absolutely love helping Ella Ruth with all the work there is to be done with self-publishing. The marketing alone is a full-time job," James chuckled. "I enjoy doing it, and that frees up more time for Ella Ruth to write."

"We both know I'm still not so great with computers, so yes, we do make a great team." Ella Ruth grinned at her husband. "I have to admit it is amazing to see my book in the window of the local bookstore." She sighed. "It's a dream come true. I have been going there for years to buy books and always imagined my book on display in the window."

"And I'm sure it will be in even more stores soon," Amanda said.

"I'm so glad you'll be living right here in town," Esther said.

"Yes, we bought a house right near the Amish community so I can visit my family often. I'd love to have all of you over once we get back from traveling Europe," Ella Ruth said, beaming, grateful that one of her friends had also left the Amish to marry an *Englisher*—now she had someone to talk to about their experiences.

On their honeymoon, Ella Ruth and James would travel to Germany, England, and France—another dream come true.

"How do you like your new teaching job?" Xavier asked James.

"I love it. My students are wonderful," James said.

"You have definitely found your calling," Xavier said with a grin.

Everyone sat down to eat. After the wedding meal, their Amish guests gradually left the wedding, which she had expected. Irvin and Priscilla approached her.

"It's getting late, so we're going to take the children home," Priscilla said, giving them both a hug, then Irvin, Debra, and Seth followed suit.

"Congratulations to both of you." Irvin turned to James. "You take good care of her, you hear?" Irvin put on his best stern face, but he couldn't hide his smile long.

"I will, *Daed*. Don't you worry." James smiled and put his arm around Ella Ruth.

"Ah, you'll understand when you two have children of your own," Irvin said, waving his hand.

"That won't be too far off, hopefully," Ella Ruth said with a grin.

A few moments later, upbeat music started, and Ella Ruth pulled James onto the dance floor. She knew she was a terrible dancer, but she didn't care. As she laughed while dancing with her new husband, her mind went back to the first time she had danced with him at the gala.

Even though she had felt awkward at first that night, he had made her laugh, which she knew he would continue for the rest of their lives. Thankfully, she had been wrong when she'd thought she'd never see him again after the gala.

At the end of the night, they climbed into James' car that said *Just Married* on the back, and James turned to her. "Here's a wedding gift for you," he said, handing her a small black box.

"Another ring?" she asked, laughing.

"No, not quite."

She opened the box to see a sparkling silver pumpkin charm to add to her charm bracelet which she now wore on her wrist. "Oh, it's gorgeous, James."

"It symbolizes that day at the fair when I realized you were my Cinderella, the one I'd been looking for," James explained, taking the charm from the box and fastening it to her bracelet. "And our first kiss."

"Oh, I remember." She smiled, a blush heating her cheeks even though they were married now. There was also a note with the charm. She opened it and read:

My dearest Ella Ruth, my Cinderella and my love,

I am so happy that all my dreams have been coming true since I met you. I am now a teacher, I have a stronger family bond with my parents, and today I am marrying the love of my life. Our future together is full of promise. This little pumpkin reminds me of our early journey together, and you already have a glass slipper shoe on your bracelet, so I thought it was fitting. I hope I can add a few more charms to your keepsake bracelet in years to come.

I have been praying for you for years even though I hadn't met you yet. I was waiting for you, my wife. I love you so much,

-James

Ella Ruth's eyes filled with tears as she read the note. She would now be able to add her own memories to this heirloom. She was marrying such a thoughtful and loving man, she couldn't be much happier.

James took her hand in his, and she leaned closer to kiss him.

She'd had no idea where their journey would take them in the future. All she knew was this was the happiest day of her life, and she had a feeling even better days were ahead.

GET 4 OF ASHLEY EMMA'S AMISH EBOOKS FOR FREE

www.AshleyEmmaAuthor.com

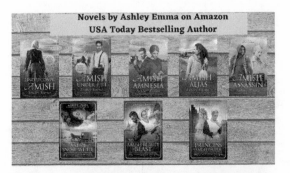

ABOUT THE AUTHOR (ASHLEY EMMA)

Visit www.AshleyEmmaAuthor.com to download free eBooks by
Ashley Emma!

Ashley Emma wrote her first novel at age 12 and published it at 16. She was home schooled and knew since she was a child that she wanted to be a novelist. She's written over 20 books and is now an award-winning USA Today bestselling author of over 15 books, mostly Amish fiction. (Many more titles coming soon!)

Ashley has a deep respect and love for the Amish and wanted to make sure her Amish books were genuine. When she was 20, she stayed with three Amish families in a community in Maine where she made many friends and did her research for her Amish books. To read about what it was like to live among the Amish, check out her book Amish for a Week (a true story).

Ashley's novel Amish Alias was a Gold Medal Winner in the NYC Book Awards 2021. Her bestselling book Undercover Amish received 26 out of 27 points as a finalist in the Maine Romance Writers Strut Your Stuff novel writing competition in 2015. Its sequel Amish Under Fire was a semi-finalist in Harlequin's So You Think You Can Write novel writing competition also in 2015. Two of her short stories have been published online in writing contests and she co-wrote an article for ProofreadAnywhere.com in 2016. She judged the Fifth Anniversary Writing Contest for Becoming Writer in the summer of 2016.

Ashley owns Fearless Publishing House in Maine where she lives with her husband and four children. She is passionate about helping her clients self-publish their own books so they can build their businesses or achieve their dream of becoming an author.

Download some of Ashley's free Amish books at www.AshleyEm
maAuthor.com.

ashley@ashleyemmaauthor.com

EXCERPT OF AMISH ALADDIN

CHAPTER ONE OF AMISH ALADDIN (BOOK 4 OF THE AMISH FAIRYTALE SERIES)

Chapter One

Aladdin Samuels' eyes shot open at the sound of a loud truck on the bridge overhead, and when he realized it wasn't a threat, he took in a deep breath and slowly sat up on his sleeping bag.

Aladdin Samuels' eyes shot open at the sound of a loud truck on the bridge overhead, and when he realized it wasn't a threat, he took in a deep breath and slowly sat up on his sleeping bag.

His German shepherd, Abe, yawned and stretched beside him, his long pink tongue extending past his sharp teeth. Though the mild-mannered dog seemed sweet, he was well-trained. On Aladdin's command, he would attack anyone who threatened them. Ever since Aladdin's time overseas in the military had ended, Abe had been his lifeline, not only for protection on the streets but as a friend. In fact, Abe was more of a friend to Aladdin than any human had ever been.

"Good morning, Abe," Aladdin said to his companion, scratching him behind the ears. Aladdin looked around at where they had spent the night, a grassy spot under a bridge in Unity, Maine. At least it was summer now and not winter, which is when they would have to face possible frostbite.

"Let's go," Aladdin said, rising to his feet. He let out a low whistle, and the dog followed.

He'd never been to Unity, Maine, before, although he was originally from Maine. For now, he was just passing through the town. Aladdin didn't exactly know where he was going, but he liked it here in Unity so far. It was a quaint town with classic diners and old bookstores, and people actually greeted each other on the street.

At twenty-four years old, this was not what Aladdin had envisioned his life would look like. After growing up with an abusive stepfather and a mother who clearly hadn't cared enough about him to keep him safe, he'd left as soon as he was old enough to join the Army. After three tours in Afghanistan, his time in the military was over.

His friends hadn't been so lucky.

Lucky? He scoffed, glancing down at his tattered clothes and running a hand over his long, scruffy black beard that desperately needed shaving. His fingers subconsciously traced the scar that ran down his arm, hidden by his tattered sleeve. It wasn't from combat but had been done by his stepfather—another part of the past he'd rather forget.

His stomach rumbled, reminding him that he hadn't eaten in two days. As he walked down the street with Abe, he received a few wary glances from shoppers on the sidewalk, but he ignored them. He was used to it by now—everyone avoiding the young homeless man and his dog. For all they knew, he was on drugs.

But he wasn't. No, he'd given that up quickly. After getting out of the military, it had been his only way to cope at first, but then he'd overdosed. Coming that close to death once again finally convinced him to give it up. There was still a gaping hole in his heart, and he longed for something—or someone—to fill it, but he knew that might never happen. At least now he knew that drugs would never fill the void.

"Street rat," an older man mumbled, glaring at Aladdin as he walked by. Aladdin ignored him, continuing on down the street. What if that person knew Aladdin had fought and risked his life for his country? Would he still treat him the same way?

"There's so much more to me, Abe," Aladdin murmured as they walked. "If people took a moment to talk to me, I think they'd realize that."

As Aladdin approached the farmers' market, the smell of baked goods and other homemade foods made his stomach growl again. He reached into the pocket of his worn camo jacket, feeling a few coins and one dollar bill between his fingers. Not nearly enough to buy enough food for the day for him and Abe.

He let out a long breath, glancing at his dog. He was going to have to steal their breakfast...again. It wasn't his first choice, but after searching in dumpsters for two days, he was desperate.

As he looked around, he noticed several Amish people since there was an Amish community just down the road, and many of them sold their goods here at the market. People bustled about, filling their shopping bags as vendors called out their goods to get the buyers' attention.

"Sugared dates and pistachios!" one vendor called, turning Aladdin's head.

Aladdin wandered over to a booth displaying Amish homemade cheeses, and his mouth watered just at the thought. He stepped up to the booth, and the elderly Amish couple gave him polite smiles and nods.

"Good morning. What a sweet dog you have there," the woman said.

"Thank you. This is Abe." Aladdin turned to the dog. "Abe, turn."

The dog quickly walked in a circle, spinning.

The couple laughed. "Oh, how charming," the woman added.

As the couple watched Abe do more tricks and draw the attention of everyone nearby, Aladdin swiped a block of cheese off the table and stuffed it into his sleeve.

"That's an impressive dog," the man said.

"Thank you." Aladdin nodded and turned. "Abe, come."

He knew Abe could smell the cheese in his sleeve, but the dog followed him obediently as they moved on to the next booth, not noticing the curious young woman who watched him.

Chapter Two

Jasmine Byler watched the strange young man with the performing dog from several booths away. As the dog covered his eyes with his paw and spun in circles, she watched as the man deftly pulled a block of cheese from Mr. and Mrs. Schuler's table and hid it in his sleeve.

So, he was a thief, and he used his dog as a distraction. She crossed her arms, eyebrows raised. Clever. Well, if he tried that at her booth, she'd be ready. She wouldn't let him steal baked goods from the Miller's Bakery.

"Cute dog, isn't he?" Laura Miller, Mae's younger daughter, asked enthusiastically.

"Yes, he is," Jasmine agreed.

"Seems to me like you're more interested in his owner." Laura wiggled her eyebrows.

"I am not." Jasmine turned and busied herself with straightening the tablecloth.

"He looks like he's homeless," Lydia, Laura's older sister, added. "Probably a common thief and pickpocket."

"Maybe," Jasmine said, studying the man as he moved from one booth to the next. His dark eyes darted back and forth as he moved through the crowd cautiously. His dog stayed right by his side, obeying his every command, whether verbal or through gestures. "He seems...lonely."

"Really?" Laura put her hands on her hips. "I knew it. You think he's handsome."

"Have you seen him?" Lydia asked. "His clothes are ragged, and he probably hasn't bathed in weeks."

"You're right, but underneath all that..." Jasmine stared at him again from across the market. If his beard was gone, what would he look like? His eyes were so mysterious that they drew her in, even from a distance. She found his deeply tanned skin handsome, and something about the way he moved intrigued her. "I think he really is good-looking."

"Me too." Laura nodded and smiled.

"You two are hopeless." Lydia threw her hands up and turned to help a customer.

"Don't listen to her. She doesn't have a romantic bone in her body," Laura whispered. "Do you think he will come to our booth?"

"How can he not? You can smell your cinnamon buns a mile away." Jasmine laughed.

Laura smiled and nodded. "True. I bet that dog can, at least."

As more customers arrived, Jasmine focused on boxing up donuts, pastries, pies, and cinnamon rolls and taking their payments. The line of customers finally ended, and Jasmine let out a breath of relief and leaned forward, resting her hands on the edge of the table.

Suddenly, the mysterious man and his dog stood before her. At the sight of his tan face and dark eyes so close to her, she drew in a sharp breath, her heart racing as adrenaline spiked through her veins.

"Good morning," she said breathlessly.

"Good morning," he said in a low voice.

Laura looked at the man, then at Jasmine. She turned to her sister. "Lydia, those vegetables over there look so good. Let's go buy some. Come with me." Laura grabbed Lydia's hand and pulled.

"We have vegetables at home, Laura," Lydia said dryly.

"Come on." Laura continued to drag her sister away, who rolled her eyes. Why was Laura leaving her alone with this man?

"I saw the tricks your dog can do," Jasmine said, turning to him. "He's very well-trained. Did you train him yourself?"

"Yes, I did," the stranger said. "I found him abandoned as a puppy. He truly is my best friend."

"He's blessed to have you. You probably saved his life."

"More like the other way around." The man looked down at his dog as though he meant the world to him, scratching behind the dog's ear. The sight was so tender that her heart flooded with warmth.

Jasmine smiled and met the man's eyes as he looked back up at her, and her stomach flip-flopped. Why was she feeling this way? She didn't even know this man.

The man turned to the dog. "Up."

The dog sat back on his hind legs and lifted his two front paws in a begging pose.

"Aw." Jasmine couldn't help but smile at the sight. She handed the dog a homemade bagel. "Here you go, buddy."

The dog devoured the bagel in two bites, then looked up at her with his tongue lolling out, the corners of his mouth turned up as if smiling.

"What kind of dog is he?" she asked.

"I'm not sure. He's a mutt, I guess." The man shrugged.

"A very cute mutt."

"Turn," the man said to the dog, and he did his spinning trick again. As the dog spun in circles, Jasmine watched the man instead of the dog, who discretely stole two bagels off the edge of the table and tucked them into his jacket. Jasmine raised one eyebrow. That trick might work on other people, but not her.

As the dog's trick ended, the man met her eyes again. "Thank you for his bagel. I'm sure he enjoyed it."

"You're welcome...for both his and yours." She crossed her arms.

His eyes widened, but only for a split second.

"I saw those bagels you stole while the dog was doing his trick. That's very clever."

"I...I'm sorry. I don't have any money. I'll go now." The man quickly turned away, and his dog followed.

"Wait." Jasmine quickly packed more bagels, cinnamon rolls, and donuts into a box and came around the table, handing the box to him. When their fingers touched, electricity shot up her arm, straight to her heart. "Please, take these."

"I couldn't. I've already taken too much from you." His warm eyes searched hers. "I don't deserve this."

"I want you to take this. Please, don't worry about it. We might not sell it all anyway."

"Really?"

She nodded.

"Thank you, miss..." he said, fishing for her name.

"Jasmine. My name is Jasmine."

"I'm Aladdin."

"Hmm. I've never heard that name before."

"I'm pretty sure my mother was high when she chose that name." Aladdin chuckled, then stopped himself. "Sorry. I shouldn't have said that in front of you."

"I don't live in a bubble, contrary to what you might think." She took a step back and crossed her arms again. "I hope you two have a nice day."

"Thank you, Jasmine." Aladdin smiled at her, causing heat to creep into her cheeks.

"You're welcome," she said softly, watching as he and his dog walked away.

"What just happened?" Laura's voice suddenly sounded behind Jasmine, causing her to jump.

"Were you standing over there the whole time?"

"Ja," Laura said, nodding rapidly.

"She was eavesdropping." Lydia rolled her eyes.

"Maybe I was. So, what happened?" Laura asked.

"Not that much. He tried to steal some bagels, so I gave him a box of baked goods," Jasmine explained.

"You what?" Lydia's eyes went wide.

"Aw, that's so sweet." Laura clasped her hands together in front of her heart.

"You can take it out of my pay," Jasmine said. "I felt bad for him and his dog, even though he tried to steal."

"Hmmm, I think it's more than that." Laura elbowed her playfully.

"I don't even know him." Jasmine turned to hide the blush heating her cheeks. "He must have been really hungry, and he said he didn't have any money."

"Right. You don't even know him. He could be a serial killer," Lydia snapped.

"Oh, you're no fun." Laura waved her hand.

"Someone has to be logical here." Lydia shrugged.

"No, I think he has a good heart." Jasmine stared as the man disappeared into the crowd.

"How can you know that from only meeting him for a few minutes?" Laura asked.

"I just have a feeling," Jasmine said, her eyes still searching for him, but he was gone.

***

If you liked this excerpt, check out Amish Aladdin here on Amazon:

https://www.amazon.com/dp/B09RF7Y3NX

OTHER BOOKS BY ASHLEY EMMA

Looking for something new to read? Check out my other books!

www.AshleyEmmaAuthor.com

GET 4 OF ASHLEY EMMA'S AMISH EBOOKS FOR FREE

More books by Ashley Emma available exclusively on Amazon in ebook and paperback

UNDERCOVER AMISH

(This series can be read out of order or as standalone novels.)

Detective Olivia Mast would rather run through gunfire than return to her former Amish community in Unity, Maine, where she killed her abusive husband in self-defense.

Olivia covertly investigates a murder there while protecting the man she dated as a teen: Isaac Troyer, a potential target.

When Olivia tells Isaac she is a detective, will he be willing to break Amish rules to help her arrest the killer?

Undercover Amish was a finalist in Maine Romance Writers Strut Your Stuff Competition 2015 where it received 26 out of 27 points and has 455+ Amazon reviews!

Buy here: https://www.amazon.com/Undercover-Amish-Covert-Police- Detectives-ebook/dp/B01L6JE49G

AMISH UNDER FIRE

After Maria Mast's abusive ex-boyfriend is arrested for being involved in sex trafficking and modern-day slavery, she thinks that she and her son Carter can safely return to her Amish community.

But the danger has only just begun.

Someone begins stalking her, and they want blood and revenge.

Agent Derek Turner of Covert Police Detectives Unit is assigned as her bodyguard and goes with her to her Amish community in Unity, Maine.

Maria's secretive eyes, painful past, and cautious demeanor intrigue him.

As the human trafficking ring begins to target the Amish community, Derek wonders if the distraction of her will cost him his career...and Maria's life.

Buy on Amazon: http://a.co/fT6D7sM

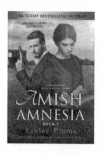

AMISH AMNESIA

When Officer Jefferson Martin witnesses a young woman being hit by a car near his campsite, all thoughts of vacation vanish as the car speeds off.

When the malnourished, battered woman wakes up, she can't remember anything before the accident. They don't know her name, so they call her Jane.

When someone breaks into her hospital room and tries to kill her before getting away, Jefferson volunteers to protect Jane around the clock. He takes her back to their Kennebunkport beach house along with his upbeat sister Estella and his friend who served with him overseas in the Marine Corps, Ben Banks.

At first, Jane's stalker leaves strange notes, but then his attacks become bolder and more dangerous.

Buy on Amazon: https://www.amazon.com/gp/product/B07SDS FV3J

AMISH ALIAS

Threatened. Orphaned. On the run.

With no one else to turn to, these two terrified sisters can only hope their Amish aunt will take them in. But the quaint Amish community of Unity, Maine, is not as safe as it seems.

After Charlotte Cooper's parents die and her abusive ex-fiancé threatens her, the only way to protect her younger sister Zoe is by faking their deaths and leaving town.

The sisters' only hope of a safe haven lies with their estranged Amish aunt in Unity, Maine, where their mother grew up before she left the Amish.

Elijah Hochstettler, the family's handsome farmhand, grows closer to Charlotte as she digs up dark family secrets that her mother kept from her.

Buy on Amazon here: https://www.amazon.com/Amish-Alias-Romantic-Suspense-Detectives/dp/1734610808

AMISH ASSASIN

When nurse Anna Hershberger finds a man with a bullet wound who begs her to help him without taking him to the hospital, she has a choice to make.

Going against his wishes, she takes him to the hospital to help him after he passes out. She thinks she made the right decision...until an assassin storms in with a gun. Anna has no choice but to go on the run with her patient.

This handsome stranger, who says his name is Connor, insists that they can't contact the police for help because there are moles leaking information. His mission is to shut down a local sex trafficking ring targeting Anna's former Amish community in Unity, Maine, and he needs her help most of all.

Since Anna was kidnapped by sex traffickers in her Amish community, she would love nothing more than to get justice and help put the criminals behind bars.

But can she trust Connor to not get her killed? And is he really who he says he is?

Buy on Amazon: https://www.amazon.com/gp/product/B084R9 V4CN

AMISH FOR A WEEK

Ever wondered what it would be like to live in an Amish community?
Now you can find out in this true story with photos.
Buy on Amazon: https://www.amazon.com/Ashleys-Amish - Ad-
ventures-Outsider-community-ebook/dp/B01N5714WE

AMISH SNOW WHITE

An heiress on the run.
A heartbroken Amish man, sleep-walking through life.

Can true love's kiss break the spell?

After his wife dies and he returns to his Amish community, Dominic feels numb and frozen, like he's under a spell.

When he rescues a woman from a car wreck in a snowstorm, he brings her home to his mother and six younger siblings. They care for her while she sleeps for several days, and when she wakes up in a panic, she pretends to have amnesia.

But waking up is only the beginning of Snow's story.

Buy on Amazon: https://www.amazon.com/Amish-Snow-White-S tandalone-Fairytale-ebook/dp/B089NHH7D4

AMISH BEAUTY AND THE BEAST

She's an Amish beauty with a love of reading, hiding a painful secret. He's a reclusive, scarred military hero who won't let anyone in. Can true love really be enough?

On her way home from the bookstore, Belle's buggy crashes in front of the old mansion that everyone else avoids, of all places.

What she finds inside the mansion is not a monster, but a man. Scarred both physiologically and physically by the horrors of military combat, Cole's burned and disfigured face tells the story of all he lost to the war in a devastating explosion.

He's been hiding from the world ever since.

After Cole ends up hiring her as his housekeeper and caretaker for his firecracker of a grandmother, Belle can't help her curiosity as she wonders what exactly Cole does in his office all day.

Why is Cole's office so off-limits to Belle? What is he hiding in there?

https://www.amazon.com/gp/product/B089PR9ML

HOSEA AND GOMER'S AMISH SECRET

Gomer is not your typical Amish woman.

On the outside, Gomer seems like a lovely, sweet, young Amish woman, but she's hiding a scandalous secret. She sneaks out at night to sing in downtown bars, lying to her entire community while leading a double life.

Hosea hears from God in a dream, telling him to marry Gomer.
Should he follow his heart and risk getting it broken?
https://www.amazon.com/Hosea-Gomers-Amish-Secret-family-eb
ook/dp/B09GQVCBM9

Made in the USA
Las Vegas, NV
06 September 2023

77155444R00208